THE PROSPERO CHRONICLES
I
SPLINTERS

D0925318

First Paperback Edition: September 2014

For information on subsidiary rights, please contact the publisher at rights@jollyfishpress.com. For a complete list of our wholesalers and distributors, please visit our website at www.jollyfishpress.com.

For information, write us at Jolly Fish Press, PO Box 1773, Provo, UT 84603-1773, or info@jollyfishpress.com

Printed in the United States of America

THIS TITLE IS ALSO AVAILABLE AS AN EBOOK.

Library of Congress Cataloging-in-Publication Data

Titchenell, F. J. R., 1989- author.
 Splinters / F.J.R. Titchenell, Matt Carter.
    pages cm. -- (The Prospero chronicles ; 1)
 Summary: ""Sixteen-year-old opposites, Ben Pastor and Mina Todd, must forge an unlikely friendship to protect their small town of Prospero, California, from its shapeshifting alien invaders' secret takeover"-- Provided by publisher.
 ISBN 978-1-939967-39-8 (paperback)
 [1. Extraterrestrial beings--Fiction. 2. Monsters--Fiction. 3. Friendship--Fiction. 4. Horror stories. 5. Science fiction.] I. Carter, Matt, 1985- author. II. Title.
 PZ7.T522Sp 2014
 [Fic]--dc23

                                        2014019114

10 9 8 7 6 5 4 3 2 1

*To John, George, Sam, Wes & Eli—Thanks for all the nightmares!*

Also by F.J.R. Titchenell:

*Confessions of the Very First Zombie Slayer
(That I Know Of)*

# THE PROSPERO CHRONICLES
# I
# SPLINTERS

## F.J.R. TITCHENELL & MATT CARTER

JOLLY
**FISH**
PRESS
Provo, Utah

# 1.

## THE FUNERAL CRASHER

### Ben

I'd never been to a funeral without a casket before. Then again, I'd never known a missing person before. This trip was full of firsts.

The funeral home had managed to fit about eighty folding chairs into their cramped, stuffy parlor, and they were all full of mourners and well-wishers. This wouldn't have been so bad if the funeral director's promise of having the air conditioning fixed in twenty minutes had actually been true. The mid-summer heat had transformed the room into a pressure cooker that smelled heavily of sweat and flowers. I couldn't leave. I wanted to, maybe just for a minute so I could clear my head, but I couldn't because I had to be there for my mother, and she had to be there for the dead girl's mother.

*Missing. Not dead. Missing.*

They didn't have a coffin, but they did have a large year-book picture of a pretty blonde girl wearing a nice, not-too-fancy dress. Her smile was gorgeous and hopeful, unaware that less than a year after the picture was taken it would be blown up and surrounded by more flowers and teddy bears than you could count.

Haley Perkins.

We were friends once upon a time. Not close friends, not even good friends—when we were both six, we'd liked each other well enough, and, since my mother was best friends in college with her mother, we got used to playing together during my mother's infrequent trips to Prospero. It didn't last long since we each soon entered the age where playing with the opposite sex was considered gross, but we were nice enough to smile and say hello and spend a few polite minutes together whenever our mothers would force us to.

I wasn't *that* choked up about her death *(disappearance)*, but there was still something surreal about actually knowing the person whose funeral you're attending.

The program said that the services were set to begin in ten minutes. Some of Haley's friends and my mother would deliver eulogies about how lovely and special a girl she was, about how she had brightened all of their lives, and about how the world would be a much worse place for not having her in it. Standard stuff. The kind of stuff that would break any audience into a chorus of tears and moans of grief.

Any normal audience at least. This audience's behavior was anything *but* normal.

Don't get me wrong, there was plenty of sadness to go around. About half the audience, mostly high school-aged, probably Haley's friends, were emotional and, if not already crying, were on the verge of tears. The older members of the audience, on the other hand, the parents, the select representatives of the Town Council who had decided to attend . . . their reactions were a bit off. While most of them put their best sad faces on, more than anything else there seemed to be an air of fear, even frustration as they occasionally whispered amongst themselves. Even stranger, I could swear that a few of the older people looked *happy*, as if this were a day of celebration instead of mourning.

This is why I never really looked forward to Mom's trips to Prospero. The place is just oozing with small town strange. Big city strange I can deal with—you expect it; at least in all the noise and anonymity, I can avoid it. Small town strange is another beast entirely, that kind of strange where you know, you just *know* that everybody's watching you and judging your every move . . . I don't know how anyone could handle that for long without going completely insane. Top it off with Prospero's tourist-friendly reputation for the bizarre . . .

I needed some air. I tugged on my mother's sleeve.

"Mom?"

She looked at me, daubing her puffy eyes with a tissue, "Yes, Ben?"

"Can I go get some water?"

She smiled, faintly, looking to the woman wrapped in her arms. "Sure. Could you get a cup for me and your Aunt Christine as well?"

"Sure," I said as I got up and walked down the center aisle. Late arrivals milled around the back, trying to find an available seat. Among them was a gawky-looking girl in a long-sleeved black dress that might have belonged to her grandmother. She looked like she had only been told how dresses worked just in time for this memorial service. Her curly red hair hung haphazardly around her face, a striking contrast against her pale skin. A pair of thick, black-framed glasses made her eyes look enormous.

I couldn't be sure, but she seemed to be staring intently at me as I walked into the next room. I'd have been unsettled even if the town itself hadn't already put me on edge.

In the next parlor over, a buffet table had been set out with a selection of hors d'oeuvres, a punch bowl, and bottles of water in ice. I grabbed a few, cracked one open, and took a long, grateful sip.

When I turned to head back to the service, the red-haired girl was standing in my way. I was startled, almost dropping my bottle to the floor. Up close, I could see that she stood barely five feet tall, and if it hadn't been for the intensity of her gaze, I could almost have tripped over her before noticing she was there. She didn't move.

"Hi," I said.

"Hi," she replied. An awkward silence followed. Though I could already tell she was hardly the world's greatest conversationalist, given the day, I wanted to be polite.

"I'm Ben," I said, holding out my hand.

She didn't take it. She only said, "I know."

Again, that unsettled feeling was grabbing my stomach, but being too polite for my own good, I couldn't act on it. "Well, then you've got me at a disadvantage?"

"Mina. Mina Todd," she said quickly, her eyes leaving me for a moment as if she were worried someone might overhear her. Satisfied that she was clear, she smiled briefly. As odd-looking as she was, she had a radiant smile.

"Did you . . . did you know Haley well?" I asked. Though this could have been a minefield, it did seem like the safest conversation topic.

"Better than she knew me," Mina said, shrugging. She did not elaborate on that statement.

This was getting a little too weird for my tastes. I could have doubled back into the parlor easily—considering the stifling heat, I decided on a different approach. I reached for my pocket, pulled out my cell phone, and forced a surprised look on my face.

"My phone's vibrating, I'll be right back."

"No, it isn't," she said simply.

"It's very quiet," I explained, starting to turn away from her to make my escape.

"No, it isn't," she repeated. She looked at me, worried, clearly wanting to say more. She was weird, I understood that, but something really had her on edge.

Still, I quickened my pace. Thankfully, she didn't follow.

It was nice outside. Hot, but nice. A faint breeze brought in the scent of the redwood trees that surrounded Prospero. I realized then that, Prospero's strangeness aside, I could probably deal with summer in Northern California, better than a lot of the places we'd lived at least. Better than Virginia and Texas, and those three weeks we spent in Phoenix. That quick escape was one of the few times I was glad my mom likes to move around so much.

I sighed, took another sip of water. This trip was another excuse. I knew it. Mom wasn't happy with her job and she hated our landlord. When she said we were coming up here to offer comfort to Aunt Christine and she didn't know how long we'd stay, I knew, I just *knew* that it would be her way of quitting her job. Something would happen, she'd decide to stay longer, and then, the way she had at least once every two years since Dad had died, she'd say it was time for a change.

If it had been funny, I'd have laughed. Instead, I kicked a stone across the funeral home's parking lot. It bounced harmlessly off the tire of a Jeep parked near the exit. I watched it skip out into the street, wondering how far it would go.

Then I saw her.

There was a girl walking down the middle of the street, dirty and barefoot, wrapped in a tattered old Army blanket. She looked like a zombie, unmindful of the cuts on her feet, how little the blanket covered up her probably naked form, and the car that was barreling down the road toward her. It was going too fast, and the driver wouldn't see her in time around the blind corner ahead.

I didn't think; I just ran for her. The car rounded the corner. The squealing of brakes filled the air. I collided with the girl, knocking her off her feet. We fell into a ditch full of dry pine needles by the side of the road. The car swerved, missed us by inches and ran into a lamp post in front of the funeral home. Its hood crunched inward and glass lay everywhere. I don't know what was louder, the unending blare of its horn after the impact, or the sound of the lamppost falling down and crunching another car in the parking lot. Someone screamed.

I looked down at the girl, rolling off her when I realized, shamefacedly, that she had broken my fall.

"I'm sorry," I said. "I meant to do that better. Are you all right?"

She was coming out of her trance. The vacant gaze was soon replaced by the look of a person coming out of a deep slumber.

Sitting up, I repeated, "Are you all ri—"

Then I saw her face. She'd lost some weight, needed a shower and some shampoo, and was a little bloody, but there was no denying it was her.

"Haley?" I asked.

Her eyes focused on me, shocked and fearful. Letting out an animalistic scream of grief and fear, she wrapped her arms powerfully around me and wept. Comforting crying girls had never been one of my strong suits, let alone beautiful girls who'd been missing for two months and declared legally dead and then showed up naked outside their own memorial services. I like to think I did my best as she hung on to me.

People from the service had started filing outside, checking out the accident. Some were already on their cell phones calling 911, which gave me one less thing to do, thankfully.

"Can you walk?" I asked, getting only loud sobs in response. I took that as a no.

Carefully, I cradled Haley in my arms and picked her up, making sure the blanket covered her. She was so light. Too light. As quickly as I could, I made my way to the accident site and the crowd that had gathered around it.

"We need help here!" I called.

With a moderately impressive car accident to look at, they noticed us slowly, but when they did, we were swarmed. There were all the reactions you'd expect on an occasion like this. Shock. Excitement. Elation. I set her down, and though she regained her footing for a moment, she soon sat down on the curb, holding the blanket around her protectively as people hugged her, questioned her, or just stood around crying. People called for her mother, and soon she came running out with my mom in tow.

Aunt Christine screamed in surprise, tears of joy running down her cheeks as she wrapped her arms around Haley and me powerfully. She babbled incoherently as she kissed first Haley, then me on the cheek, and though I was soon pulled aside by the crowd for congratulations from a couple dozen strangers, I did catch her saying the words "Thank you" and "hero."

Within minutes, there was a police car parked in front of the funeral home and five minutes after that, an ambulance to take Haley and the driver to the nearby medical center. By then I'd had my hand shaken and my back pounded so many times I was thinking of asking for a ride over there with them.

It was right around the time they started to load Haley into the back of the ambulance that I felt the insistent poking on the back of my shoulder. I turned around, expecting another well-wisher or congratulatory handshake.

Instead, I got Mina Todd. She looked at me, almost frantic, as she wrote furiously on her funeral program with a marker and thrust it into my hands.

"We can't talk here. It's not safe. Just . . . call me, okay?"

Before I could ask what she meant, she darted off into the crowd and disappeared. I looked back to Haley as she was loaded into the ambulance. She smiled at me, grateful, and for a moment, it almost looked like she said, "Thank you."

I was a hero. A *hero*. I gotta say . . . it felt pretty good. They wouldn't call me a hero for much longer, not the guy who just saw her wandering in the street and decided to help. I was going to enjoy it while they did.

It was almost an afterthought when I finally looked at the message Mina had scrawled on the back of her funeral program. Beneath her phone number, in large block letters, she had printed three simple words.

*THAT ISN'T HALEY*

## 2.

## CHANGE OF PLANS

Mina

I am probably not crazy.

More importantly, I am almost certainly not *wrong*.

Strange things happen in my town. Most people at least agree on that. If you haven't already heard of Prospero, California, you only have to walk down Main Street, take a lap of the glorified gift shop we call a cryptozoology museum, and stop for a Cherry Timewarp at the Soda Fountain of Youth to know that it's that kind of town.

Everyone has heard the stories about the monsters in our woods and about the people who come here with Parkinson's or cancer and then live to be a hundred. Some even know they're true.

Very few know the two are connected.

I do. I know what happens to people here, what the Splinters do to them. I've seen it.

And I am one of the few resistors working to stop it.

Most of the people I've lost along the way have not received the last respects due to them. The ones being used by the Splinters are not quite dead, and few realize that they're missing, but I've been to more than my share of funerals as well.

I don't like them.

All those people sitting so still and quiet, so eager to be offended. It's even worse than school. Mentally alphabetizing and spelling the periodic table can only keep you occupied for so long.

This one had been a necessary evil, an investment I hoped would pay off.

Back in the basement bedroom that served as my office and sanctuary, I could finally think.

My room was as organized as the space allowed while keeping everything I needed easily accessible. Most of the walls and table space were taken up with amulets of various sorts, a salt lamp and Eye of Osiris, plenty of different hex marks, a vial of holy water, a few garlands of garlic, and bundles of sage. There's a handmade broom over the door, and the top of the dresser was covered with different crystals and herb sachets.

They all looked silly, took up valuable workspace, and didn't smell too pleasant mixed together, but some of their combination seemed to be working, so I'd had to learn to tolerate the rest of them, for as long as it would take to isolate the active ingredients. And if the combination failed, I had plenty of flammable materials for more aggressive defense.

There was room for the things I needed to keep my mind in working order, the electric keyboard and headphones, the ceiling-high shelves of jigsaws, puzzle books, puzzle boxes, and half-finished lanyards. The closet had a chin-up bar over the door and just enough space kept free to hide something the size of a small human when necessary, less comfortably but also less obviously than in the tiny adjoining bathroom. The reference books were under the bed. At least, the good ones were.

Over the desk was the bulletin board containing the essentials of my life's work. My map where I marked all the sightings, my schedule of the most important bits of watching and listening to do, my ever-shifting top five leads, and, most importantly, my lists of names.

Effectively Certain Non-Splinters (ECNS for short), Probable Non-Splinters, No Useful Information, Probable Splinters, and Effectively Certain Splinters (or ECS).

I'd crossed Haley Perkins off the Probable Non-Splinters list when she'd gone missing, and she hadn't been anywhere since then. Suddenly, she needed a place again.

I selected a Java Monster from the case of assorted energy drinks in my closet, turned on the computer monitor, selected a playlist, and turned to a fresh Sudoku page to clear my head.

*One, four, eight . . .*

*"I am the very model of a modern Major-General . . ."*

All the nicely ordered thoughts crowded Haley securely into the part of my brain where I could handle her, like packing peanuts.

*Two, three, nine . . .*

Haley had been missing for two months. Like everyone else, I'd thought she was almost certainly dead.

I'd even started to consider the possibility that she was

just the ordinary kind of missing person, left in a shallow grave somewhere by some depraved human, and the fact that she'd happened to disappear from Prospero was just a wild coincidence.

As unpleasant as that option was, I'd hoped, for her sake, that it was true.

Haley and I had never exactly been close. She had been popular, forever absorbed in some social function or event, surrounded by questionable people.

But she had never been unkind to me, and that was more than I could say for most of the Prospero High student body. I was quite sure she was intelligent, if a little naïve, and a far greater talent than the school's Theatrical Society knew what to do with.

As the weeks had passed with no sign of her, I had sincerely wished her the dignity of death.

*Seven, nine, two, five, six, one, eight, four, three vertical . . .*

I penciled her name onto the Probable Splinters list. It's one of the longer ones, but I gave hers a double asterisk so it wouldn't get lost.

*"And many cheerful facts about the square of the hypotenuse . . ."*

I didn't like the idea of my potential new ally living under the same roof with someone on that list, but I wasn't ready to write him off just for that. Ben was the most promising prospect I'd found in a long time. I'd picked apart every tweet and status update from both his family and the Perkinses for the past five years, every signature in the museum guestbook that every visitor *had* to sign, every page of the set of Haley's yearbooks that had been on solemn display in front of the school since her disappearance, until I couldn't find any reasonable way he could have been in Prospero recently enough for it to be a problem.

His local and school newspapers had never reported any miracles connected with him, or anything remarkable about him at all, unless you counted taking AP World History or announcing his Eagle Scout project a year early, and I hadn't been able to identify any unexplained contact between him and any of the Effectively Certain or Probable Splinters.

He'd been living under uncertain circumstances all his life, ever since leaving his childhood home in Wisconsin after his father's death, and he had remained strong.

I can't overemphasize the importance of that. What I do isn't easy.

He already knew the Perkinses and was likely to want answers about what had happened to Haley. He wasn't going to be in Prospero permanently, so once I'd taught him the basics, I could send him on his way to safety, to research, consult, and preserve the knowledge from afar, without my having to watch him every second to ensure his continuing humanity.

*"And whistle all the airs from that infernal nonsense, 'Pinafore . . .'"*

It was going to take—

"Sweetie, are you down there?"

My brain jammed up completely, the way it always did whenever I heard that voice on the stairs going down to my basement bedroom. It makes me feel like I've been thinking out loud, and that shuts me up fast.

"Yes," I called back.

"I just warmed up some pizza bagels! I know it's not exactly post-funeral food, but since it wasn't exactly a funeral—"

"No, thank you, Dad."

"Are you sure?"

"No, thank you, Dad," I repeated.

I clicked the pause button so I could listen to him backing away into the living room. Once he had gone, and my head churned back into motion, I didn't start the music back up—I was functional enough. Instead, I checked my daily download of the important times and places. It had almost finished. I selected the clip of my mother's meeting from the previous morning, adjusted the volume a little so that if anything important had been said, it would catch my ear, and opened Skype. As usual, Aldo was online.

Aldo's one of the longest standing names on the Effectively Certain Non-Splinter List and one of the most useful. He's a tech genius, and his dad runs the one computer repair shop in town.

He also has a sizeable crush on me. I know this because I've been informed by multiple sources, on separate occasions, all with strong track records of detecting such things and with no likely shared ulterior motives. I've asked him repeatedly if this has any significant chance of interfering with our work under any conceivable set of circumstances. He refuses to acknowledge the issue but he assures me that, if it *were* the case, it wouldn't be a problem.

"Did you hear the news?" I asked him.

His face appeared onscreen. Every time I saw it, I expected to see his first pimples finally standing out. I don't know any other fourteen-year-olds who've avoided them, at least none who like chili cheese fries so much and showers so little—but, like the promised growth spurt that still had not come and the baby-fine white-blond hair he could never find the time to trim, his skin made him look even younger than he really was.

"About Haley Perkins going Romero on us?"

"Going what?" I waited, as usual, for Aldo to translate, wondering if he'd ever stop making me ask.

"Returning from the dead. And no, I didn't hear. I decided to spend a nice afternoon in my NASA-grade isolation chamber."

"It's *not* Haley Perkins," I reminded him. There are few enough people I can talk to about these things. I don't like not knowing that we're clear on them.

"Effectively certainly not," Aldo agreed in the tone he thought I hadn't identified as mocking yet. "What are you listening to?"

I could see him squinting to listen to the recording playing faintly on my end. It had taken me forever to figure out why he did that, act as if his eyes and ears ran through the same temperamental fuse box. I think his brain doesn't need as many packing peanuts as mine.

I saved him the trouble. "Council meeting."

"You're still listening to the ones at Town Hall?"

Aldo had made so many bugs for me that he tended to forget that I didn't always lose interest in them as soon as he had moved on to his next project.

"The Council's involved, even if they don't talk about it explicitly," I insisted for the sixty-seventh time. That's a precise count. "But they're not the richest source," I agreed. "I'm going to need some more. Something I can fit in—"

My phone vibrated in my pocket, and I pulled it out. Restricted.

I've only seen that a few times before. People in Prospero don't have restricted numbers. It's seen as unfriendly. I held up a finger to ask Aldo to wait and answered the call.

"Ben?" I asked.

The voice that answered wasn't his. It wasn't even really a voice. It's what Splinters sound like when they don't want to be recognized, a clicking, popping, rasp. I'd only heard it a few times before, on the same occasions when I'd seen a number show up restricted. It made my stomach clench, but this time I was ready enough to hit speaker phone.

"Stay away from Ben Pastor," it said before I could hold the phone to the computer mic and find the right record button. Luckily, it said it again.

"Stay away from Ben Pastor, or history will repeat itself."

"Who *is* this?" I asked. Not that I expected them to answer. They never had before.

"Stay away from Ben Pastor. He belongs to us."

Then the call ended. Aldo stared at me out of my screen, waiting for me to say something.

"They're after him," I said, even though that was obvious. "Warning him isn't going to be enough. I need a link to his GPS."

"Uh . . . yeah," Aldo gave me one of his awkward, sympathetic smiles that I dreaded. "Did you happen to catch his account number, PIN, last four of his social, and the name of his first pet?"

# 3.

## PERKS OF BEING A (LOCAL) HERO

### Ben

We were only supposed to be in Prospero for another two days after the memorial service.

One week later we were still taking up two of Aunt Christine's guestrooms. Mom had already called her office saying that she would need to take an indeterminate amount of time off due to a family emergency. She said they were okay with it. I didn't entirely believe her.

Same old, same old, really.

I'll say this, though: if you're going to be stuck somewhere, and you don't know how long you're going to be stuck, it helps to be a local hero.

Those first few days were just one long stretch of people coming in and out of the house, dropping off congratulations and more baked goods than I imagined were possible. Some of them were even good. Since Mom spent most of her time with Aunt Christine, and Aunt Christine spent most of her time at the medical center with Haley as she recuperated, I was pretty much left to my own devices.

For the first few days, I hung around the house, taking in gifts and messages for Haley from well-wishers, chatting online, or reading by the pool.

Three days of this kind of nothing will give you a case of cabin fever quick. And so, as much as the town weirded me out, I began to wander.

At first it was strange when people on the street would thank me and congratulate me for saving Haley, especially given how little attention her disappearance had gotten in the media. After the first few handshakes though, it started to feel pretty awesome. Especially when they started giving me free stuff. The diner cook at The Soda Fountain of Youth, this burned-out surfer dude with a grin on his face that said he never graduated high school and a pair of drumsticks jammed in his belt, gave me a bacon cheeseburger and fries on the house.

BILLY, his ketchup-splattered nametag read.

"The world doesn't have enough cute cheerleaders in it. Good on *you* for saving one of the last of 'em, Superman," he said.

I tried to pay for it, I really did, but he wouldn't let me. The same thing happened later when the guy who ran the hobby shop, Foxfire Collectibles, sent me on my way with a model kit for a P51 Mustang and some comic books. And when I stuck my head in The Prospero Museum of Unnatural History just to see what it was like, they wouldn't let me leave until I'd signed their guestbook and taken a complimentary t-shirt. I grabbed "PROSPERO—PROUD HOME OF 'THE HOOK!'" with a picture of a metal hook hanging from a car door. Compared to the other t-shirts of urban legends that Prospero claimed to be the "Proud Home of," it seemed the most benign.

The attention was fun while it lasted. I won't try and be noble and say I had to suffer through it, though, when I heard that they were finally going to release Haley from the medical center, I was glad to pass the torch. She was the survivor; she deserved the attention.

According to my mom, Haley barely remembered what had happened to her. The best the police could figure, she had sleepwalked out of her room and had probably gotten lost in the nearby woods. She survived off of whatever she could find, probably finding an abandoned hermit's shack—if the blanket was any indication—before wandering back to town. They said it was a miracle, but they sounded unsurprised.

After all, Prospero's supposed to be a town of miracles.


The night she was released from the medical center, we all went out to dinner at The Grey Lodge, which was the nicest restaurant in town by default since they served steaks and were known to have lobster on occasion. While I wouldn't exactly call a place with faux-log cabin walls covered in taxidermy animal heads and what I'm guessing was nineteenth century brothel art fancy, it did have pretty decent food.

Of course, since Haley was the latest town miracle, what felt like the entire town showed up to join us.

The week in the med center had done wonders for her. Though she was still underweight and had some odd cuts and bruises, she looked less skeletal than she had when I first found her and had a nice glow whenever she smiled. Wearing a new sundress, she was actually quite pretty. Though a little jumpy, she did keep a pleasant smile on as she talked with everyone who came to see her. Every so often she would shoot a nervous glance my way, as if asking me if I'd been getting the same treatment. I would respond with a slight shrug of confirmation.

With a line of people trying to catch her attention, I guess I should have figured that those who couldn't reach her would come to me instead.

On my way back from the bathroom, a powerful arm wrapped around my shoulder and pulled me off to the side. The arm belonged to a short, wiry, middle-aged man with a mane of greasy black hair that fell below his shoulders and a pale, perpetually uncomfortable-looking face, who looked up at me with a smile that lacked any trace of sincerity. Even if he hadn't been wearing sunglasses at night, his breath loudly proclaimed that he had been drinking heavily recently.

"Oh, hello!" he said in a thick, strange accent. His vowels all stretched out too long for me to guess exactly where he was from. "You are the hero boy? That is so fantastic! How are you? I am Alexei Smith, the drama teacher. Please, let me buy you a drink!"

"I'm sixteen," I said. I tried to get out from underneath his arm, but he was surprisingly strong for his size.

"Oh, that is too bad! I used to be sixteen once! Haley is such a gifted and beautiful girl, I was afraid when she was gone that she would not audition for my show!"

I took the bait, "What show is that?

"My Youth Shakespeare program show! We do it in the park at the end of every summer. This year is *Titus Andronicus,* it will be a laughing riot! She is a good actress, one of my best, I think. It would not be complete without her there. You should try out, too. Very handsome you are; you must be a great actor!"

He twitched faintly, darting his head to the side and whipping me in the face with his hair. He then looked at me with an apologetic smirk.

"I am sorry. I must flee so I can talk to a man about a mustache!" He laughed.

I didn't know how to respond to that, so I just said, "Well, I hope that goes well."

"That's the idea!" He laughed as he wandered away into the crowd.

"Welcome to Prospero," I muttered to myself. Before I was certain whether I meant that as a joke or an insult, another hand grabbed me by the wrist.

It was Haley. She looked up at me with a forced smile.

Through her teeth, she said, "Please, get me out of here."

"Are you all right?" I asked.

"I won't be if another person asks me that exact same question," she said. "I'm tired of everyone wanting to talk to me. I just want to go home. Is that too much to ask?"

"No. No, it isn't," I replied. Relief flooded her face as she dragged me back to our table.

"Mom?" she said, "I'm getting real tired. Do you think it'd be okay if Ben and I walked home now?"

Concern flooded Aunt Christine's face. "I'll get the car ready."

"No!" Haley cried. Catching herself in the outburst, she put a hand to her chest and giggled. "What I mean is, I've been cooped up in that med center room for so long, I could just use some fresh air."

Her mother looked skeptical; I couldn't blame her. Haley had had quite a bit of fresh air recently.

Looking desperate, Haley took my hand in hers. "I just need to be out, and I'd like a minute to thank Ben for saving my life. I know if he's there with me, nothing bad can happen."

She was laying it on pretty thick, but her mother bought it readily enough. She smiled knowingly at both of us before waving us on our way through the crowd.

When we stepped outside, she let go of my hand. She smiled as she twirled around daintily, enjoying her freedom.

"Thank you, for that," she said.

"No problem," I replied.

"I'm just sick and tired of people asking me how I'm doing, telling me I can talk to them if I need someone to talk to, or asking me what happened while I was missing," she said.

Putting my hands in my pockets, I laughed a bit, "Well, since I was gonna ask you the first and third things you mentioned, I guess it'll be a pretty quiet walk."

She laughed, "Well, at least it's a short walk."

The house was only five blocks away. She was a bit unsteady on her feet. I had to catch her once by the elbow, balancing her. This time her smile was real.

"Thanks," she said. She looked at me, biting her lip. "So . . . the second thing?"

"Only if you want to," I said. "I've been told I'm easy to talk to, so if you want to, the offer's there. If you don't want to, that's cool, too."

She wrapped her arms around herself protectively and said nothing. There was laughter up ahead. I could see a few men standing by a car under a light across the street, talking and drinking. As we walked around a fire hydrant on the edge of the narrow sidewalk, I made sure to switch sides with Haley so I was closer to the men. Just in case.

When she dropped her arms, she snapped with a ferocity I did not know she had in her.

"I'm tired of people telling me what happened. They're just guessing, they're just trying to put together a picture that fits in a situation that doesn't so *they* can move on. There are *two months* of my life missing. I missed the last month of my sophomore year of high school, and nobody seems to care. It's all just, 'Well, we're glad you're back. Now let's pretend nothing happened and get on with our lives.' I get the feeling that nobody *wants* to know what happened to me. They don't want to know if I was kidnapped, or if I was crazy, or if . . ."

She was silent for too long. I tried to fill the void, "So you don't remember anything?"

She shuddered. "Bits and pieces, but none of it makes sense. I'm not even sure if any of that is real."

She fought through a sudden wave of tears, covering her face and breathing heavily. She was strong. Stronger than I'd have thought someone could be after going through whatever it was she had gone through. I put my arm around her shoulders. She looked up at me and started laughing.

"Way to make a guy feel special," I said, trying to laugh it off to cover my bruised pride.

"I'm sorry," Haley laughed. "It's just . . . if my mom saw us, she'd be going nuts. After what you did, I think she's already planning our kids' names right now."

I wanted to laugh with her, but a sharp exclamation followed by dead silence from across the street caught my attention. The three men had stopped laughing and were standing as still as mannequins, staring at us as we passed. Two were covered in shadow, one wearing a hoodie, another a postman's uniform, their faces obscured. The third was unquestionably Alexei Smith. They made no move to follow us as we passed and began laughing again after we got a good distance away. It was creepy.

Haley, thankfully, had not seen them.

"I just don't think I could handle that," Haley continued. I realized that she'd been talking the entire time I was watching the men stare at us.

"I'm sorry?" I said.

"I just don't want to be with anyone right now. Before any of this happened, I'd just gotten out of a bad relationship, and the way I am right now, I really don't want to try for anything. Does that make sense?"

I nodded noncommittally. Haley looked at me nervously, quickly adding, "It's not that I don't think you're a nice guy, it's just—"

"Relax," I said. "Don't worry about it. I came up here to go to your funeral. It's not like I was expecting anything more from you. I'm gonna be stuck here for a while, it looks like, probably in your house, and probably with both of our moms under one roof. Even if we did want to make a go of dating, it would be—"

"—weird," she finished.

"Yeah, weird," I agreed, wanting to add, *But not as weird as this town.*

We could see the lights of the house coming up. Our moms had probably driven back while we walked. This moment of peace would be over soon.

"Are you okay with being friends for now?" she asked, looking up at me hopefully. As if for dramatic impact, she pulled herself out from under my arm and held out her hand (though it was hard to miss the emphasis she had put on *"for now").*

For a brief, fleeting moment that I couldn't understand, I remembered that strange girl, Mina, I'd met at the memorial service. I thought about the words she'd written, "THAT ISN'T HALEY," on the back of one of those gaudy, giant programs they'd given out to everyone. Thinking of that program, sitting somewhere on the desk of the guest room I was sleeping in, I vowed to throw it away once I settled in for the night.

I took Haley's hand in mine and gave it a firm shake. "Friends."

# 4.

## NEW APPROACH

### Mina

Of all the things I have to do to protect the humans of Prospero, explaining myself to potential new assets is easily the one for which I have the least talent, the one task that makes me more nervous and prone to stalling than any other.

Usually, I prefer to wait until I can get my hands on a fresh Creature Splinter from the woods before making my pitch. People find it harder to brush me off while they're watching a furry, oversized dragonfly trying to grow itself human arms and legs, but such things are hard to find, harder to catch, and hardest to keep alive long enough for any particular use. The threats against Ben, and the return of the thing I will henceforth refer to as "Haley," purely for convenience's sake, had forced me to move up my schedule considerably.

The bug in the program I'd given Ben hadn't died yet, and he hadn't thrown it away, or at least, if he had, he hadn't emptied the guestroom wastebasket since, so at least I had a muffled ear in his room at the Perkins house. Haley had finally left her purse unattended in a locker behind the park amphitheater long enough for me to fit another temp bug in her wallet, download a good teen tracker app to her phone, and get Ben's number out of it—it still wasn't nearly enough.

My network is small at the best of times, and some of the members leave town for summer vacation. Fewer ECNSs in Prospero means fewer people to worry about, but it also leaves any work that comes up to Aldo, Billy, and me. Mostly me.

Keeping Ben accounted for every minute of every day without his help was costing me an unsustainable amount of sleep.

For his own safety, he needed to know.

I stood for a while outside one of the windows of the Soda Fountain of Youth, preparing myself.

It was nice, knowing it was a human sitting inside, laughing at Billy's jokes. It was nice not worrying about whether the way Ben folded his long limbs might include slightly unnatural angles, whether they had the ability to twist into new shapes at a moment's notice. He had what Aldo had always referred to, not so affectionately, as "heartthrob hair," exactly the color of wood varnish, cut short up to the middle of his ears and left just long enough on top to fall into his eyes.

I'd never had an opinion on the style one way or another before, but, on him, it gave me the bizarre, persistent urge to brush it behind his ears with my fingers and then staple it there. Or something.

Human.

I wanted him to stay that way, an ECNS, forever. He was *my* asset. I wanted him for *my* side. I didn't want to have to cross him off the list and wonder if it had been my attention that had brought theirs on him, too; and most of all, I very earnestly didn't want to end up having to kill him.

That made it just a little easier to open the Soda Fountain's front door, walk up to the booth Ben currently had to himself, and say the most straightforward thing I could think of.

"May I join you?"

Ben froze when he looked up at me, and for a moment I thought he might bolt for the door.

"Um . . . okay."

I slid onto the bench opposite him and grabbed one of the menus from the clip on the wall, partly to look normal, partly so I could rearrange the letters of the menu items in my head while I gathered together what I'd been planning to say. Somehow it had already gotten muddled on the way from the door to the booth.

Ben still had a menu open in front of him as well, and he showed signs of discomfort with the silence after just a few seconds.

"So . . . uh . . . what do you recommend here?" he asked.

"You come here a lot," I noted, trying to arrange my argument. "I thought you'd know what you preferred by now."

In a town as small as Prospero, a person's movements, particularly those of a recent local hero, aren't exactly secret, even to those who pay less attention than I do, but judging by the look on Ben's face, this wasn't a good start. I picked a recommendation at random to try to fix it.

"Do you like cherries?" I asked.

"I don't *dislike* cherries," Ben responded.

Right on cue, Billy's hazy voice called out to us.

"Hey, what's happening?" He wiped his hands on his stained apron as he walked up. Seeing us both at the table, he smiled broadly. "Jailbait and Superman? How'd you two get together?" His eyes were more red-rimmed than usual. It was hard to tell if he was feigning ignorance of my plans better than usual or if he'd really forgotten.

"He calls you Jailbait?" Ben smirked.

"Billy enjoys nicknames," I explained. "He finds them amusing."

"And Mina can sometimes use reminding that she's not a withered old cat lady just yet," Billy added.

"We're here on business," I cut off this counter-productive thread of conversation. "Get me a Triple Chocolate Malt, Loch-Ness sized, double shot of espresso, dark and white chocolate chips, no milk chocolate, extra whipped cream, and a Cherry Timewarp for Ben here."

"You know him?" Ben asked as soon as Billy retreated to the kitchen.

I nodded and seized the topic. At least this was something we had in common. "Billy Crane. He's part of my Network. My driver, mainly, but he does a little bit of everything. He owns a van, and he drives it less negligently than you'd think. He's also good at breaking things, fixing things, he's a competent drummer, and he's studying to become a licensed hypnotist."

"Hypnotist?" Ben asked, poorly suppressing a smile.

"He insists it's a good way of meeting girls at parties," I explained.

"Does it work?" he asked.

"If I ever go to one, I'll tell you. He can also buy alcohol, if that matters to you."

"No, not really," Ben laughed.

"Good. This isn't a place where you'll want to dull your reaction time."

Billy returned from the kitchen and, with one of his standard flourishes of ill-conceived humor, arranged two straws in the malt he set in front of me.

Once he'd gone again, Ben eyed the bright red, fizzy, pink whipped cream-adorned Cherry Timewarp skeptically for a moment before taking a sip. The set of his jaw muscles when he swallowed it didn't suggest that he found it anything less than pleasant.

In any case, he continued to drink from it, watching me warily but expectantly. I had to get to the point.

"Do you believe in UFOs?" I asked.

This caused Ben to inhale some of the Cherry Timewarp and slip into a discouraging coughing fit.

The fact that he'd developed such a fondness for the Soda Fountain of Youth had been one of the few good signs since he'd arrived in Prospero. It's one of the only places that actually cashes in on the town's paranormal reputation, with its jukebox full of 50s sci-fi TV soundtracks and collection of framed UFO photographs and stuffed cryptids. Little of it had anything to do with the truth, but I'd thought that maybe if it held any appeal for him, it might be a good place to start.

"What?" he finally choked.

"In aliens? Bigfoot? Angels? Ghosts?" I tried.

When Ben could breathe again, he answered, quite firmly, "No."

"No to one, or no to all?"

"No to all," he said. "If any of those things existed, I think you'd probably find one stuffed and mounted in the Smithsonian somewhere."

So much for that angle. I took a spoonful of my malt and concentrated on crunching the frozen chocolate chips for a moment to keep my head clear.

"Okay," I said. "I was hoping for a frame of reference you might understand. Instead, I'll just cut to the chase."

"I like the chase. I can totally cut to that," he said, with the nervous kind of smile people wear when they're trying to calm someone down. It didn't do much for me.

I took one long draw from the malt, and then I told him.

"For more than a hundred years, Prospero has been ground zero for an invasion from another world of shape-shifting beings who seek to take over our minds, bodies, and lives, and there is every possibility they have designs on the world as well."

For some reason, the Theremin riff that emanated from the jukebox at that moment seemed to amuse Ben.

"The so-called miracles and monsters of this town are mere side effects of this invasion. When things go according to their plan, it's almost impossible to notice they exist, but sometimes there are accidents, sometimes they experiment, and sometimes things leak through from the other world that aren't supposed to. The abnormal activity in Prospero has gotten some attention from the UFO chasers and crypto enthusiasts of the world, as you can see."

I gestured around the Soda Fountain's convenient décor.

"But instead of welcoming the publicity and the tourist dollars that come with it, like Roswell, Point Pleasant, and Port Henry, the Prospero Town Council does its best to suppress any information about anything out of the ordinary. It does this because it has been collaborating with the invaders, possibly from the very beginning. In exchange for their silence and their help procuring humans to be copied and replaced, its members are protected and kept in their positions of wealth and power. I have made it my life's work to combat these creatures and all that they do. Many have come before me. I'm here to invite you to join the fight."

I sat back and waited for the answer. I could tell a moment before it came that I wasn't going to like it.

Ben laughed.

"You think this is funny," I said as agreeably as I could.

"Well, this is some kind of a big joke, right?" he asked, barely suppressing his laughter. "I mean, there are hidden cameras filming this somewhere, right? And at any minute they're gonna just jump out and say, 'Hey, you're on Monsterville: The Reality Series, please sign this release form so we can make you look like a jackass on network TV.' Right?"

"I don't have any hidden cameras here," I told him,

calmly, seriously, the only way I'd ever convinced anyone of anything. "And I assure you, this is no joke."

He stopped smiling. "You . . . you really believe this stuff, don't you?"

"The way UFO chasers 'believe' things on faith alone? No," I told him. "I've *seen* it."

"And of all the people in the world you could share it with, you decided to tell me?" he asked.

"You were a logical choice. Almost everyone in town is potentially a Splinter—"

"Splinter?"

"Not my term," I explained, "but it fits. From what I've studied of the resistors who came before me, that's been the word for these things for at least fifty years. But as I was saying, anyone, and I mean *anyone* in town, or who has even visited, is potentially a Splinter and cannot be trusted completely."

"Well then," he said, "I hate to break it to you, but I have been to this town, many times before. How do you know I'm not one of them?"

This part would require some finesse. I hoped I had enough to spare.

"Because the last time you were here, you were eleven years old, and unless you were an early bloomer, they couldn't have replaced you then," I said.

Ben's fingers went whiter than they already were against the cold glass of the Cherry Timewarp. Again, it looked very much like he might run, and again he didn't.

"How do you know when I was last here?"

I was honest. To a point. "*Status Update: July 9th,*

*3:46 p.m. Ben Pastor is going to be attending a funeral up in Monsterville, USA. First time we've been up there in five years. Hopefully the last.* If you don't want the world knowing your life story, you really shouldn't be posting it on—"

"Thanks for the tip," he stopped me, looking as annoyed as he did relieved, but he still made no move to get up. "So you looked me up because you didn't know me, and because of that you thought you could trust me?"

"Yes."

"Has anyone ever told you you should get your head examined?"

"Many times," I said. They had, and the conversations had never been productive. "Are you prepared to discuss anything with me other than my mental health?"

Ben needed a few seconds to consider this. "Yes. Fine. I'm listening. You want me to help you fight shape-shifting aliens, and—"

"I never said—"

"Okay, okay, you never called them aliens," he backtracked. "Suppose I believe you. What exactly do you want to do?"

A helpful question. "First of all, I want you to be on your guard," I said. "The Splinters have taken a particular interest in you, and with you living in the same house as one of them—"

"You mean Haley." Ben set his now empty glass down with a *clink,* all helpful inquisitiveness instantly closed off. "You're saying that while Haley was gone, she was actually being transformed into some kind of . . . pod person out in those woods?"

"She's a Probable Splinter, yes," I said. "A very, very Probable Splinter, actually, and the process does seem to be executed in the woods, although I haven't been able to pinpoint the location."

Ben glanced around for eavesdroppers. A good instinct, one that could be channeled into usefulness, if he'd allow it.

"I can't believe that," he said.

"Can't, or won't?"

"Does it matter? I've known Haley for my entire life. I can't say we're close, but she *is* my friend. I can believe that something terrible, something nobody wants to talk about, happened to her. Maybe it's even something involving someone in this town, someone connected, someone who could afford to keep this covered up, I don't know. I believe that whatever it was caused enough stress to make Haley want to forget it as some kind of defense mechanism. But the idea that she's been replaced by some kind of body-snatching monster is . . . impossible."

"Impossible?" I repeated. "Maybe on a global scale it's *improbable,* but you've been willing enough to believe more improbable things than that recently. How many people can you name, real people, not characters on TV or in movies, who've disappeared, only to reappear *two months* later with no ill effects other than some scratches and a convenient dose of amnesia?"

I could hardly believe it. I thought I'd lost him after the reaction Haley's name had gotten, but something in what he'd seen of Prospero so far must have already brought him closer to my line of thinking than he was letting on because this actually made him look thoughtful. I drank from the malt to keep my focus while he processed it. Finally he asked the question I'd been hoping to hear most of all.

"Maybe . . . maybe if you just had some *proof* of something paranormal, something more than this . . ." He waved his arms at the pictures and the stuffed Jackalope in the case behind him. "Maybe—"

"I do! Not about Haley personally, but I do!"

It wasn't the proof I liked to have, the living, breathing kind that I could put in front of someone at almost any level of denial and have them consider it, but when people *ask,* it's different. When people *ask,* sometimes videos will do the trick. I'd loaded my best one, the one I'd captured of Alexei glitching up when a stage light fell on him a couple years earlier, onto my best phone for just this purpose. I hurried to queue it up and passed it across to Ben.

He watched, a little skeptically, but he watched, and I watched the reflection in the Jackalope case over his shoulder. The light would fall at fifteen seconds in, and as the time approached, I found myself much more anxious than any person who's actually *fought* Splinters should ever be about anything else.

At four seconds to go, the phone vibrated. A text message. Before I could even think of snatching it back, I caught the reversed words scrolling along the upper menu, over the video, next to Aldo's name.

*Pics from morning shift. He's been visiting your Splinter-dad's shop again.*

Ben's eyes narrowed, and—with an information-need that I had to respect, as inconvenient as it was—he swiped the message open, filling the screen with the latest candid shots of himself.

After a few seconds of very uncomfortable silence, he started with the easy part of the message. "You think your own *dad* is a pod person?"

"A Splinter," I said. It was time to start getting terms straight. "And I'm effectively certain he is. I saw him."

"Jeez, do you think the worst of *everyone?*"

"No," I said. "There's Billy, Aldo, uh, a few you haven't met, and . . . you."

He was still scanning through the photos.

"Tell me," he said, "exactly how sick a stalker are you?"

He was angry. I'd been the object of a lot of anger, but for some reason this time it made my stomach twist in on itself so hard it hurt.

"I'm not sick."

"How long have you been following me?" he asked.

The hurt in my stomach was filling up my brain, not in the helpful, packing peanut way. "I needed to know you were—"

"Never mind." He put the phone down, opened his wallet, and slammed what little was in it (twice as much as the drinks and tip demanded) on the table without looking at it. "Don't come to me again, Mina," he said slowly and clearly, stepping out of the booth. "And I don't care what you think she is. Stay the *hell* away from Haley."

## 5.

## THE USED CAR PRINCE
### Ben

"Are you all right?" Haley asked as we walked down Main Street, shopping bags hanging lazily at our sides. She'd caught me looking over my shoulder again. I told myself not to be so jumpy, so *paranoid,* but it was hard not to be.

"Yes," I lied. When that didn't feel right, I quickly amended, "No . . . I don't know."

"Do you want to talk about it?" she asked.

"No," I said firmly. Anyone else would have pushed the point, tried for more detail, but after all she had been through, Haley had gained a great appreciation for people not constantly asking her how she was doing. At the moment, I liked it.

I looked again, then forced my eyes forward, cursing myself. She was out there, somewhere, and I just had a sick feeling in my gut that she was watching me. She'd already forced her way into my life, she already knew more about me than I felt comfortable with her knowing, and I wasn't entirely sure she wasn't insane. But there were enough points hiding in what she'd said to make me paranoid.

I was sure she would have loved that.

After I ran away from her in the Soda Fountain, I spent the next few days inside, staying away from my phone, the internet, the windows, any possible way that she could have been looking in on me. That first day I even began tearing the room up, trying to look for hidden cameras or bugs, stopping only when I realized I didn't know what hidden cameras or bugs actually looked like.

The Perkinses were another issue entirely. I got by those first few days playing sick. Mom bought that readily enough. Haley, for her part, kept a respectful distance, but I could tell she didn't entirely believe the excuse. Aunt Christine was the real problem. Haley was right about her mom trying to play matchmaker for us. Every opportunity she got, she would try to arrange family nights out at the movies, or make suggestions for new places for Haley and me to check out, saying she wanted a review. She bought me so much cold medication, vitamins, and cough syrup, I thought I'd spontaneously catch something just from being around all of the bottles.

It was Haley who finally got me out of there. She'd said her mother had been driving her crazy, and that she needed an escape.

It was not a good time for my knight-in-shining-armor problem to kick in, but it did, so I spent the better portion of the afternoon wandering around downtown Prospero helping Haley carry supplies for the upcoming block party. Being a gentleman, I offered to carry the two canvas bags that held watermelons.

I regretted this offer after the second block.

"So is this going to be a big party?" I asked.

Haley shrugged. "It's big for Prospero, if that's what you're asking. Almost everybody brings food. They set up a few games. You might even get to see Mr. Smith dressed as a clown."

She shuddered dramatically. I laughed for the first time in a couple days. It felt nice.

"Sounds like something to see," I said.

Haley chuckled. "I know he's weird, but he's mostly a nice guy when you get to know him. Have you noticed how he sometimes doesn't seem to know how things are supposed to work?"

I hadn't spent much time around him, though it seemed as decent an assessment as any. "Yeah."

"Well, the same goes for his perception of appropriate clown makeup. I think he gets most of his makeup tips from scary movies," she said. Again, I laughed and it felt great. At least it made the bags feel slightly lighter, the day slightly cooler, though a Cherry Timewarp was beginning to sound pretty good. . . .

No. I couldn't think about it. I liked the Soda Fountain of Youth, I even loved bantering with Billy, but it was one of *her* places. I couldn't chance running into her again.

"I could see how that would be a problem," I said. Then, on inspiration, I said, "You know, you're pretty easy to talk to."

Sympathetically, Haley reached down for my hand, stopping when she remembered the bags I was carrying. She smiled. I smiled back.

It was a good moment, at least until she looked up the

street. Her eyes went wide, and the smile completely disappeared. She darted away from me, then half-turned on her foot to look back.

"I don't think he saw me. You haven't seen me either today, okay?" she said urgently.

"What?" I asked.

"You haven't seen me. Please?" she said quickly, opening the door to the nearest business and jumping inside.

"All right." That was weird. I looked up the sidewalk, trying to follow her gaze. Aside from the usual street traffic, I could only see a boy on a bicycle. He was blonde, tall, and lanky in a muscular sort of way, wearing a faded t-shirt and soccer shorts. His shaggy, tied-back hair and poor attempt at starting a beard made me first take him to be lazy, but as he came closer I could see his eyes held steely focus. He almost paid me no mind, almost passed me by. I thought Haley had overreacted.

Then he saw me.

He looked away, then did a double-take, skidding sideways slightly as he turned the bike to me. Jumping it up onto the sidewalk, he smoothly lowered the kickstand and dismounted, walking my way.

"Are you Ben Pastor?" he asked, never letting up his deliberate pace. Like his eyes, his voice was focused and clear.

"Who wants to know?" I asked, suspicious.

This was all the confirmation he needed as he quickened his pace. He raised his arms. I dropped the bags to the ground, preparing to fight, hearing the sickening sound of one of the watermelons breaking open on the sidewalk.

Then he smiled a disarmingly crooked smile and wrapped his arms around me in a powerful bear hug.

"Thank you, brother. Thank you so much for saving Haley," he said, letting me go. He grabbed me by the shoulders hard, laughing. "You need anything, and I mean *anything*, you just call me up, okay? Anytime."

"Thanks?" I said, more than a little confused. I'd gotten used to strange people in this town congratulating me; they just rarely did so with this level of exuberance. He looked down at the bags I had been carrying, at the one that now steadily leaked watermelon juice.

"Oh, man. So sorry, so sorry," he said. "I'll totally get you a new one."

He reached into his pocket, pulled out a wallet, and rifled through a surprisingly large stack of cash before pulling out a business card.

"It's not necessary," I said. "I got it on sale—"

He put a hand up dramatically as he pulled a pen from his pocket and started writing on the back of the card, "Stop. I insist. You wouldn't have dropped it if it hadn't been for me. And after all you have done, it is the least I can do."

He handed me the card. The front had a jaunty cartoon of a man driving off into the sunset in a new sports car with text reading, "BRUNDLE'S AUTOS—IRWIN BRUNDLE, THE USED CAR KING—YOU'LL SAVE BUNDLES AT BRUNDLE'S!" On the back he had written what was presumably his phone number. Something about that name . . .

"That's my dad's card, but my number on the back. I know Haley's dodging me right now. With what happened, I'm totally cool with that, but just gimme a time and a place when you're free and I'll bring you a couple watermelons to make up for that one. Organic ones, the good stuff, I swear," he said with a smile.

I could tell he wouldn't back down easily, and though I wanted to politely get rid of him so I could get back to Haley (even though part of me was curious about why the son of the "Used Car King" rode a bicycle), I said, "Thanks. I didn't catch your name?"

The boy smacked himself on the forehead theatrically before offering his hand, "Sorry, brother. Kevin Brundle at your service."

A slight, cold chill went up my spine as that name fell into place.

Haley had mentioned Kevin only a few times when we had been hanging out. They had dated for almost a year, breaking up only a couple weeks before she disappeared. She said he had taken it badly. After she had been declared missing, he was one of the primary suspects. Considering the fact that his younger brother had disappeared two years ago under similar circumstances, he made a pretty good one. His dad, in addition to being the Used Car King, was also an influential member of the Town Council and got Kevin out of the Sheriff's custody after just under a week. There was no evidence against him, and nothing more than coincidence to tie him to either of the disappearances.

The boy standing before me was not entirely what I expected.

"Thanks, Kevin," I said. Looking for an easy exit, I motioned down to the bags, "Listen, I really gotta get these—"

He nodded sympathetically as he walked back to his bike. "I hear ya. Get the good one on ice, the bad one on the compost heap. Just remember, hit me up when you're free and I'll get you a new one!"

As he rode off, he waved to me. I didn't wave back. So far, Kevin wasn't the complete jerk that Haley had made him out to be, but she had known him longer and had to know more than the façade he put on to the public. I was willing to trust her judgment on Kevin.

*What if he's one of them?*

The thought came and went quickly, and I was angry at myself for letting it in at all. I thought of Mina—her damned Splinters—and I laughed.

I took the dripping bag of crushed watermelon and dropped it into the nearest trash can I could find. After inspecting the other melon I had dropped, I began looking for Haley.

I didn't have to look far.

She'd retreated into Foxfire Collectibles. It was a small shop with aisles upon aisles of model kits, comic books, magic tricks, remote control vehicles, and hundreds of ornately painted, custom-sculpted, role-playing miniatures locked in glass cases. It was hard to see Haley through the aisles, but I could hear her talking to the owner by his well-hidden desk.

" . . . I think I'm adjusting well. I mean, I'm still a little shaky, but I'm getting used to it," she said.

"Good. It was a traumatic experience. It will take some

time yet to recover, but you are doing remarkably," the owner said. "Now, I believe your escort has arrived."

"Thanks," Haley said. She walked around the aisles to greet me, followed by the middle-aged man who ran the shop. With a smartly-shaved beard, precisely-parted reddish brown hair and thin, wire-rimmed glasses, he looked more like a college professor than the man who ran the town's hobby shop. The patched jeans and black t-shirt that read, *"It Goes to 11"* were the only things that gave him away as probably the town's biggest kid-at-heart. I'd met him a few times during my walks through town.

"Hey, Ben!" he said when he saw me. "Good to see you again! Getting the newest issue of *The Gamemaster* in tomorrow. They promise someone's gonna die, but I doubt it's gonna stick."

"I'll have to pick that up," I said.

"Is he gone?" Haley asked.

"Yeah," I said. "We talked for a bit, but he left."

"I'm sorry," Haley said simply.

"Don't worry about it," I replied.

Haley looked up at the owner, smiling politely. "Thanks for letting me hide out in here, Mr. Todd."

"Anytime, Haley," he said, patting her on the shoulder.

Mr. Todd. Mina's dad. The man who raised her, the man she thought was a monster. He smiled pleasantly, *humanly*, and only then could I understand how truly crazy she was.

Haley took my arm with a smile as we exited the store. "Seems I owe you again."

Looking down into her eyes (her *human* eyes, I reminded myself again), I knew what I had to do. I had to stop thinking about Mina Todd, stop thinking about her "Splinters" and just try and enjoy the rest of this trip, however long it turned out to be. It was not a bad realization to come to.

Accepting Haley's arm, I asked, "So, where to next?"

# 6.

## Mina

I wasn't sure why Aldo had insisted on working on the new containment chamber in my room instead of his. Neither of us was in any heightened danger of abduction, I was no great assistance when it came to engineering matters, and he was even less fond of the smell of all my mismatched herb sachets than I was. I asked him four times if he and his parents were having one of the "rough patches" that usually caused him to shelter at my place, but he insisted that they weren't, and I couldn't catch even a hint of the nervous little tic in his left anterior auricular muscle that those "patches" always gave him.

I'd tried to talk him out of it. I wasn't eager for company while I was dealing with the stomach pain Ben's outburst had given me. It had since spread to my throat, and when I'd gotten home from the soda fountain, it had forced me to spend nearly three full minutes in the bathroom with the mat shoved under the door, waiting for my eyes to stop watering so I could get back to work.

I couldn't account for it. Ben wasn't the first person to

decline Network membership, and he was far from the first to call me sick. He wasn't even the first to do it while in serious, imminent danger of replacement. I wasn't due for a major hormonal fluctuation for almost two weeks, and raising my blood sugar didn't seem to have any effect.

This had me even more worried than Ben's answer itself. I'd had a similar physical reaction to just one ally before. It hadn't ended well. I would have to proceed with even more caution than I'd thought.

I'd spent the three days since my failed approach with a different recording in each ear and Ben's cell phone tracker open on the screen (it had only taken Aldo six calls to cell phone stores to find a sales rep dumb enough to activate it for us), trying to catch up on general info and keep on top of all possible threats to him at once.

"I'll need you on him on Thursday," I told Aldo when I reached it on my schedule.

"Huh?"

"Thursday," I repeated. "Haley has another follow-up appointment, so he might not be in range of her wallet. He could get separated from his phone and we wouldn't be able to hear a struggle."

"Sure. Okay. Have a look at this!"

Aldo scooted back on the carpet, away from the containment chamber, to show me his progress. I wasn't even sure why he'd chosen this week to build it. It wasn't going to be much help with the immediate Ben Pastor mission, and he'd been promising me he'd make one for months ever since my last specimen had oozed its way out through the corner of a sandwich bag before I'd gotten it home.

This chamber was about two feet cubed, made of aquarium glass, laminated and layered four panes thick, with a rubber seal from a pressure canner around the lid, rattrap springs in the hinges, steamer trunk locks soldered to the front, and a tangle of wiring threaded through it that I was sure Aldo would explain.

He was holding a universal remote and grinning.

Before explaining anything, he pulled out an LED, touched the contact points to two of the wires inside the container, and pressed a button. The "volume up" button, to be precise. The diode glowed so brightly green I thought it might burn out on the spot. Even though I hadn't been reaching for the chamber, I jerked my hand away from it.

"It's electrified?"

I have a "thing," as Aldo would put it, about electric shocks. Even when I was little before I had better things to do, I refused to use the park playground equipment because of how the static builds up on those plastic surfaces and then discharges the moment you brush against one of the metal bolts. Unfortunately, electricity also happens to be one of the only things that consistently bothers Splinters. Tasers and stun guns, both real and improvised, make up a large, vital portion of my arsenal. I keep them aimed away from me even more carefully than I do with real guns, on the rare occasions when I've been able to gain access to those.

Aldo snorted. "'Is it electrified?'" he mimicked. "In case you have to subdue one quickly without opening the lid! And you haven't seen anything yet."

He hit "play," and a set of lights embedded in the bottom

of the container started turning on and off in sequence, illuminating a selection of protective symbols hidden in the second layer of glass.

"Wait for it . . ." he told me, then slid a little farther back and pressed "pause."

The lid slammed shut with the force of, well, as I said before, a rattrap, and latched by itself.

"Just in case we ever figure out how to set a lure," he explained. "So . . . how awesome is that? Go on, you can say it."

"It's perfect," I said, and I meant it. I turned back to my schedule. "I might need you Friday, too," I told him. "And of course Saturday we've got the damned—"

"And then what?"

"I'm getting to that," I said. "Monday might be a bit of a challenge, but—"

"That's not what I mean."

I put down the schedule and turned my chair away from the desk to wait for him to speak. He preferred it when I avoided looking at other things even though that made it harder to listen. It didn't make him spit it out much faster this time, though. He just kept picking at a spot of cold solder on the side of the iron, not even looking back at me.

"We . . . we keep watching him, and we keep watching him, and we interrupt when they try to take him, and then we keep watching him, and . . . what's the plan here? I mean, I'm really, really sorry I screwed up the last—"

"It wasn't your fault," I told him for the third time. "I should have anticipated that problem."

"I'm still sorry. But it doesn't sound like he's going to

change his mind. How long are we going to keep doing this?"

I'd known this question was coming. According to my standard policies, Ben was already a loss. I didn't spend resources watching ECNSs who'd already heard my side and told me to go to hell. I couldn't force someone into the Network, and I couldn't afford to protect people who wouldn't help me protect other people. I could think of a hundred reasons why Ben was an exception, but I could also name plenty of reasons to make exceptions for people I'd already written off.

"He'll be out of Prospero soon anyway," I reminded Aldo. "This is a small battle. It's not permanent."

"You don't know that. There's no date set. It could be months. How far are you planning to take this? Until he calls the cops on us? Until we have to kidnap him and keep him in a closet to stop him from wandering into the woods? Until we have to take shifts on the roof with a sniper rifle to keep Splinters *and* humans away? I mean, I know you put in a lot to get him on the list. I know. It's a lot of time—"

"It's not about the time." I said this without thinking about it first, which, as a rule, is something I don't do. I said it without having a clue what I meant.

"So, what is it about?"

I turned back to my schedule and started factoring in rest breaks just to make a secure enough thinking space to look for an answer.

*What is it about?*

I thought about the first night of research when I'd seen Ben's face on my screen before I'd ever seen it in person.

I thought about how well I knew him, even if he never wanted to know me; how everything he wrote read as if he had been laughing as he typed it, even the parts that hinted that he might be crying, too; how he had made me want to know so badly what it was like to be where he was.

I pictured him running out in front of that car to save what he'd reasonably assumed to be another human being, and I tried to take stock of exactly what I could say I'd accomplished in the past seven years if *they* could still take all of that away from the world and there was nothing I could do about it.

In my right ear, Ben was laughing at something Haley had said that I hadn't been able to catch. The sound was so much happier than I knew how to be. The pain in my stomach was rising again, but I held it down.

I didn't want to take that away from him. I didn't *want* to force him into the Network, and if crying fits and incompletely rationalized decisions were what happened when he was around, it was probably best not to prolong our contact anyway.

But the threats against him had been delivered directly to me. If there was even a chance I was the reason, I couldn't just walk away from a very viable chance of putting things right.

"Until school starts," I proposed. "I probably got him into this. The least I can do is *try* to get him out. We maintain his protection until school makes it impractical, or until we can get him out of town—whichever comes first."

Finally, Aldo nodded his concession. "Okay. And then that's it?"

"That's it," I agreed.

My throat was feeling tight again, but before it could become seriously troubling, a name of interest came up on the feed in my left ear. My own name.

" . . . How *is* Wilhelmina, by the way? Getting enough sun? Showing any interest in . . . anything?"

I plugged the player into its speaker dock and turned up the volume.

"She's fine," my mother answered warily. "Why the sudden interest?"

"The client's concerned that you might not be the best person for the job. It is *family* law, after all."

"Put that away. Now!"

That last voice was mine.

"Here, help me get things cleaned up, get the decoys back in place."

"Now?" Aldo asked, but he helped me as he did. "But she's all the way over in Town Hall."

"The recording's two hours out of—"

I couldn't even finish explaining before the front door opened and my mother did what I knew she would, the thing she almost never did. She maneuvered her high heels down the narrow stairs, gave my door a token knock, and opened it.

I fumbled with the speaker and turned it off just before the door was finished interrupting.

"Hi, Mom," I said, pretending as usual that this was a normal interaction. I scanned the room once more to make sure we'd put everything she was most likely to comment on out of sight, remembered the other surveillance feed still in my right ear, and bobbed my head a few times as if it were music.

"Hi there," my mother said, pretending even harder. "Hi, Aldo. What are you kids up to today?"

My mother was very, very probably human, and she very probably cared about me. She used to enjoy playing chess with me when I was little, and once, when I was twelve, she blackmailed my principal into letting me switch from a class with a Probable Splinter teacher to one with a Probable Non-Splinter teacher even though she never admitted that was why.

I always did my best to remember those things when I had to see her, to remember anything other than that she had collaborated. It made it easier to play along.

"The usual," Aldo and I answered her together.

She knew what had happened to my father. I was effectively certain of that.

She knew about me, too, about what I did with my time, and even though she refused to acknowledge to my face that Splinters existed, my crusade had been a constant point of contention between us. In the beginning, she had forbidden all forms of investigation. There had been daily shouting matches, and she had wiped my hard drive more than once. Luckily for me, my brain permanently stores all the information I see or hear. Unluckily, that information often doesn't make much sense, all jumbled together in my head like that, not the way it does when I put it in front of me so I can reorganize it with my hands. My mother's early interference caused me enough delays that I'd eventually had to sniff out some of her more mundane underhanded dealings to hold over her head.

Now I was allowed to continue my work without interference on two conditions. I was pretty sure that if I failed at either, she'd take her chances with the bits of her reputation that hinged on the security of my off-site data storage.

The first condition was unspoken. I could never actually get too close to the truth. That was what the decoy leads were for, pinned all over the board whenever she might walk in on it.

The second was that I always had to make her look good any way she needed me to.

"Don't you two feel a little cooped up down here?" she asked, still wobbling on the bottom step instead of coming in, probably less out of manners than the desire to preserve the chemically sterilized fragrance of her crisply ironed suit and more-crisply-ironed hair.

Aldo was about to give the normal response, that there was no reason to feel cooped up when there was no reason to go anywhere else, but I knew where the question was leading. I tried to make it easier for all of us and followed her lead.

"Yeah, actually, we were just going for a ride, probably going to grab some tacos from that place across from Town Hall. Want us to bring something back?"

*Look at me, Prospero!* I prepared to proclaim silently from the seat of my bike. *Look at the happy, well-adjusted spawn of Diana Todd, enjoying a wholesome, carefree evening with a real, living, human companion! See me laugh too loudly! See me babble inanely! See me not obsess over the world's impending doom at all!*

Mom wasn't Aldo's biggest fan, but she usually hid it well. She thought it looked odd for me to spend so much time with someone two years younger than myself, but compared with the time I spent with Billy or with no one at all, Aldo was her favorite option.

"Sure, just let me get you some cash." She dug through her purse, one of an inconveniently large rotating set, and pulled out enough to feed the three of us plus Dad for two nights with a generous tip, even without accounting for my mother's freakishly small appetite, but she didn't give it to me. "I had a thought," she said.

I waited for it.

"Irwin was just saying how much harder it's been this year to get people together to get the block party off the ground."

I tried not to let my panic show and kept waiting.

"He's worried it's a dying tradition. I said how silly that is, but I thought it might be fun for you two to help out, show off your . . ." She glanced awkwardly around the room. "Town pride. Pick up the torch for the old generation."

I couldn't go to the block party.

Ben was going to the block party.

My mother kept smiling, one hand holding the money, the other toying with the brush of the broom I'd secured back over the door.

"Um," Aldo tried to help me. "We were sort of thinking—"

"That's okay," she told him. Only him. "I just thought

Mina might like the company, but I'm sure she'll manage. She'd never make a liar out of me."

Mom kept smiling.

I had to go to the block party.

"No, it's fine," said Aldo. "I'm there."

"Wonderful!"

For a while, we all stood there, Aldo and me waiting for her to leave so we could figure out how we were going to pull this off, and then I remembered the money. She was finally holding it out to be taken. On top of the party, she was still going to make us waste an evening biking across town. I reached out and took it, already planning out the equipment I was going to buy Aldo with every cent of the change.

## 7.

## THE BLOCK PARTY
### Ben

The McMurdo Avenue Block Party was a lot bigger than I'd expected. I figured they would close off a street, set up a few tables of potluck food, maybe even have someone rig up a few speakers to a boom box to get some music going. Simple stuff. What I hadn't accounted for was that, like many small towns, Prospero is generally starved for entertainment, and when the opportunity for some fun presents itself, they'll take it with gusto.

The party itself stretched for two blocks, the ends cut off by parked police cars. The first block (the only one actually on McMurdo Avenue) was lined with card tables covered in more food than I had ever seen. It seemed everybody in town had brought at least one dish in a show of neighborly competition, each trying to outdo the last. The street itself was filled with rows of picnic tables where it seemed half of the town milled about, feasting.

The second block was an odd combination of a farmer's market and a low-budget carnival. Most of the major businesses and many local farmers had booths selling everything from fresh ears of corn to poorly-printed t-shirts. A few more booths held some basic games, a BB gun shooting gallery, a "Dunk the Mayor" booth, a face painting pavilion, and a fortune-teller. The intersection between the two streets had a crude stage flanked by large speakers in the middle of it. Signs by the stage promised a couple of local bands and a magician from two towns over as entertainment.

It wasn't the grandest party the world had ever seen, not by a long shot, but it was what I needed. It felt normal.

Mom and Aunt Christine mingled with some of the other people from town down by the potluck, so after Haley and I had taken our share from the buffet, we wandered down through the ad hoc carnival.

Haley treated me to a caramel apple that looked almost as big as my head, and I did my best to return the favor by winning her the biggest teddy bear imaginable at the shooting gallery. I was one shot off from the big prize, but she cooed approvingly all the same at the stuffed green bunny I won her.

It felt good to be out with Haley. More and more I found her smile real and unforced, though I knew she still had her bad days. There were some nights I could hear her having bad dreams in the next room, tossing and turn-ing, occasionally crying out in fear. She would always look embarrassed the next morning, but I never questioned her. If she wanted to talk, I'd be there. Until then, I was happy just to hang out.

That happy feeling did not last long.

We were walking past the Dunk the Mayor booth when

I got that feeling again. Like I was being watched. I turned around, expecting to see a flash of red disappearing behind a booth.

Instead, I found we had an audience. There were three of them, standing around the Dunk the Mayor booth, a stout, balding man with glasses, a tall, skeletally-thin man in a Hawaiian shirt, and a cold-looking middle-aged woman who tried to look casual and only pulled off business-casual. The portly man in the dunking booth was soaking wet but still managed to look almost jovial. At least, I think he was *trying* to look jovial because, much like the other three, he stared at us with a look on his face that might have been fear.

Haley turned, saw our audience and waved to them cheerfully. The men waved back, though they clearly didn't want to. The woman just stood there, observing us, appraising.

Like a bird of prey.

"Who are they?" I asked.

Haley laughed. "Just some of our Town Council."

The woman looked familiar to me. Something in the eyes. When she moved slightly and the fading sunlight illuminated the faint, reddish highlights of her dark hair, I realized she just reminded me of Mina.

Great.

"Why are they staring at me?" I asked.

"At us?" Haley replied. She looked thoughtful for a moment, then shook her head, "I wouldn't worry about them. They're harmless."

She grabbed me by the arm and dragged me to look at

one of the Farmer's Market booths. For now, at least, she was carefree. Happy. I wanted to be with her, I wanted to have fun again.

But those eyes . . . Mina's paranoid ramblings . . . they just wouldn't go away.

## Mina

"They're at the southwest corner," Aldo informed me. "Moving east one stall . . . two stalls. The way's wide open."

I kept wanting to tie my hair back, or at least put it behind my ears, but even my smallest Bluetooth was as obvious as an old-fashioned hearing aid, and I needed to keep it out of sight as much as possible.

Aldo often told me that if my mother and I had only one thing in common, it was our knack for precise, detailed instructions. He never meant it as a compliment, of course, but I was grateful to her for not making me guess what would satisfy her.

I was to arrive in time for the late cosmetic phase of setup, spend no more than a hundred and fifty dollars, and not leave before 8:30 or before I had been seen by a minimum of five Council members or immediate family members of Council members and made small talk at every one of her list of the dozen most gossipy vendor booths.

There was just one I'd really been putting off all day. It wasn't as if he was going to try to abduct me in the middle of a crowded event, but small talk with Alexei Smith still wasn't something I could exactly look forward to, even by the standard of my mother's favors. The logical part of me wished all human Splinters could be so glitchy and obvious, but that didn't stop his obviousness from turning my stomach. Mom had hardly made an excuse for why I had to see him, something about his influence on the children of the Council—we both knew the real reason. As a person, he was nobody, but as a Splinter he was somebody, and that meant, as far as my mother and the rest of the Council were concerned, his opinion mattered.

At least getting his attention was easy. All I had to do was walk past the information booth of the Prospero Society of Theatrical Recreation without trying to hide. He took it from there.

"Oh, hello, Meeenaaah!" he dragged out my name like a tongue twister, throwing his arm around my shoulders. "I hoped you would stop by!"

The way he said "stop by," like he was expecting some kind of congratulations for mastering a non-literal turn of phrase, made me even more aware (if that was possible) that it was not a human hand squeezing my shoulder. I smiled at him and did my best not to shudder.

"You were?"

"I have to talk to you," he said very seriously, "about trying out for the troupe! I cannot give special treatment, you know thaaaat, but I fear you are the only one in all of town who can be the true spirit of Miraaaanda!"

The society's traditional production of *The Tempest*, performed every January 3rd, rain or shine, workday or weekend, on what Alexei falsely believed to be the anniversary of the founding of Prospero, was easily the worst of its regularly scheduled performances—which was surprising considering how much practice most of the cast had. The last Miranda had just graduated out.

A couple of Alexei's students stood to one side, a little more than ten feet apart, tossing an empty water bottle back and forth. I tried to focus on it and wished, not for the first time, for a bit of Aldo's mental exclusivity.

"Really?" My smile was becoming painful. "I thought you were going to use Haley for that."

"Oh, no!" he said. "She is much too tall!"

Such was the nature of Alexei Smith's theatrical wisdom.

"Oh." I couldn't think of a small talk reply to that.

The water bottle hit the ground at our feet.

"Twenty-five yet?" Alexei asked his students.

"Nineteen," a girl answered.

At least it was a conversation starter.

"Twenty-five what?" I asked.

"Oh, twenty-five catches, of coooouuurse! You should definitely try. Twenty-five is the perfect number!"

I didn't ask what made it perfect.

"He's on in five minutes," Aldo reminded me. "Are you going?"

I'd added just one thing to my agenda for the day without my mother's prompting. Billy's band was playing from seven until eight, and I knew how glad he'd be to have at least two people there who'd cheer no matter how bad it was, even if only for the first half.

"I guess so. Is it safe?" I muttered back to Aldo.

Around anyone else, I might have been a little more discreet, but Alexei and his minions didn't exactly have the upper hand when it came to acting normal.

"Oh, it is very saaaafe, Meeenaaah! Look!" He picked up the bottle and tapped me on the head with it to show how harmless it was, as if he thought I might not have seen a plastic water bottle before.

"Um, yes, that's okay though," I said, backing out of the booth toward the bandstand just across the way, my small talk successfully made. My goodbye might not have satisfied Mom if she'd seen it, but I was sure it was more polished than anything Alexei had ever done.

## Ben

As we slowly made our way down the farmer's market stalls, I caught a familiar face I'd rather not have. I sighed. I hated unfinished business.

Haley was looking intently at a stall that sold handmade bead crafts. I asked her if she was all right for the moment, and then made as stealthy a path to Kevin Brundle's Earth Brownies as I could.

There was no line at his booth. I assumed the words "All-Natural," "Organic," and "Proceeds Go to Charity" written on the booth had something to do with that, or maybe it was the fact that his brownies looked more like granola bars than brownies. All the same, the guy had brought by three massive watermelons this afternoon and refused to let me pay him back. I figured buying a few brownies (even if I had to throw them away later) would even out our books some.

He saw me walking up and smiled. "Ben, brother, what's happening?"

"Not much, just taking in the sights," I said.

"Enjoying our fair town's hospitality?" he asked.

Thinking about Mina and those people in the Town Council staring at me, I almost said no. Then realizing I'd be better off lying, I said, "Yeah."

Kevin nodded with a knowing smile, "I know it's a small town with a lot of small minds . . ."—he waved at his nearly full display and nearly empty money jar for emphasis—"but it's got its charms."

"Look, I just wanted to thank you for—"

He held up a hand. "As I have said before and will say again if necessary, we're cool. My fault entirely."

Okay, time to try a different approach, "Well, can I at least buy some brownies?"

He brightened at that. "Certainly, brother."

He talked at length about how awesome and good for Mother Earth the brownies were, and I dutifully nodded as if I were interested. In the end, I bought a bag of six for ten dollars and took a free one "for the road" at Kevin's insistence. To my surprise, they actually almost tasted like brownies.

It was as he was packing up the brown paper bag that he finally asked, "So, does Haley talk about me much?"

Again, figuring lying would be the best approach, I said, "Some, but not really in detail."

He nodded, a little sad. "I wouldn't think so. We had something real good there for a while. I've made my mistakes, I'm not gonna deny that, but I'm not bad, not like everyone thinks. I would've taken care of her."

He sighed. "Be careful, brother. She's one of the good

ones. She knows how to make you feel more special than anyone in the world. If you lose that, sometimes, maybe, it's better not to know what you're missing."

"Why are you telling me this?" I asked.

He shrugged and laughed slightly. "Because I want you to know what you might be getting yourself into. Because, despite all this, I don't think I'm ready to give up on her. Call me a masochist, but I still love her. If you want your chance with her, I will not stop you, but if you don't, I'm gonna try my best to salvage something."

There was no polite way to get out of there, not that I was sure I wanted to be polite to him at that point.

"Thanks for the brownies," I said, snatching up the bag and stalking away.

"Anytime, brother," I heard him calling behind me.

I walked out of sight as quickly as I could and tossed the bag of brownies into the nearest trash can before catching up with Haley at the bead crafts booth.

## Mina

I cheered appropriately hard at the first gap in the band's music, though their tinny, staticky sound system and rudimentary understanding of harmony and rhythm made it nearly impossible to distinguish one "song" from the next. Billy winked at me from behind his drum kit, with their logo and name printed on the front of it. The Twist Endings, they called themselves. He was a very good drummer, though I wouldn't have known it if I'd only heard him play with the rest of the band at events like this.

I'd successfully smiled and applauded for nearly twenty minutes before I felt someone standing closer than was necessary behind me. I reached into my bag and secured my hand over a flamethrower before turning to check who it was.

It was Aldo.

We both hurried to hang up our phones before they could get close enough together to convert the awful music into even more awful feedback.

"They're far enough away?" I asked.

"A seven minute walk with no reason to hurry," he confirmed instantly. "And not moving, last I saw."

I double-checked the time. A seven minute walk made a collision acceptably improbable, under normal circumstances. With Ben involved, I would have preferred impossible, but I let it go, rather than try to find a reason he should make circumstances anything other than normal.

After Alexei and the rest of Mom's army of chosen contacts, Aldo was welcome company, but being close to him under the circumstances, knowing that he couldn't see any farther away than I could, made me feel like I was trying to walk a tightrope with one eye covered.

There was another gap in the sound at 8:29, and I was more than ready to run directly home from where I stood, even if it meant crossing the party's outer curb before my promise was officially fulfilled. That's when Billy took the mic.

"This next one's my personal favorite."

I might have done it anyway if he hadn't been looking right at me when he said it.

The beat of this song was a little more complex, probably the reason for Billy's preference, but with the distortion of the speakers, it couldn't help occupy my mind much. Without thinking, I brushed back my loose, distracting hair.

The first thing I saw in my newly unobscured range of vision was a head of blonde hair jogging toward Alexei's booth.

No reason to hurry.

Then another figure diverging from the path of the blonde one, wandering toward the bandstand.

I leaned toward Aldo's ear.

"Run straight ahead. Don't look back. Find a safe place. Call you later."

Aldo hesitated only a few seconds before stepping around me without turning his head and disappearing behind the next row of booths. The sudden movement drew attention.

I'd planned to try ducking behind the bandstand, but Ben turned, looked, and recognized before I could move.

He hadn't seen Aldo's face. I'd managed that much. Instead, he saw me standing there, looking at him, Bluetooth visible for a full two seconds before I remembered to cover it again.

I saw him glance at it for a moment, wondering what sick stalker purpose it served, no doubt, and then he walked away as if he hadn't seen me.

No, not as if he hadn't seen me. He was fine when he hadn't seen me. He was much more agitated now. He turned back toward the theater booth, saw Haley engrossed in some kind of group theatrical exercise, and broke off in another direction. For a moment I thought he might just make a circle of the party until she finished, but he hadn't learned to be nearly that sensible. Moving in a hurried, distracted pattern, he turned again and wandered straight out into the empty streets.

I reached for my phone and opened the app to track his, but that couldn't make him any safer. Even in the best case scenario where he was never separated from it, all it could do was tell me where they'd take him once they found him alone.

That thought warranted a moment's consideration. But only a moment.

*Moving, not in the woods, checking in within the hour.*

I sent the message to Aldo one-handed before reaching the curb, then pocketed the phone and ran after Ben.

He was headed back toward the Perkins's house. Not a good thing in that it was on the isolated, wooded edge of town. Not a terrible thing in that it was predictable and some distance uphill, so I wasn't likely to lose him on the way. He wasn't used to walking on an incline. I could tell by how far he leaned into it. There wasn't much chance of going unnoticed, so I took advantage and let myself gain on him during the steepest parts. He kept walking and tried to ignore me for a while, and then changed his mind when the road started to skirt along the trees, closer to the house, as if I wouldn't know where he was going as long as he didn't lead me all the way.

"Go away, Mina." He was out of breath, but it didn't soften his tone.

"I can't do that," I said. "You're not safe."

"I'll take my chances."

"You don't know what you're saying."

He stopped and turned around so that I had to stop, too.

"I know what you think!" he snapped. "You told me! I listened! You got your say! Now you can leave me alone!"

He didn't seem to notice the ominous rustling in the bougainvillea in the yard behind him.

A deer stumbled out of the yard onto the sidewalk, an enormous buck as tall as I was, taller, counting its impressive rack of antlers.

"Ben," I hissed.

Ben turned and stared at the deer for a few seconds, warily and with what looked like suppressed awe. He skirted carefully around it and continued scaling the hill away from us both. I followed, but didn't take my eyes off the deer.

It took an unsteady step forward, as if it were still getting the hang of being a deer, even though it was full grown. On the next step, it tripped slightly, and there was an unmistakable ripple of unearthly shapes under its skin.

"Ben!"

I plunged my hand into my bag, but I hadn't quite grasped anything useful yet when the deer lowered its head to charge, so I reached for the sleeve of Ben's shirt instead.

"Ben, look out!"

# 8

# WHAT WAS THAT?

## Ben

You know, it's amazing the things that come back to you when you think you're about to die. In this case, staring at the massive buck that stood in the middle of the road, it was my Wilderness Survival merit badge.

One of the main requirements involved describing in detail how to protect myself from insects, reptiles, and bears while surviving in the wild. Given the fact that I was something of an overachiever when it came to merit badge attempts, and the fact that I really, really had this thing about not being eaten alive by a wild animal when I was little, I studied up on how to avoid pretty much every animal in North America.

Including deer.

Generally docile deer will only usually attack if they believe you are a threat to them. If they think you are boxing them in, or might be after one of their young, they will come after you without hesitation. Bucks, like the one we were facing down, were generally more aggressive, but would only really attack unprovoked during rutting season.

Since that usually runs from October to December, I hadn't been too worried when I first saw it. Once it had lowered its head and begun grinding one of its front hooves into the pavement threateningly, I'd started to wonder if the wilderness textbook rules could be applied to the kind of deer that wandered willingly into suburban streets.

Mina grabbed my shirt and cried out. I didn't listen. I was trying to remember what to do in this situation.

"Don't run," I said. She looked at me as if I were insane.

"It's not—"

"I know what I'm talking about," I said. "Don't take your eyes off of his. Back away slowly with me, and make as much noise as you can."

"That won't work," she said vehemently.

"Trust me," I said, taking a slow step backward. I raised my arms, started hollering at the top of my lungs at the deer. Mina stood still and went back to rooting through that giant bag slung over her shoulder. I reached for her, ready to pull her back.

Then the deer charged. For a split second I cursed the books I'd read for never actually mentioning how to deal with a deer that was actively running at you, antlers poised to gore. Then instinct took over, and I'm pretty sure I forgot what books were for a good five minutes or so.

The deer could beat us in a flat-out sprint, and I was at least mostly sure that Mina didn't have a hunting rifle in that giant bag of hers, so the best options I could see would either involve calling for help or hiding. The street was open with only a few parked cars nearby, and almost every house dark.

There was a silver SUV parked on the street maybe fifteen feet away from us. It would have to do.

The deer was upon us with frightening speed. I grabbed Mina by the arm and pulled her to the opposite side of the SUV, putting the car between us and the buck. The deer slammed into the side of the vehicle, rocking it back and forth violently. The animal was dazed, shaking its head slightly. We only had a few seconds. I had to make them count.

"Get under the car," I said, forcefully.

Again, she looked at me like I was insane. "What?"

"Get under the car and call the cops. It won't be able to get you down there, and I'll try and lead it away," I said.

"That won't work, it's not—"

I cut her off, "Just shut up and let me try to get us out of this. You said you thought you could trust me, well, trust me on this!"

The deer had regained its footing; it would walk around our crude barricade in no time. I was prepared to push her under the car if I had to, but for some reason Mina actually listened to me.

One problem down. Now for the other.

I'm a fast guy. Not an Olympian by a long-shot, though I could probably compete on a school track and field team if I really put my mind to it and trained. Looking down the darkened street, I figured I could maybe jump over one of the fences into the houses' backyards. With any luck, there'd be enough protection to keep the deer from following. It'd lose interest, or the cops would come when Mina called, and this'd be just another Prospero story.

It was a stupid plan, I knew, but since I couldn't fit under the SUV with Mina, it was about the only plan that sounded like it might work.

I turned on my heel and ran for the corner of the block, watching the few lights in houses blur past me, hearing only the wind whipping and my heart pounding. For fear of my last sight on Earth being a set of giant antlers pointed at me, I didn't dare look back until I'd made it as far as the end of the block. Then I turned my head slightly.

I wasn't being followed. In fact, the deer seemed to be trying to dig for Mina under the SUV, gouging its antlers into the side of the vehicle, trying to tip it over. I'd never seen anything like it, though, to be fair, I hadn't really been around deer that much. I had to get its attention.

I yelled. Nothing. There were a few rocks in the grass near me. I picked one up, threw it at the deer, hitting it in the side. This got its attention a lot faster than I would have liked, actually. It whirled on me and closed the distance in just a few seconds. I was able to turn around and take one long stride before I felt the searing, hot pain of its antlers digging into my back, and my feet lifted off the ground.

It tossed me into a white picket fence, wooden stakes breaking around me as I rolled right through it. The wind was knocked out of me, my back felt as if it was on fire. With what strength I could muster, I rolled over, trying to avoid a killing blow that did not come.

When my eyes cleared, I saw that it had gone back to the SUV. Mina stood near the front of the car, pulling out a large, red cylinder from her purse and . . . talking to the deer? Yes, she was definitely talking to it. The beast stared her down, ready to charge her at any moment.

I grabbed one of the fence stakes that I'd knocked loose. It felt sturdy, and its end was pointed and sharp. It would have to do. Holding it like a spear, I ran toward the deer. Mina held it distracted, trying to start a lighter for some reason. It did not see me coming, not even as I thrust the fencepost eight inches deep into its side. The deer bleated and struggled, trying to pull itself free from the stake, yet still trying to pull itself forward to Mina.

In some faraway place, I could hear her calling out to me, trying to tell me something. I knew that if I didn't finish this, the deer would do everything possible to kill us both. With this grim thought, I ripped the fence stake from the deer's side and thrust it in deeper.

At that, the deer finally hobbled away from Mina and the SUV, letting out pitiful, painful bleats as it went. Blood dripped steadily from its muzzle and the wounds I had gouged in its side. I felt bad, no, *terrible* for what I had done to such a beautiful animal. It had wandered into the street, confused, probably hungry, and now it was going to die in pain because of what I had done. It looked at me accusingly, its beady eyes almost glimmering in the faint glow of the streetlights. For a moment, it almost looked human.

After that, things started happening extremely fast.

The deer cocked its head with a sound like snapping wood. It opened its mouth, I thought to let out another pitiful bleat. Instead, it let out a high-pitched, warbling roar that sounded like an unholy cross between a bird of prey, a rattlesnake, and a pig being slaughtered, punctuated with more loud, wooden-sounding cracks and pops. The deer's whole body shuddered violently, and shapes that looked like several different, angry animals trying to escape shifted beneath its fur. Its neck contorted horribly to the side. It opened its mouth for another roar, too wide, its bottom jaw seeming to detach completely before splitting in two like an insect's mandibles.

Each separate prong of its antlers opened at the tip like a carnivorous tropical flower, and when I found myself looking into the glowing buds of a dozen-odd eyes, some segmented like insects, some horribly human, I felt ready to go completely insane.

Thankfully, Mina kept a clearer head. Without fear or hesitation, she approached the deer monstrosity with the lighter and red cylinder she'd pulled from her purse at the ready. Calmly, almost mechanically, she used them to aim a stream of flame at the beast. It dodged easily, barely singeing its fur as it let out another of its terrible roars. The deer beast turned its head to me, the thing now lopsided with large, tumorous growths, opening its mandibled mouth wide.

I stood in shock, transfixed by the horror before me as it spat a black, gecko-like tongue at me. It wrapped around my legs like a snake, pulling me to the ground. Hitting the asphalt brought me back to my senses somewhat, enough to have me clawing at the ground and crying out for help as the powerful tongue dragged me closer to the monster's mouth. I could feel its mandibles closing around my shoes, the stinking slime of its mouth dripping on my bare leg.

Then there was Mina, pulling a large knife from her bag and darting over to me. With practiced precision, she forced both of her hands into the deer's mouth, hacking at the tongue and dropping me to the ground. The beast let out an indignant howl as it backed away, and, for a brief moment, I felt relief.

The next thing I felt was the tongue, still wrapped around my ankles, growing hundreds of centipede-like legs before it started to crawl quickly up my body toward my mouth.

"Get it off, get it off of me!" I cried as I fought with the powerful creature.

"I'm trying!" Mina said as she knelt down beside me, helping me wrestle with the tongue-centipede. After we broke its death grip around one of my legs, she scrambled back to her bag, picking up her improvised flamethrower.

"Throw it!" she yelled, motioning to an empty section of street. She didn't have to tell me twice. With all my strength, I hurled the writhing monstrosity onto the street's double-yellow line. A jet of fire spat out of her flamethrower, engulfing the tongue-centipede, which crackled and screamed and skittered toward the forest.

The deer monster let out another of its roars. I turned, watched as its body stretched and contorted with that same terrible snapping wood sound. The fencepost I had rammed into its side wobbled about, was sucked into its body, and rocketed out the other side, clattering bloodily into the street. The gaping wounds I had made in its side began to stretch and widen, splitting open as the deer monster ripped itself in half.

The two halves toddled about unsteadily at first, but new limbs soon grew in to remedy that problem. Three giant spider-like legs burst from the back of the front half, while the back half grew one large, thick leg that ended in what looked like a clawed hand. Where organs should have been, the back half grew a toothy, triangular mouth rimmed with black eyes and tentacles ending in vicious-looking hooves. Two large, crab-like arms burst from the side and clicked threateningly as the creature tested out its new limbs.

"One for each of us," Mina said. She looked scared. I didn't know she *could* look scared. She went to her bag, pulling out the goo-streaked knife she'd saved me with and what looked like a disposable camera with two muted metallic spikes sticking out of one end. She put each weapon in one of my hands before picking up her jury-rigged flamethrower.

"What's this?" I asked.

"Improvised stun gun. You'll get one or two shots at most, but it should help. Creature Splinters are very hard to kill, but they are not very smart, and they can feel pain. Hurt it, keep it distracted while I kill the other one with fire, then I'll deal with yours," she said simply.

"That'll work?" I asked.

"Probably," she replied humorlessly.

As I looked at the two monstrosities standing before us, finally finished transforming, I thought it was a task that was easier said than done. Then they charged us, and I didn't have much time for thinking.

It was not an organized fight, nor was it a clean one. We didn't choose our targets, we didn't decide the terms of engagement, we just fought for our lives. I mostly fought the back half, dodging the clumsy swipes of its claws as I tried to get in every stab I could with Mina's large knife. Jamming her improvised stun gun into a particularly soft part, I watched the creature go rigid and shudder violently, howling in pain. Then it knocked me back to the ground. Without even thinking, Mina helped me to my feet. A moment later, I was doing the exact same for her after the deer-front sent her rolling roughly on the asphalt.

The ground was streaked with whatever it was this creature considered blood and stray bits of flesh as I hacked at it and Mina kept it at bay with the flames. With the way the creature grew new body parts and shifted its old ones whenever we hurt it, it was impossible to tell what progress we were making. I looked to Mina to see if she knew what was happening—her face only showed determined ferocity.

Still, we must have been doing something right. After only a few minutes of fighting, the two limping, shuddering halves of the deer monster limped back together, reconnecting in a mess of distorted limbs and hastily-grown tentacles. Though it looked fully capable of healing itself, we had clearly hurt it badly.

With our backs to the SUV, the panting, grunting deer-monster stood before us, looking fully ready to charge again. Though hobbling about on no fewer than nine mismatched legs, it darted for us with startling speed. We jumped out of the way, watching it hit the SUV like a freight train, crushing in its side and smashing all of its windows. I expected it to turn on us at any moment, ripping through the SUV like tissue paper, but something unexpected happened.

It was stuck.

Its antlers, so wide and jagged, were lodged tightly in the shattered remains of the car. It thrashed about and howled its unholy howl as it struggled to get out, and, in a moment, it would probably just shed the antlers and be back to chasing us down.

Then I smelled it. The rich, unpleasant smell of gasoline. A puddle was forming beneath the car; it must have ruptured the gas tank when it hit.

"Mina," I said, pointing at the puddle.

She knew what to do. Aiming her crude flamethrower beneath the car, she let out a quick, short blast of fire. It caught quickly, and we began to run down the street.

I didn't see the car explode, but I saw the night sky light up, could feel the heat licking at my back and the pieces of debris raining down around us (the SUV's jaunty vanity plate reading CATDOC nearly clocking me in the back of the head). The creature's horrible, strangled screams filled the air. Lights came on in the house the SUV was parked in front of, and a bald, middle-aged man in glasses came running outside. I watched him grabbing at his head, screaming about his car, blissfully unaware of the horror that burned to death inside of it. If the last ten minutes had been any less terrifying, I would have felt guilty about what we had done to him.

We ran around the corner. I was panting and ready to fall over. Despite some scrapes and bruises, Mina looked surprisingly composed.

Finally gathering myself a bit, I said, "You were right."

"I know," Mina said, without adding, *I told you so.* "You're bleeding," she said, eying the gash on my back.

"So are you." I pointed at the scrapes on her forearms.

She looked at them idly, as if just noticing she had arms. "So I am. I've got a very comprehensive first-aid kit in my room. If you come with me, I'll help fix you up."

It wasn't a request. She began walking, and though I still didn't entirely trust her, it's hard not to follow someone after sharing an experience like that.

# 9.

## WHAT THAT WAS

### Mina

I was stuck working by a strongly scented ginger candle perched awkwardly on the windowsill. It had been between that and turning Ben around so the injury faced the light by the doorway. There was no telling when Mom might come home, open that door, and ask me for a rundown. At least the flame made a convenient place to sterilize the needle.

Not for the first time, Ben's phone and mine announced almost simultaneous incoming messages.

Haley.

Aldo.

Neither of us looked. We'd each answered once that we were safe, full details to follow, but we still hadn't discussed what those full details were, so there was nothing more to report.

There had been no time to rearrange the room for his benefit. It was slightly guarded against Mom, with the decoys prominently displayed on the board and mentions of the Council minimized, but the shots of Ben and other subjects who had obviously not been saying "cheese" at the time were hard to miss.

"You haven't stopped watching me for a moment, have you?"

"No."

He didn't try to pull the needle away and run for the door, but I still felt like I should try to justify myself.

"I couldn't just leave you unprotected."

It looked at first like he might protest, but he didn't. Maybe the gaping Splinter-inflicted hole in his back had something to do with that.

"You're . . . not bad at this." He changed the subject. The position of the gouge seemed to have him more worried than the severity because it prevented him from supervising my work. "You've, um, done it before? For real?"

"As often as I've had to. More often than I'd like," I answered. "We don't go to the med center if we can help it. Too isolated, too many potential Splinters, too many excuses to get someone alone for long periods of time."

He didn't jump on this opportunity to contradict me. He even looked like he might be thinking about all the time Haley had spent there, not that it had mattered for her by then. I kept stitching as quickly as I could, trying to get it over with the way Aldo always asked me to while squirming and slowing me down.

Ben, on the other hand, had turned down both the whiskey and the biting stick I kept for Aldo, didn't comment on my pace, and barely winced when I pushed the needle through. If he hadn't been gripping my bed frame so hard,

I would have wondered if he could feel it at all. I couldn't see his hand, but I could feel it shaking all the way through the mattress.

"If you *could* go to the med center, would they know how to handle it?" he asked with a forced smile. "I mean, do you do anything special to it?"

"No, just the usual things. Garlic. Aconite." I broke a bulb off one of the garlands around my bed and hit it against the wall to break off a few cloves. "You'll probably want a buddy to remind you when to reapply it for the first few lunar cycles, but the condition's perfectly manageable with proper education."

The shaking spread beyond his arm for a moment, and he let go of the bed just long enough to run his hand nervously through his heartthrob hair, setting the sweatier parts on end.

"S-seriously?"

"No."

It took him most of the length of a stitch to respond.

"Did you just make a joke?"

"Yes."

He waited for the space between stitches where I was in less danger of slipping before throwing the loose cloves over his shoulder at me.

"That's not funny!"

"It isn't? Huh. I was sure it was." I let him wait while I brushed the garlic skin out of my way. "They've sliced me up plenty of times," I admitted. "There aren't any side effects, and they don't seem to be able to copy humans without getting them to wherever it is they take them." I pulled the next stitch through maybe harder than I needed to. "But of course, if I hadn't been cornered under a gas tank and a layer of flammable residue, I could have taken care of it faster."

"If you hadn't been under that car, I'd be the one sewing *you* back together!" he snapped. "And I didn't hear you arguing when it was charging you!"

"I didn't have much choice when it was *charging*," I pointed out, "after all the time you wasted getting in the way, comparing how tall you were!"

"That would have made a real deer back off!"

"Well, it *wasn't* a real deer, was it? And if you'd listened to me, you would have known that it wouldn't *care* how big you were or what you stabbed it with or how bravely you can stand your ground!"

I expected him to argue back again, and when he didn't, I thought back over what I'd said and wished I'd said it another way.

" . . . Brave?"

"I don't mean it was a good thing to—"

"Thanks for not letting it get me."

I took a stitch to find what felt like the correct answer to this. "Thanks for trying not to let it get me either."

"You're welcome."

I waited until I was tying off the suture to ask the next question, to make sure it was definitely my best possible guess. I wanted to get it right.

"Are we bonding now?"

He glanced back at me, as far as he could with the needle still attached, as if checking. "I'm not sure."

I cut the thread, poured an extra splash of rubbing alcohol over the finished job, topped it off with a layer of Neosporin, and covered it with one of the extra-large adhesive bandages in the kit I keep under my bed. He tensed harder against the sting for a moment before finally letting go of the bed again.

He turned around to look at me, and even though his was just an ordinary, genuinely human body, something I'd spent hours upon hours researching, hoping to find some detail that the Splinters couldn't replicate, I had some difficulty looking at him until he'd untangled his shirt and pulled it back on.

Even then it wasn't effortless.

I'd washed my hands and the places where the skin was missing from my arms before getting to work on Ben, and I'd told myself the rest could wait until I could hear him on the program bug, safe as he could be in that guestroom bed.

I'd have to get in and plant some better bugs soon, I realized. Its battery had to be on its last legs.

I was arranging my kit for storage when Ben pulled it across the bed toward himself before I could close the lid. He stretched one of my arms across his leg, and started to roll back my sleeves. I pulled away.

"You'll feel better when we get it over with."

He said this as firmly as he kept his grip on my right hand, thinking I might be hesitating over the pain. I hoped, when he peeled the fabric away, that the abrasions might be bad enough to stop him from noticing anything else.

They weren't.

I'm a quick healer. Everything from fractures to the flu, I can shake off in well below-average time. My skin is very difficult to scar, but the life I live has been more than up to the challenge. A particularly deep gash circles my right arm just below the elbow, branching down toward my wrist in a few places. Ben startled slightly when he saw it and then politely tried to look at any other part of my arm as if he hadn't noticed it at all.

"This isn't my first Splinter attack," I explained.

"What was that one pretending to be?" Ben asked, glancing back at the twisted, bone-deep, purplish trench in my skin. "A cougar?"

*Yes,* I should have lied.

"A bear?" Ben gave me another chance, but I didn't take it.

" . . . A *person?*"

I could see him already trying to come up with a rational explanation, probably imagining some ordinary human hurting me badly enough that I'd had to construct the Splinter-filled hell I live in just to process it, before his eyes shifted back to the fresh scrapes, remnants of the very real Splinter attack he'd just lived through with me. What exactly he made of this, he didn't say. He just doused my tweezers in alcohol as easily as if he handled them every day and started picking the leftover bits of mulch and stray asphalt out of my skin. I didn't object.

"So what now?" he asked.

"Now nothing," I said. "Now you go back to your mom and the Perkinses and enjoy the rest of your visit, and I go back to keeping the Splinters off of you until you can make a safe distance, and maybe I'll be able to do it a little better if you don't make me pretend I'm not doing it at all."

"No lecture?" he asked. "No Splinters 101: There's More to Them than Killer Deer?"

"No."

"Then why did you bring me here?" he asked.

"You would have gone to the center if I hadn't."

"What happened to 'you need to hear this whether you believe it or not?' What happened to 'I need you to join my crusade?'"

"You turned me down," I reminded him.

"Oh, so now you're done talking to me?" He sounded hurt, as if I were accusing him of making the wrong choice instead of the right one. "Okay, fine. I'll start, and you can tell me when I go wrong." He selected every word slowly and carefully while he collected all the little unidentified fragments from my arm in an old Petri dish that had never been able to contain a specimen for any useful length of time. "I think . . . I think we were attacked by something I've never seen before, or heard about, or read about, something that's not in any textbook, and I think you're maybe the only person who can tell me what it was. I think there's something freaky as hell going on in this town and a lot of people in it creep me out." He started on my other arm. "I think you know something other people don't know, or won't say, but I *don't* think that's proof that there are things like that passing for human, never mind that any of the *particular* humans I know are like that. That's what I think," he concluded. "How am I doing?"

"From what you have seen, that sounds fair," I said as indifferently as I could.

"Go on," he prompted me. "Your turn. Why am I wrong? What was that thing?"

Less than a week earlier, I would have given almost anything for him to ask me that and be so ready to hear the answer.

I really wanted to say something while he smoothed on the antibiotic, if only to clear up my thinking. My brain was doing something odd. It was mostly hazy, the way it always is when I have nothing to do, but, for some reason, Ben's face and his hands on my arm were in perfect focus.

And I could still remember that saying less would be better, for him and for me.

When he tied off the bandages, he did an even tidier job than I could have myself, though I wouldn't have told him so. He waited a few seconds afterward before asking, "Well?"

I went back to packing up my kit, though it was nowhere near enough to make me clear. The energy drink I'd quickly gulped down before getting started was already wearing off, and after the look Ben had given me when I'd offered him one, it felt awkward to go get another one even later in the evening.

"Is that what you want?" I asked. "To belong to my Network? To be the Splinters' enemy every minute of every day?"

He took a long time trying to find an answer, so I stopped him.

"I'm sorry I dragged you into this."

He looked more like I'd accused him of something rather than apologized.

"I'm sorry I called you a creep."

"A sick stalker," I corrected him. "And it's fine."

"Then what? Is it because I'm not drinking the Kool-Aid? Because I like evidence? Just because I won't promise to take it all as gospel truth, you're going to keep me in the dark?"

The kit was back in order, so I started piecing the garlic cloves back into a bulb to keep the train of the conversation. "What do you want from me, Ben?"

"To know what I'm *doing!* I want to know what you know and what you're basing it on, so I'll know how to handle myself!"

"I said I'd protect you," I reminded him. "And you're still here so far."

"You've been protecting *me,*" he said. "Look, just because I don't think Haley's like that deer . . . that's all the more reason for me to be worried! People act weird around her as much as me whether they're really people or not! You think this place is dangerous—I agree with you there. And I have to assume it's just as dangerous for her until I know otherwise. I know what you think, why you don't care about her, but she's human until proven Splinter to me. And what about my mom? What about *Haley's* mom? I'm sure you've got this down to a science and everything, but you can't protect everyone, can you? I need to know what to do on my own."

I was getting that feeling again, the one I'd had just before my worst failure to date, the one I had to avoid at all costs. Not tears this time, but the same feeling, in the form of unexplained warmth in my fingers and erratic pacing in my pulse.

I really needed to hear him laughing again like a normal, safe, happy human to remind me of the other reason I'd changed my mind, why I had to say no, that laugh I'd never had to hear out loud from him before he'd arrived in Prospero, the one I knew no Network member would ever have time to achieve. He was nowhere near laughter now, and no matter how hard I squeezed the garlic in my hands, I couldn't quite recapture the sound in my head.

I *could* hear him asking me to tell him everything two years ago. I could see something else that looked like him listening so earnestly in his place. I could feel that thing taking me to be replaced, leaving me with two broken bones and an assortment of second-degree burns in the attempt.

Except that hadn't been Ben, and the face that *did* belong in that memory wasn't allowed in my thoughts anymore.

Ben was different—would be different—in every way.

Because I was too strong to let that feeling take me over ever again.

Remembering my conviction that had been so solid before he'd actually arrived, there was nothing left in my head strong enough to stop the offer from slipping out.

"First thing tomorrow, after Mom goes to work, I have to go back to where it attacked us to check for evidence and document the cleanup. You could meet me there . . . if you want to."

It looked like he was considering arguing for more, but he also kept glancing at his phone, the late hour of its clock and the growing tally of messages.

"And then we can talk about this?" he asked.

"We'll talk about whatever you want," I agreed. "If you still want to."

Ben stood up stiffly, carefully testing the movement in his right shoulder. "I'll see you tomorrow, then."

It felt like I was supposed to do or say something more before letting him leave. I couldn't think of anything.

Just as the front door closed behind him, my phone vibrated once more, and this time I answered.

"I'm fine, Aldo. But something's come up."

# 10.

## LEFTOVERS

### Ben

I found Mina Todd the next morning, crouching down by the curb near where we had been attacked by the deer. As usual, she was dressed in plain black with long sleeves in spite of the heat, with that hideous bag over her shoulder. Less usually, she also had a large glass box strapped to her back. She looked at me, more than a bit irritated. I was hoping the paper bag I had brought would smooth things over.

"You're late," she said.

Looking to counter, I quickly replied, "You're outside."

"You've seen me outside before, several times," she said.

I had to keep reminding myself that she didn't always register jokes like normal people.

"Haley's mom took my mom out shopping, so I had to walk her to play practice before coming here," I explained.

"It shouldn't have taken you that long to get from there to here," she said. Once again, she said it not as an accusation, but as a simple statement of fact. I had to tell myself not to get defensive.

"Hence the bag," I said, handing her the paper sack. She opened it up, pulling out the six-pack of energy drinks I'd bought. For a fraction of a second, I caught some of that radiant smile. It didn't last long.

"Tell me what you see here," she said.

They'd cleaned up nicely. The fence I'd been flung through had been repaired, the blood on the street was gone, and a brand new SUV with that same "CATDOC" vanity plate that had nearly decapitated me the night before was parked on the curb. Even the grass by the curb had been replaced, probably to cover for the fire. It was almost as if nothing had happened. I don't know why, but that almost felt worse than having actually been attacked by an alien deer.

Almost.

"Is this what you meant by 'document the cleanup?'" I asked, motioning to the SUV and trying very hard to hold my fear in check.

"They're fast," she agreed. "Come on, let's see if there's any of it left. Usually the bits go back in the direction of the forest."

"What bits?" I asked.

"Bits of the deer," Mina said.

She talked about this as if it were completely normal. It took me a moment to remind myself that to her it *was* completely normal.

"Where do you get a perfect replica of a car, even a common car, in the middle of the night?" I asked.

"I've told you how much of the town they've taken over," she said, kneeling down and rubbing her fingers lightly across the asphalt. "Many of the town's more affluent citizens help the Splinters maintain their anonymity. Mainly the Town Council. That includes the fire chief and the 'Used Car King.' And my mother."

I got a flash of the night before, that woman whose steely gaze looked so familiar. That explained a lot.

"I have listening devices at all their meetings. They're good at hiding what they're talking about, but I've been able to determine that they have a treaty of sorts with the Splinter leadership. In exchange for keeping their families safe and the Council completely human, they help the Splinters cover up any problems, like the fire, while the Splinters themselves take care of any *people* who might be problems," she continued. That reminded me of the man we saw running from the house last night, screaming and yelling about his car—a car that had come back from the dead overnight.

"You know, if the car's here, the guy who owns it probably still is, too. Maybe we should . . . I don't know . . . apologize?" I suggested. It was a silly, stupid notion, but honor dictated that I at least put it out there.

"You can try if you want," she said, "when we're done."

I lowered my eyes. This next part was not something I had been looking forward to.

"So you're going to make me ask again?" I asked. "What attacked us last night, and what are we looking for now?"

"Last night, we were attacked by a Splinter," she said quite simply.

Okay, maybe I would have to get a bit more specific on this. "What are Splinters?"

"Figuratively, they are perhaps the greatest threat unknown to mankind, a plague that seeks to replace us with otherworld duplicates so they can live our lives. Biologically, they are, in many ways, like any other organism. They consume, they rest, and they fight to survive."

"And reproduce?" I proposed, going down the checklist of natural functions I remembered from biology.

This gave her a moment of pause. "I'm uncertain as to whether or not they reproduce as we know it."

"Then what do you call those pieces that broke off last night and came after us? They looked pretty alive to me," I asked.

"Smaller Splinters," she said. "Are you all right with me entering the realm of speculation for a moment?"

"Please do," I said.

"From what I've seen, each piece of a Splinter can survive as an independent organism, or they can rejoin into the original piece. I have also seen human Splinters transfer *thoughts* through physical contact. Based on this, I think it's likely that all Splinters come from some larger consciousness, probably even one large organism that is capable of breaking itself into infinitely smaller parts, hence the name. I'm not sure yet about the parts' exact level of independent thought."

I nodded, trying to ignore the way my skin was beginning to crawl with imaginary microscopic aliens.

"What attacked us last night was what we call a Creature Splinter. Creature Splinters are bits that break off into Prospero without having a human body already brought to them. They grab and copy the first living thing that walks by and do what they can with it. And you saw the result. When they're too broken to re-form, the pieces wander off, probably where they came from, but sometimes a few get left behind. Hopefully we'll find one in time."

"In time for what?"

"Creature Splinters use a cruder copying technique than human Splinters do. It makes them more . . . unstable. They have a harder time holding onto their form, and they only live for a few days, maybe even hours before dissolving away."

"So, if there *are* Splinters that are smart enough to pass for human—"

"There are," she said without hesitation.

"If there are, then the thing we killed, if we killed it . . ."

"It wasn't like them," she confirmed. "It couldn't think like a person. It couldn't even think like a deer."

That was comforting. Slightly.

We worked our way down opposite sides of the driveway, searching flowerbed edges of the yards on both sides along the way before we had to walk around the garage and into the woods. I could tell that Mina would have preferred we split up to cover more ground, but I had too many questions that needed answering.

"Do you know where they come from?" I asked as we began to walk into the forest. "The Splinters, I mean?"

"Not precisely, but again, I can speculate," she said. "Do you know of The Miracle Mine Incident?"

I nodded. The Miracle Mine Incident is about the only thing Prospero is actually proud of. Prospero was founded as one of the many Gold Rush boomtowns, the earth around it pockmarked by dozens of crisscrossing mines. As mines often do, one of them caved in, trapping eight miners underground. The men had been thought dead after two weeks of fruitless rescue efforts, but then surprised the world when they walked into a nearby tavern, no worse for wear, and ordered a round of drinks.

When I thought about it, the story sounded a little too familiar for comfort.

"You think it happened down there?" I asked.

"Before the incident, nothing out of the ordinary happened in this town. All the reports of monsters and other paranormal phenomena began shortly afterward, so, yes, I would say there is a likely correlation between the two. Since every Creature Splinter I have seen is based around something found in the forest, something that may very well have wandered by accident into an old mine, I would say it is very likely that the transformation process happens out there."

"So they can't just take over anything anywhere?"

She shook her head, "No. I've seen smaller pieces try. They're not very smart, but for a complete transformation to take place, I think the person needs to be taken to someplace special, most likely within the mine, where they are stored and replaced. It's a pretty quick process. I've seen cases where I am almost certain someone has been taken and replaced overnight."

"They're stored?"

"Yes," she said.

"Why would they need to store them?" I asked.

Mina looked at me, almost hesitant, "To answer that, I have to speculate again, is that all right?"

"Yes," I said. "And feel free to speculate all you want, you don't need my permission."

This didn't seem to calm her any. "Well . . . from all I have been able to piece together, from my sources and investigation, Splinters are incapable of existing in our world for long on their own. In order to exist here, they need a link to both the living person they have taken over and their own world, and if you kill the body of one, the other will die."

She wouldn't meet my eyes as she said this. Before I could stop myself, I asked, "You've seen this, haven't you?"

Mina stalled for a moment, kicking the grass as if to flush tiny Splinters out of it, her left hand wrapped unconsciously around her right arm, over that stiflingly covered scar, and then spoke as if she were pulling off a Band-Aid. "I have it from a reliable source that that is what I saw."

Her strong façade faltered for a moment, and I saw true sadness in her eyes. I didn't push her further.

"All right," I said. "So if we kill either one, the other dies. I get that. If we can't kill them, how do we fight them?"

Mina waved to the town dramatically. "We watch, we gather information, and we do everything possible to undermine and sabotage their efforts."

"We can't take the fight to them? What if we were to find this place where the humans are being kept prisoner? If we were to free them from the source, what would happen?"

She shook her head vigorously, "Nobody knows where

the Miracle Mine is for sure. Well, no human does, as far as I know. Accurate records from the era have been lost, and with all the accidents and lawsuits stemming from people trying to find it, thinking it has some fountain-of-youth kind of power, the Town Council has found it very convenient to keep any information there *is* on the location of the mines confidential. *"For the public safety."* I've been hoping to dig something up for years."

She crouched down, tracing her fingers through a faint indentation in the dirt and leaves.

"Find something?" I asked.

"Maybe," she said, following the faint trail farther into the woods. There was one question. One *big* question that still lingered here. It was the one I had been avoiding, the one I had been dreading most, but it was another one that we had to get out in the open.

"So what does all this mean for Haley? If this transformation can happen overnight like you said, why was she gone for two months?" I asked. I wanted to stump her, for this to prove that, somehow, Haley couldn't be one of these monsters Mina feared so much.

Instead, Mina shot back, "Because sometimes they have a hard time taking someone over. Sometimes . . . it doesn't take properly."

There was no uncertainty in this remark, no question in her voice.

"This has happened before, too?" I asked.

"Decades ago," she replied, and when I looked to her for more information, she explained, "I'm not the first person to resist the Splinters. There isn't much left of the ones who came before me, but I've learned what I could. Technically, this information is secondhand, so bear with me. Last time their secret got out on any noticeable scale, it started with a guy they couldn't replace because of some preexisting brain damage. I learned a lot from his notes, in the beginning."

"So that means Haley wasn't taken?" I proposed.

"It could mean anything," she said. "Haley not being taken is one possibility, but unless she managed to survive a gunshot to the head at some point without me hearing about it, it's unlikely. It is also possible that they know that I know about this process, and they delayed her release to cast doubt in me. Or it could be something that I haven't seen before. There's nothing to suggest, just yet, that she's anything but a Probable Splinter," Mina said.

I wanted to tell her she was wrong, that there was no way that Haley could be a Splinter, that in all the time we'd spent together since her reappearance, never once had I seen any indication that she was anything but the girl I'd known most of my life. I wanted to tell Mina this, but I didn't because at that exact moment she shrieked.

"Open the box!"

She unslung the glass case from her back and thrust it into my arms, pulled some long metal kitchen tongs from her bag, and knelt next to the fragment.

"Oh, sweet Jesus." My stomach turned when I saw it.

It was part of that tongue that had gotten away, still with most of its improvised legs attached. It had anchored one end of itself to a tree root and wrapped the other end around a small rat, which was struggling for its life half-heartedly enough that it had probably been doing so unsuccessfully for most of the night. The tongue was repairing itself in the middle where small slivers of it had recently been gnawed off, and it had sprouted a few patches of brown fur and tufts of coarse whiskers at random intervals.

"Box!" Mina reminded me. I had almost as hard a time looking away as I did trying to figure out how the box was supposed to open, but I managed it somehow. Forcefully, she fit the tongs around the tongue-rat combo and began to pull it from the roots.

The tongue's tail, if that was the right word, ripped off when she pulled it hard enough. When she held the rest of the squirming tangle just out of reach, it let go of the root to jump up and reattach itself. I held the box open for her to toss the whole thing in and then latched it shut. It fought viciously inside, scrabbling up the glass and hissing at us with two . . . no, make that three new mouths.

"It's horrible," I said.

"It's a means to an end," she clarified as she shook the box slightly. "I've built up a collection of talismans that have somehow kept my father out of my room. At least one of them appears to have an effect on Splinters. I've been hoping to test just which item or combination of items it is."

"Maybe he just respects your space," I proposed.

She shrugged, "Possible, but improbable."

We'd made it back to the sidewalk when I heard the front door of the house behind us open and close. I looked back to see the same bald man from last night, smiling and waving at us in a neighborly fashion from across his immaculate yard before unwinding a garden hose to water his roses.

"That's the guy from last night," I said.

She nodded, "Dr. Westlake. Our town veterinarian."

He smiled, looking at the sky and breathing in the fresh summer air as if he didn't have a care in the world. This wasn't the same man who had been shouting and cursing at his flaming car last night. Now there was something undeniably spooky about him.

I had to know for sure. I walked to him despite Mina's protests.

"Uh . . . hi," I started out. Dr. Westlake had been about to turn on the faucet but stopped to listen. "I heard there was a . . . commotion here last night. Did you see it?"

Dr. Westlake looked thoroughly bewildered. "Commotion? What commotion?"

"Uh . . ." I looked back at the car. "Wasn't there a fire around here?"

"Fire? Not here, I'm afraid. If you're mistaken and there was a fire somewhere else, I certainly hope everyone is all right," he said. Then he smiled, as if this were all some good-natured joke. He didn't glance at the glass case behind Mina, not even when the rat inside gave an extra high-pitched squeal.

He wasn't afraid.

This man had been freaking out about his car the night before. Not the deer or the blood on the street, just his car. He definitely hadn't been in on some plot about more important things then. And now he couldn't care less about what had happened, and not because someone was bribing him or blackmailing him. That kind of "cleanup" would have left him at least a little nervous. He was absolutely calm on a pure biological level.

He was a Splinter now.

"Oh. Sorry. You . . . have a good morning, then." I backed away to join Mina. We walked away slowly down the sidewalk, and it took everything I had to avoid looking back at him to see if we were being watched.

Once I was sure we were a safe distance away, I blurted out, "I believe you! About humans being Splinters, I mean."

"Good," she said simply.

"We *have* to find the Miracle Mine."

She looked at me, exasperated, "I told you, I've tried. Being in the forest is dangerous at the best of times, obviously, and searching it without the records is like looking for a needle in a stack of needles. And I can't get the records."

I smiled. Mina had a good head on her shoulders when it came to analyzing whatever information she had in front of her, but I could tell she wasn't used to more creative problem-solving.

"Have you ever tried asking nicely?"

## 11.

Mina

I didn't exactly have the most extravagant hopes.

Finding the Miracle Mine had been one of my highest goals for as long as I'd known what it really was, just a few notches below ridding the world of the Splinters altogether. There was nothing in the National Mine Map Repository beyond the tourist info—I'd searched the obvious places thoroughly enough to be kicked out of most of them— and I'd stolen just enough time in the Historical Society database to realize how much more time I'd need there to find any decent new leads.

Ben had more experience in the woods than I did. That much was true, but it seemed like such a small advantage against such steep odds that I hadn't even taken it into consideration when I'd selected him to maintain as an ECNS.

On the other hand, if I didn't take whatever advantages I could when it came to finding the Miracle Mine, it would just be poor prioritization.

So I followed behind Ben on our way to one of Prospero's

few publically advertised tourist points of interest, the Prospero Historical Society and Museum.

Quite a distance behind him, actually.

Mrs. Voorhees smiled her enthusiastically noble, volunteer, housewife smile at him from behind her desk, the way she did at anyone who opened the Society and Museum's front door.

Well, almost anyone.

"Hello!" she chirped at the exact same discordant interval she always used for the word. "New to Prospero?"

"Almost new," Ben agreed.

"Welcome! You're definitely going to want a copy of the—"

Her eyes revoked the "welcome" when they found me in the doorway.

"She's not allowed in here."

Technically, any volunteer at the Historical Society was required to point this out, but Mrs. Voorhees had been the particular volunteer dumb enough to use her birthday as her password and then leave me alone at the reception desk, and she had taken it very personally.

I stayed at the door, holding it open without crossing the threshold. Ben looked over his shoulder at me as if only just remembering I was there, as if I hadn't warned him about this complication five times over, and then looked excitedly back at Mrs. Voorhees.

"Really? What did she do?"

"Blatant disregard for the integrity of local records," Mrs. Voorhees said stiffly. I doubted that was a specific charge, even as far as the Prospero Historical Society was concerned.

Ben laughed agreeably. "Yeah, that sounds like her. Blatant disregard for a lot of things. I can sympathize, believe me."

Mrs. Voorhees smiled and looked back and forth between us, as if she expected to find writing on one of our foreheads explaining what brought us there together, if we were there together by more than chance at all. "What did you say your name was?" she asked.

"Ben Pastor," Ben introduced himself, as agreeable as ever, any hint of how inconvenient or unpleasant he might find this woman perfectly hidden.

"Ben Pastor?" she repeated excitedly. "Ben Pastor who saved that poor Perkins girl?"

Ben blushed very convincingly for someone who'd been milking that impression all over town.

"People make it sound like I found her in a dragon-guarded castle or something," was the way he said, "Yes, that Ben Pastor."

This was probably among the most exciting things ever to happen during Mrs. Voorhees' volunteer shifts.

"Well, what can I do for you, Ben Pastor?" she giggled, though I didn't get the joke. "Have you had a chance to look through the museum yet?"

The museum was a single room full of black-and-white photos and a few dioramas of the town from different time periods.

"Oh, just you, I'm afraid." Her desire to be nice to Ben

wasn't quite strong enough to make her look apologetic about me.

"I completely understand," Ben hurried to assure her. "And I would, but I'm kind of stuck with the babysitting thing if I want to get out and see the place while I'm here at all. Package deal."

Even from behind, I could tell that he was rolling his eyes at me in a gallant, put-upon way.

I hurried to add up Mrs. Voorhees' immediate network of contacts in my head. We were lucky. She almost certainly didn't know how little connection there was between our families, so as long as we got in and out before she had the opportunity to check, this ploy would be no problem. I made a mental note to remind Ben later how verifiable things like that were in a town as small as Prospero.

"I'm sorry to hear that," Mrs. Voorhees said with excessive emphasis. "Guidebooks, then?" she offered, opening the large filing drawer next to her desk. "We've got the real insider look here, not just the stuff you get from the Auto Club. Or a brief local history? Ancestry guides—"

"Actually," Ben interrupted her the way I was trying to teach myself not to do, but she looked at him more as if it were a charming expression of interest than a breach of etiquette. "I'm more into hiking. I like to make time for a little nature exploring whenever I'm in a new place, and I know Prospero's supposed to have all these old mining sites—"

"You don't want to go looking for those!" She was warning him very earnestly, but she glanced at me, too, and I wondered if she still remembered what she had once caught me looking at. "We've got a couple restored for public viewing, but you take one wrong step next to one of those old—"

"Exactly!"

That weird flattered look from Mrs. Voorhees again. I really needed to learn Ben's style of interruption.

"No, I was hoping you had a map of places to stay away from! My cousin slipped into an old well when we were six—well, I was six; he must have been seven. It had been mostly filled in over the years, thankfully, but it still scared the hell out of me—pardon my French, ma'am. I wouldn't risk it at all, but . . . I mean, look at this place!" He gestured at the gift shop's helpfully labeled "Vista Window," and Mrs. Voorhees looked out as proudly as if she'd designed Prospero herself, surrounding landscape and all.

"Beautiful, isn't it?" she agreed. "Our Adventure Guide points out the popular trailheads."

Ben looked like he was trying to hide his disappointment. If he had actually been trying, he would have done a better job.

"Yeah," he said wistfully. "I remember my dad helping me get certified for those beginner trails. I guess that's kind of where the obsession started for me."

Mrs. Voorhees had found the guidebook, but she didn't make him take it, just gaped at him like this was the sweetest thing she'd ever heard, which, if true, almost made me feel sorry for her.

"He was so happy when I started asking him to show me the bigger challenges," Ben hinted.

Mrs. Voorhees glanced at me, apprehensive again. "I

can't endorse reckless behavior," she said. I think that's a direct quote from the Prospero Historical Society Volunteer Handbook.

"Of course, not." Ben leaned on the counter, closer to her. I was sure she would never have let me get anywhere near it without a lecture on leaving finger smudges, even before I was banned. "But if I wanted to be reckless, I wouldn't need a map at all."

I was sure this was the point where his plan would fall apart. This was where she had to say yes or no, and as hard as he'd pulled on the "yes" side of the scale, "no" would still win, and "no" was just as big an obstacle whether it was said with single-minded conviction or not.

Trust Ben to find a third option.

He didn't ask for her answer.

"You know, if I did want to have a quick look around the museum . . . it wouldn't take too long, would it? I mean, I've always heard Prospero's had some really interesting things happen here. . . ."

He glanced over his shoulder at me, and I tried to look as if I'd be annoyed if she gave him a good reason to stick around with her any longer.

"No, it wouldn't take long, not at all!" she answered.

"You don't mind, do you?" he asked me.

I pretended to sulk harder against the doorway, and he turned back to Mrs. Voorhees.

"I was so tempted by those gold rush journals when I read they were here. I'm kind of a history buff; I'm thinking about teaching someday. I know I'd kick myself if I missed them."

"Oh." Mrs. Voorhees bit her lip and drew her eyebrows together for a moment and then stopped herself before she could crack her makeup. "Most of the historical books aren't actually on display. They're very fragile . . ." Ben didn't say anything, but somehow he made her spontaneously decide that she couldn't stand to disappoint him a second time. "But the journal's in surprisingly good condition!" She dropped her voice as if speaking in anything less than her usual maximum volume might obscure her words at all. "I can close up shop for my break. If you'd be very careful and keep it to yourself—"

"Of course!" Ben saved her from saying anything more incriminating. "I mean, if it'd be okay. I can't even tell you how cool that would be!"

Mrs. Voorhees smiled unpleasantly while she shut and locked the front door to keep me away from her computer while she gave Ben the grand tour.

I set myself up under one of the stray pines in the side yard, a feed in each ear, eyes on the tracker, front door, back door, and two rearview compact mirrors for my own safety. It was an uncomfortably warm afternoon; it only took a few minutes of trying to block the sun with the pages of my observation notebook to make me envy Ben's air-conditioned project.

It took closer to an hour to make me start to worry, to start imagining a Splinter Mrs. Voorhees taking Ben straight to what he'd really been asking for, however far away it was, even though I couldn't see any way I could have missed them leaving.

After an hour and ten, I packed up my things and was

about to start knocking on the glass door when I heard another door open inside, and Ben and Mrs. Voorhees both came back into sight in the temperate reception area, both laughing, not a drop of sweat or a hint of sunburn between them.

Ben fiddled the lock on the front door open to join me on the step, slowing down for excessive repetitions of "Thanks" and "It was great to meet you," with an encouraging smugness about his smile and a thick manila folder tucked under his arm.

Once we'd descended out of Mrs. Voorhees' sight, he opened the folder to show me the topographical maps inside.

I remembered the survey team coming out when I was little and how disappointed I'd been when the results had been kept confidential. And that was back when seeing the actual Miracle Mine would have been a cool day trip to me rather than a breakthrough in my life's work.

"And I got a look at that journal," he told me, "but it'll take a lot more than a lunch to find anything useful in it."

Lunch. The word distracted me painfully, but only for a moment.

"Did you get a copy?" I asked, wishing he'd finally adopt the logical habit of beginning with important details like that.

He pulled out his phone and brought up the slideshow of thirty-four pictures, each one of them two handwritten pages wide. Whatever involuntary reaction it caused in me doubled the triumph on his face.

Cold energy drink and matching energy bar in hand, leaning against the cool, underground wall of my room, I waited
for the photos to upload and watched Ben laying out the
map pages on the floor by the coordinate markings, pointing out his errors here and there. My skin was still stinging
from the sun. The writing in the Diary of Ambrose Arkham
was small, sloppy, and smudged in places, and the lines
on opposite pages were so misaligned with each other that
it was hardly any faster to read both at once than one at
a time, and the sketches of tunnel layouts were so crude
that they took even longer to make sense of. It took me all
of thirteen minutes to get through the whole thing, but
that was okay. Ben was only just finishing laying out the
last few pages by then.

"Okay," he squinted back and forth between the carpet
of pages and some kind of reference key on his phone, the
way Aldo did when he was trying to see too many things
at once. I wished I could just see it all for him. At least
he understood the thing, in a slow, rusty way. It probably
would have taken longer for him to teach me what I was
looking for. "There are caverns that look like they were
probably mines here . . . here . . . here. . . ." He marked
sixteen places, some small enough to put in a near perfect
circle, some long and irregularly shaped.

"How deep do these three go?" I pointed out the ones
with public tours.

"Not very. Looks like they were the newest when the
mining stopped."

"Probably not those, then. I've searched the public parts,

and people have definitely disappeared while I've been watching their main entrances."

Ben put a double minus sign next to each one. I liked it. Much better than crossing them out. He was finally understanding the concept of "probably."

"That leaves a lot of options."

"He describes the place a little," I said, "before the replacement." I meant to turn back to the first half where the only useful observations were, but I was having some trouble looking away from later entries.

"You can tell when he was replaced?"

I didn't want to end up arguing more of the obvious, not when the obvious was so awful, so I just said, "You tell me," and read to him. *"21st August, 1851: Edgar claims to be drunk on his own breath despite the caverns of air beneath us where none will venture, for fear of another collapse. Others are joining in his delusion. There is no sound of rescue, yet I remain confident in the success of our escape tunnel. This paper will not be my last will, and when you wish to know how these long days have been for me, my darling, I will be the one to place the answer in your hands."*

It went on that way for several pages, all more or less the same, divided into entry breaks with sequential dates, until the gap between the third and the sixth. I pointed this out in case the numbers weren't enough.

"It stops for two days and then picks right back up again, still in the mine."

"What, like he had something better to do there?"

"Something like that."

"What if they were just trying to conserve the lanterns?" Ben suggested.

"Then it would be unlikely for the next entry to mention one of the other miners regressing to shadow puppet making and babbling about all the shapes his older brother had taught him to make, which it does. But it's not just the time that's strange."

I reread the next few pages to myself, trying to pin down what was wrong with them.

"Afterward, he's just repeating himself." That wasn't good enough. That was most of what he'd been doing from the beginning. I tried again. "He hardly mentions any symptoms from being trapped in the mine anymore after the gap, at least not as if he's worried about them. The turns of phrase are the same, but the entries are twenty percent shorter on average, he mentions his wife and daughter less than half as often, and when he does, he only uses the same terms of endearment from earlier in the book."

Ben was on his feet, leaning on the back of my chair and squinting over my shoulder. As usual, his shape was much clearer in my awareness than its level of complexity and detail should have made it.

I tried to use the space it filled in to help me think of something more to say if he proposed that Ambrose was just dehydrated or oxygen deprived or desperate. This didn't turn out to be necessary.

"He writes like he thinks he's expected to," Ben analyzed, less precisely, but somehow more accurately than I'd been able to. "It reads like a boring school assignment."

"Yes!"

"Okay," said Ben, "that's creepy, but it doesn't get us any closer to the mine."

I pulled myself away from the Splinter entries and finally scrolled further back into the human ones.

"Right. Does anything there look like 'twin peaks of twin devils' bulge?'" I asked, rereading to double-check the miner's terminology.

Ben turned back to scan the sheets of symbols and shadings. "Well, if 'devils' bulges' are anything like Devil's Elbow, he probably means outward curving formations of rock that make them hard to climb. These two look pretty likely, but you'd be able to see them from almost anywhere near Prospero."

"He says he can see them beyond the mine on his way out from town."

Ben put more minus marks next to the two sites out farther than the two highest tree-covered outcroppings. "Anything else?"

I was sure there had been one more. "He also mentions 'four miles' headway into the sun at morning,'" I read further back.

"Okay . . ." Ben leaned closer over the sheets. "Relative to the town, the main forested area is north by northeast." He put another double minus next to the one site to the west of the interstate. "So, assuming the town hasn't gotten smaller, he lived somewhere inside it; he took the straightest possible path, walking within forty-five degrees of due east; didn't go farther than the 'devils' bulges,' and 'four miles' in old-timey prospector speak means at least 'three to four miles' . . ." He put single minuses next to the four northernmost sites, leaving six unmarked.

"It's a start."

## 12.

# A MIRACLE WOULDN'T BE SO BAD RIGHT ABOUT NOW

### Ben

A few weeks before, I'd have found a hike in the forests around Prospero something to get excited about. Peaceful even. When you get past the city limits, you've nothing but redwood trees as far as the eyes can see, trees that stretch so high into the sky they blot out the sun in some places. The air is clean and crisp and smells richly of pine, and every clearing where the sun shines through looks like it belongs in a nature club calendar.

That was before I knew about Prospero.

Knowing the horrors this town hid underneath its surface, even a day hike in the woods had me on edge. Every snap, every birdcall in the distance would put me on the alert. Every shadow seemed to hide a monster, and even the trees seemed wrong, like the light didn't fall through them correctly, or they leaned just slightly in the same direction.

The first of the bigger scares came when we were investigating the second mine site and were nearly knocked over by a group of a dozen bicyclists rocketing through a forest trail. I wasn't surprised when Kevin Brundle skidded to a stop, apologizing for almost running us over, and recommended some better hiking trails than the one we were on. I politely nodded, saying I'd consider his suggestions, then sent him back on his way.

That guy was really beginning to annoy me.

In her own odd way, Mina tried to be reassuring, saying there wasn't *much* to be afraid of, that most Creature Splinters only really came out at night because they had a hard time with the light.

It didn't help.

The only thing that really helped was knowing that if things got bad, rescue wouldn't be too far away. Billy had an evening shift and no Twist Endings practice, so he'd spent the better half of the morning driving us up the various access roads that would get us closest to the mine locations. Even though our first two stops yielded disappointing results (one mine was caved in after fifty feet, the second was covered in steel shutters that hadn't been disturbed since the 1970s), he remained as upbeat as ever, still drumming on the wheel to the radio whenever he wasn't enlightening us on his own unique philosophy of the world or showing off the ancient revolver he kept in his glove compartment "in case things got hairy, man." Normally, being in a windowless van with a strange guy who wants to show me his gun would be one of those things I wouldn't do—with Billy I just took it as part of the experience.

We were on our way to the third mine location, holding

on for dear life as the seatbelt-free van jolted back and forth violently with every minor bump in the road, when Billy suddenly swore loudly and slammed on the brakes. The engine groaned and squealed in complaint, and the van stopped with a lurching jolt. I braced myself, catching Mina as she was flung out of her seat. She looked up, annoyed, and walked up toward Billy.

"What is it?" she asked.

"A problem," he responded. I walked up behind them, looked out the windshield.

It was a problem, all right. A wrought iron gate built across the road with several large "No Trespassing" and "Danger!" signs bolted to it. It wasn't insurmountable, we could walk around or over it easily, but I got the impression we weren't entirely welcome.

"This wasn't on the map," Mina said.

"A lot of stuff wasn't on the map," I said.

"Not that big a problem. If you're in a hurry, I got some bolt cutters that'd go through that in no time. If you're not, I got some locksmithing tools in the green satchel in back. They'll take longer," Billy said, motioning to the pile of bags and toolboxes that formed a large wall in the back of his van.

"Locksmithing tools?" I asked.

Billy smiled. "Everybody needs a hobby."

I didn't argue this point. I did argue when he and Mina started talking about using the bolt-cutters. While it would have been faster, it would also be pretty obvious that *someone* had broken in, and we wanted to keep a low profile. On top of that, well . . . I had a bit of a problem with breaking the rules. If I intended to keep up an association with Mina Todd in this battle, I knew I'd have to get past that. Still, old habits . . .

We got out of the van, stretching and trying not to think about what hid behind the trees. Mina looked out of her element, blinking heavily and shielding her eyes from the sun. I reached back into the van, pulled my old, battered "3 of a Kind" baseball cap from my backpack, and tossed it to Mina. She caught it out of the air easily but then looked at it, confused.

"For the sun," I said.

"I'll be fine," she said, staring at the cards in the hat's design.

"It's more comfortable than it looks, I swear."

"Don't waste your breath, Superman. Jailbait here doesn't wear hats any more than she knows what '3 of a Kind' really means," Billy said as he rifled through the back of his van.

Mina huffed, indignant. "I know what it means. Poker, right?"

Billy laughed. "I stand corrected."

It was hard to keep from laughing with him. "You've never played poker?"

"I haven't played a lot of things," Mina explained.

"We all keep trying to teach her to live a little, but she's one stubborn little monster-hunter," Billy joked.

"I've been busy," she tried to explain.

I was still trying to wrap my head around it. Before my dad died, one of the many things he wanted me to know was all the important card games. Some of the best memories I had were playing poker for peanuts with Mom and him. He'd gotten hats for each of us because we were "3 of a Kind." For a while at least, we were.

I felt bad for Mina. Dad had always said that a healthy understanding of gambling was a rite of passage into adulthood, and because of her crusade, she'd missed out on it.

I promised myself that if we got even a moment of downtime, I'd teach her the basics. It seemed the only responsible thing to do.

Of course, that was a pretty big *if.*

Billy went to work on the heavy padlock on the gate with his bag of mismatched, rusty locksmithing tools, humming to himself and occasionally cursing. Mina looked antsy, bobbing around on her feet slightly before reaching into the van and pulling out the compilation map we had made. At its core it was still a copy of the topographical survey map we'd retrieved from the Historical Society. Since then we had traced over it several hiking trail guides, some official, some retrieved online (mostly from sites promoting UFO and monster sightings) as well as making our own notes for things we had discovered. She traced the dirt road we had been on for the past half-hour before adding a jagged hash mark across it and writing the word GATE next to it.

"It'll take some time for Billy to pick the lock. If we start walking now, we can make it to the next location in about fifteen minutes," she said firmly, showing me the map.

"How long will it take, you think?" I asked Billy.

He shrugged. "Been a while since I've done this. Could be sooner rather than later. If I were a betting man, I'd probably say later."

"Then let's get walking," I said. I grabbed my backpack,

checked to make sure the necessary supplies were there (water, snacks, flashlights, first-aid kit), and slung it over my shoulder, pulling my baseball cap low for good measure from the sun. Mina grabbed her massive Bag of Mystery and carefully folded the map into it before joining me in climbing over the gate. Billy said he'd drive up to the trail break as soon as he could and asked us not to Blair Witch it up too much in the meantime.

As we hiked, it struck me that Mina and small talk were two concepts that were very rarely in the same room together. Given how few interests she had outside of this quest, there wasn't much for us to talk about. She didn't seem to mind, but I found the silence to be deafening. My mom was always talking, always trying to fill silences, and though I hadn't entirely adopted that trait from her, I did have trouble with uncomfortable silence. I searched for a safe subject to talk about.

"So, does that thing have a story?" I asked, pointing to the tattered, oft-re-sewn black bag that she carried everywhere.

"It's a bag. I've had it for a long time. It carries everything I need," she said.

"Like?" I prodded.

"Surveillance equipment. Weapons. Flamethrowers. Some standard purse stuff, too, I think," she said as if it were the most normal thing in the world.

"Flamethrowers?" I asked. "As in more than one?"

"Of course. In case one runs out," she said conversationally. For emphasis, she reached into her bag and tossed me a red, sixteen ounce metal spray bottle. Strangely, the words FIRE EXTINGUISHER were written in bold letters around the top.

I must have looked confused, for she quickly added, "A few years back there was a company that had the brilliant idea of selling aerosol fire extinguishers. They made very poor fire extinguishers, but excellent flamethrowers. I made sure to buy as many cases as I could before the company went bankrupt."

I tossed the can back, looking at this girl in wonder. "How long have you been doing this?"

Without hesitation, she said, "A while."

A small trail broke off from the main road up ahead. It wasn't more than a foot wide and appeared to have been abandoned for some time, but it lined up with what we had found on the map. The heavy tree cover kept the under-growth light. I still picked up a large stick and used it to beat the path ahead, making sure we didn't run afoul of any snakes (or worse) hiding in the bushes.

"How much longer do you think you'll be in town?" she asked out of nowhere.

The question hit me like a ton of bricks. Honestly, it was one I hadn't put too much thought into recently. We were creeping into August. School would be starting sometime soon, and Mom would have to get back to work, but where and when . . . that was the question.

"I could be here for a few weeks, I could be here for a few hours. It's hard to know with my mom sometimes," I admitted.

"You have moved around a lot," she said. Again, it wasn't a question.

"Yes," I said. I wanted to say more, I really did, but I still barely knew her, and the way she tended to brush off anything not directly related to stopping the Splinters didn't make her the easiest person to open up to.

For some reason she trusted me. She was telling me everything she could about what was going on here, and it wasn't information that she gave away lightly. If she trusted me, it was about time I started putting some trust in her.

"I *have* moved around a lot," I said. "I barely remember what it's like to stay in one place anymore. We move into a place, we put down roots, Mom gets a job, I make friends, and for a while I wind up convincing myself that maybe this time it will be different, and maybe this time it will stick. Then she decides that things aren't working out, and we start the whole process over again. I love her, so I follow her, and I don't fight her. I just want some stability. I just want things to be . . . normal. Is that too much to ask for?"

Mina looked at me with something that might have been sympathy, "No. No, it isn't."

She was silent for another moment, biting her lip, clearly not wanting to hold back, but unfamiliar with sharing.

"My brain's never worked quite . . . in the usual way," she blurted out. The way she said it made it sound like a major confession, so I didn't tell her I'd already figured that out. "Would you believe me if I told you there was a time when I wasn't . . . this? When I might have been *almost* normal?"

I did believe her. Stranger, though, for the first time, I felt that maybe I understood her in a way that went beyond our fight with the Splinters.

Before I could think of a way to tell her, she looked up sharply, scanning the trees.

"Do you hear that?" she asked.

I listened. I couldn't hear anything. "What?"

"Exactly," Mina said, dropping her hand into her bag. It took me a second to realize what she was getting at. As we walked farther along the path, the sounds of the forest faded. There were no more birds, no more droning insects. Just the soft rustle of the wind through the trees, and the occasional sound of a pine cone falling to Earth.

It was beginning to feel a lot more like Prospero all of a sudden.

We walked through the forest with greater caution. The wind was picking up, almost making it sound as if there were faint voices hiding among the trees, whispering, watching us. The trees were darker, thicker, letting less sun through, many of them bearing jagged cut marks on them as if some wild beast had slashed at them. Out of the corner of my eye, I could have sworn I saw a figure running between the trees. By the time I looked, it was gone.

"We're here," Mina said as we entered a small clearing.

Once upon a time, this area had been cleared, but nature had done its best to reclaim what was rightfully its own. The remains of an old, wooden cart lay overgrown with ivy off to one side, and a pair of metal mine cart tracks stretched almost into the forest from the hillside. Odd bits of garbage, crushed cans of Coke, and cigarette butts showed that this area still had occasional, if not regular, visitors.

More than any of the other mine locations we'd visited, it held a vague feeling of wrongness. The ground beneath our feet was cracked and felt somewhat unsteady. Every so often we saw a gnarled bush of thick vines, bulging and spreading across the ground in an unnatural fashion. One particularly large bush, vibrantly green and dotted with sickly brown flowers, had a bleached deer antler hanging from it. That feeling of being watched was stronger than ever, and, for a moment, I was sure we had found what we were looking for.

That hope disappeared quickly when we saw the mine entrance.

At least, where the mine entrance should have been.

The rusted metal tracks in the ground led toward the hill, and certainly would have led into the hill itself, had a massive redwood tree not grown right in the way. We could see a few ancient wooden beams that made up the frame of the mine, but they were so compressed by the tree that I doubted even a monster could find its way around.

"So we can cross this one off the list?" I said.

Mina looked at the mine entrance long and hard before saying, "Probably. It could be that—"

A car horn started beeping frantically not too far away. Billy.

Without thinking, we ran down the trail back to the main road.

Billy had gotten his van past the gate. Another car, a

Jeep better suited for these roads, was parked right behind it. I didn't need to see the "PROSPERO SHERIFF'S DEPT." decal on the side of it to know we were in trouble.

Billy stood at the front of his van, running his hands through his hair, exasperated. There were two men in sheriff's uniforms talking to him: one who looked like he'd just graduated high school, the other a stout, balding man with glasses I remembered vaguely from the block party.

"I swear, guys . . . I didn't see the signs! The gate was open when I got there. I thought it was, like, a temporary thing! I'm just trying to encourage an interest in the outdoors. Is that really so bad?" Billy pleaded. I'm sure he was doing everything possible to keep them from searching his van. He looked around desperately for help, then caught sight of us in the tree line. I half-expected him to wave us away, but the moment he saw us he called out.

"See, there they are! They'll back me up!"

I wanted a good place to hide, right then and there. Mina sighed heavily. This wasn't good for either of us.

"Let me do the talking," I said.

"If you insist," Mina agreed. "You've been pretty good at that so far." She walked down toward the gate, half a step behind me, with her hands raised, looking very ready to kneel and place them behind her head in what I could already tell would be an all-too-practiced motion.

She didn't even fake a smile when she said, "Hello, Sheriff Diaz. Deputy Arbogast. What seems to be the problem?"

The older man looked at Mina as if he wished anyone *but* her had just walked out of the forest.

SPLINTERS

"Mina Todd. What are *you* doing all the way out here?"
he asked.

"It was my fault," I said. "I'm not in town long, and Mina
was showing me some of the old hiking trails in the forest.
I gave her a hard time when she said we should stick to the
marked trails. I was looking for a bit more adventure, and
we might've gone a little too far off the map. Please, please
don't take out on her what was my error in judgment."

I was hoping that whatever little credit I still had as a
town hero would lessen whatever trouble we were in. The
Sheriff sighed, looking at the three of us.

"I'm not gonna write up anything official about this,
this time," he said. "But I have to tell your mother, Mina."

I interjected, "Now that really isn't neces—"

The Sheriff pointed at me, "I'm afraid it is, Ben. We got a
call about some trespassers, and her name was mentioned.
Her mom's gonna hear about it no matter what happens.
Besides, Mina here's got a history of sticking her nose where
it ought not be. And if my reprimand doesn't stick, you
can sure as hell bet her mom's will. I'm not bringing you
in, Ben, because people around here like you, and it'd be
a damn shame to see a boy with as promising a future as
yours get a mark on his record. Don't make me change my
mind by saying another word. Are we clear?"

"Crystal," I said.

"Good," Sheriff Diaz said. "Take a word of advice, son.
Stay away from this girl. She's nothing but trouble."

I wanted to say something cool then, something along

the lines of *I like trouble,* but fear of arrest shut me up. The Sheriff looked back to Billy.

"You make sure these kids get back to town safe, and keep a better eye out for signs next time?" he asked.

"Yes, your highness," Billy stammered, almost terrified.

The Sheriff looked at him oddly, then turned about on his feet and walked back to the Jeep, shaking his head.

Billy looked at both of us, saddened. I couldn't blame him. Just when it felt like we were making progress, we were being shut down.

## 13.

## I CAN'T ARGUE WITH THAT

### Mina

Billy drummed his fingers nervously on the steering wheel for the first few turns down the hill and back into town, keeping perfect rhythm as always.

"I can't—"

"I know," I stopped him when he tried to apologize.

"You know I love doing this for you guys—"

"I know."

"But I really can't afford to get in any more trouble—"

"I know."

"And if those police dogs get a whiff of my car—"

"*I know*," I repeated. "It's okay. It's not going to do any good, anyway, going out there again now."

Ben looked like I'd confirmed his worst fears.

"So whose place am I taking you to?" Billy sighed.

The sensible answer would have been, "Both."

The sooner I got home, the less worry I'd have to diffuse about how big a spectacle I might be making of myself in front of the cops, and I certainly couldn't have Ben anywhere near Mom when she got the call.

Ben and I could regroup later. I was free to use his number now.

But for reasons I couldn't fully explain, I just couldn't leave him looking so disappointed.

Billy must have noticed, too, because when I didn't answer right away, he retracted the question.

"Hey, how about a malt first, on me? Least I can do."

"On me" just meant he'd risk getting one of his coworkers not to charge us at all, but it was still a good idea.

I got the most challenging thing I could think of to drink, a bubble gum thick shake with a double scoop of gummy bears, and waited for Ben's Cherry Timewarp to arrive before sorting out the edible and inedible globs of sweetness in my mouth enough to talk.

"This isn't a loss," I said. He needed to know that even though I knew he wasn't going to like the reason.

"How do you figure?" Ben bit into one of the cherries more violently than usual, as if he could bite the difficult parts out of the day.

Billy stirred his root beer float a little more quietly, and I almost hoped he'd say it so I wouldn't have to, but I hadn't built my Network by delegating the most unpleasant tasks.

I took another spoonful of shake and sorted it while I sorted words.

"Someone sent the cops after us." I bit the frozen gummy bears down to a swallowable size to give my tongue room to maneuver. "That could even be a good thing. It could mean we were getting close. Now we know we *definitely* have to check the next mine over from the blocked one. We can't do that until we can figure out how to distract whoever's watching."

Ben seemed to understand this, at least for the most part. "Whoever?" he repeated. "If they're watching, aren't they *all* watching? Aren't they all part of the same thing?"

"That doesn't mean all the parts have to do the same thing at the same time. We'd be one job on a long list."

"Okay . . ." said Ben. "That's easy, then. Who could have known where—No."

He'd figured it out, and as I'd anticipated, he wasn't happy.

"So she *did* know where you were going?" I confirmed.

"Haley is *not* a Splinter!"

I'd just taken another bite, and I'm sure I swallowed at least a little gum in order to point out promptly, "You don't have proof of that."

"You don't have proof she *is*."

"It's the more probable assumption. She's been taken by them. She knew where we were."

"It wasn't her!"

"Guys," Billy interrupted us, slamming his spoon into the bottom of the glass harder than was necessary to break down the scoop of ice cream. "I'm just thinking out loud here, and I shouldn't even be talking trash to you kids about anyone for bringing in law enforcement, but just for the sake of, you know, thinking things through, is there anyone else it *could* have been?"

I seriously doubted it, though he was right that it was only fair to give it some thought. I scooped up the chunkiest lump of ice cream the spoon could hold and tried. Ben took a long sip and probably tried harder.

*Gum.*

*Gummy bear.*

*Gummy bear.*

*Gum.*

"Well, if she could have mentioned it in passing to—"

"What about Kevin?"

Ben interrupted so decisively that I didn't bother trying to finish the thought I'd had no particular faith in anyway.

"No one would have had to tell him. He was there. In fact, he's just happened to be in a *lot* of places I've been lately."

Billy raised an eyebrow at me, asking me if this didn't sound reasonable.

I folded a gummy bear into a lump of bubble gum so I could chew it back out while I tried to think of a reason it wouldn't be reasonable.

"*And* his father owns the closest car dealership," Ben continued.

"That just means his family's collaborating! It doesn't prove he's one of them!"

"You don't have *proof* about Haley either! How can you not be just as suspicious of him?"

Ben and Billy both stared at me, waiting for my answer. There wasn't a good one.

*Gum.*

*Gummy bear.*

*Gum.*

*Gummy bear.*

"I can't," I agreed.

I still believed (or wanted to believe) checking up on Kevin would be a waste of time, but there was no excuse not to, at least not one that hadn't led me wrong before.

I don't work on gut instincts.

I took out my phone and hit the first number on speed dial.

"What are you doing?" Ben asked warily.

"You're right," I explained again because he didn't seem to have understood that part.

" . . . Really?"

"Yes. So now I have to teach you how to set up surveillance."

Aldo picked up halfway through the last word.

"Wait," he said. "Let me guess what you called for. It ends with 'ail-ence.' I'll be right—"

"I'm not at home," I warned him. "Probably won't get any privacy there today at all."

Avoiding home wasn't the quickest way to get the day's bust forgotten; however it was better than trying to pick microphones apart right under Mom's nose while she was lecturing me.

"Well, we can't do it here."

When it came to Aldo's parents' moods, he never had to say more than that.

"Okay," I said. "Bring what you can and meet us at Billy's in ten."

Billy sipped his float hesitantly for a few moments after I hung up and checked his own phone. There was only another hour before his evening shift. "Fine. But if you get caught, I had no idea you went there after I trustingly dropped you off in front of a parental residence."

"Deal."

Billy lived in half an old duplex right next to the interstate. The other half was empty, which was lucky because his soundproofing attempts were more decorative than functional. There was no air conditioner, limited floor space, not much in the kitchen other than expired burger buns, soda syrup, and six half-empty jars of mustard all rescued from the Fountain, and it was going to be a steep uphill walk to the Brundle place when we were ready. At least we had a place to work.

Ben and I only had a few minutes alone after Billy went back to the Fountain, clearing the laundry off one end of the coffee table in an awkward silence I couldn't quite understand, considering the fact that I'd surrendered our last argument.

Then Aldo knocked on the door, and I began to form an idea about where the awkwardness was coming from based on how suddenly it intensified.

Aldo's arms were so full when I opened the door that he went straight to the space we'd cleared to collapse among the boxes of cell phone parts and coils of wire before looking at us.

When he saw Ben, he stood up, straightened his shirt, straighter than I'd known it could get, and held his hand out. Well, out and up, since being even a couple inches shorter than I am, he barely stood as high as Ben's chest.

"You're Ben Pastor," he said. "I know you are. Mina made me watch six hours of video of you last week," he explained.

"You're Aldo," Ben responded in kind, accepting the handshake very formally, as if it were being offered by a precocious child. That is, if Ben were the kind of person who gets extremely uncomfortable around children, which I knew from his Facebook he wasn't. "I haven't seen any video of you, but Mina's mentioned you once or twice. Her *techie?*"

He emphasized the word "techie" a little harder than he needed to, and I got the strange impression that he was thinking about other words that could almost have fit into that part of the sentence but didn't. What words they were, I couldn't guess.

"Yeah, that's me." Aldo gestured around at the equipment. He didn't start explaining what any of it was or what we were going to do with it, so I gave him a nudge.

"We haven't identified a window of time to get anything into his wallet or phone," I said, "so I'm thinking a couple basic roof cams, a good, long-term bug in his bedroom, a GPS unit for his bike, and another good bug for his father's office, unless you think you can hack his voice mail."

Normally, Aldo would have asked me if I was sure that was all I would need and if I could possibly find a use for his latest invention, whatever that happened to be, but his attention was still on Ben. He just acknowledged with a dignified nod that all those things were possible.

"Who are we . . . concerned about again?" he asked.

"Kevin Brundle," Ben said promptly.

Aldo did a double-take and turned to check with me.

Then he must have noticed Ben staring harder at him because he looked back, and I could have applauded them both for their mistrust if it hadn't been so inconvenient at that particular moment.

"How much does he know now?" Aldo asked.

"Almost everything," I said.

Both of them looked annoyed with me, Ben for the "almost" and Aldo for the "everything," I assumed.

"Everything that matters," I clarified.

"How much does *he* know?" Ben asked.

"Everything that matters," I repeated.

"Like why suspecting Kevin is such a big deal?" he pushed.

I took one of the wire coils and started re-coiling it to prepare myself. Ben was right. Now that he was a full member of my Network, I needed to break the habit of keeping secrets from him without a really good reason, and I didn't have one for this.

"Kevin knows about the Splinters," I explained.

"You told him?" Ben guessed. From there it got trickier.

"Not exactly. You know his brother . . . disappeared?"

Ben put it together pretty quickly. "The Splinters? But . . . why did he disappear? Why didn't they just replace him?"

"I caught them," I said. That was the simple version. "Kevin and I are the only ones who saw what they did to him after that. I offered Kevin a place in the Network, protection, but he turned me down. He said that he's not a fighter. And that he would prefer to try to trust people, live a normal life, and accept the end whenever and however it comes, instead of living like me. I hoped his awareness would keep him safe, but that doesn't mean it did. And he did make me promise that I wouldn't waste my time watching him for his own good. It's not for his own good this time."

Ben accepted this, but he didn't stop there. "Does 'everything that matters' include all the ways you spy on him? On me?"

I didn't fight it. I listed every method of surveillance I'd used on Ben as quickly as I could. "If you fall out of touch for long enough to be replaced, it disqualifies you as an ECNS, so if this is what you want, I wouldn't—"

"I'm not going to disable them. I just wanted to know. Does it include the fact that you don't know for sure about Haley? Does it include what you think of your dad?"

"You told him about your dad?" Aldo asked me indignantly. "You waited two years to tell me that!"

"I've had more time to come to terms with it now," I explained.

Ben was looking a lot happier, but that didn't help break down the giant blockade of awkwardness that was still stopping us from getting anything done.

After a few more seconds of Ben and Aldo staring at each other as if there were infinite visual details between them to keep them occupied, Ben got serious again—a similar kind of serious to the mysterious, disarming way he could interrupt people.

"Whatever you're going to do with those boxes, I promise, I won't tell anyone."

Aldo waited just another 2.3 seconds before kneeling to

unpack one of the boxes, handing Ben a tiny webcam, and breaking open a few cheap prepaid flip phones.

"Where do you get all this stuff?" Ben asked, turning the webcam over in his hand.

"My dad owns Prospero Electronics Repair," Aldo answered shortly.

Ben raised an eyebrow.

"He *did* promise," I reminded Aldo. I had no high ground when it came to short answers, but at least Ben had been happy with mine.

Aldo sighed. "You know the Green Caller free E-waste disposal bin in front of the shop?"

Ben hadn't been near Prospero Electronics Repair, but he looked on steadily, as if he had.

"There's no company called the Green Caller," Aldo admitted.

Ben looked equal parts impressed and frightened, something I thought should have made Aldo very pleased with himself. He changed the subject very quickly.

"Be careful with that," he told Ben. "We're going to set it up for you to plant it on Kevin's roof."

Ben set the camera down on the coffee table, almost as carefully as he asked, "So . . . you *are* going to help me? With *my* idea?"

Aldo set out one of his USB battery packs and a roll of duct tape with a stern look. It didn't fit easily on his childish face, but somewhere around the time he'd figured out how to get us all that free, life-saving electronic scrap, he'd earned the right to wear it now and then. "You're a member of the Network. You don't have to sound so surprised."

# 14.

## BREAKING AND ENTERING

### Ben

Summer. We had to do this during the summer. At any other time of the year, there would have been almost no foot traffic on the street during the middle of the day. People would be at work, kids would be in school, and the street would be doing its best ghost-town impression, minus a tumbleweed or two. It would be a perfect time to plant illicit surveillance equipment.

We had to make do in the middle of a heat wave in August. Someone next door was throwing a barbeque. Across the street two houses down, a group of kids played on a Slip 'n Slide. The faint jangling sound of an ice-cream truck's bells promised more visitors on the street in the next few minutes. I could have gone for some ice cream. Some barbeque. I could have even gone for some time on the Slip 'n Slide.

Instead I lay face down on the roof of the two-story Brundle house, trying to remain invisible as I wired together a webcam, motion detector, and battery above the front door. Nobody had noticed me so far, but I was looking forward to getting out of there as soon as possible. None of us knew how long the Brundles would be out running errands. We could have had ten minutes or ten hours for all we knew. Aldo was keeping an eye out for us, but between that and monitoring the computer, he could only do so much.

Everything looked together. I hit the "on" switch, tapping the Bluetooth Mina had given me.

"Everything working?" I asked.

"I can see your shin just fine," Aldo said. "Turn the camera a good one-eighty and it might actually be of some use."

I'd say I was beginning to think that Aldo didn't like me—to be honest that was pretty clear from the start. Still, this was his realm. I wasn't going to argue with him. I continued playing with the camera's angle until he said it was all right, checking over my shoulder every few seconds for the cop car I was sure would come any moment.

Thankfully, it didn't.

Carefully, slowly, I began climbing to the peak of the roof so I could plant the one above the back door. That would be a lot easier; you don't normally have to worry about people staring into your backyards.

I pushed the reusable grocery bag of cameras Mina had given me just over the peak and made sure it wasn't going to fall before I climbed over after it. As I reached the top, I felt a brief, fleeting moment of triumph for having done this without getting caught.

Then my left foot slid out from underneath me.

I fell face-first onto the roof and began to slide down the slope toward the yard. Ever since that night with the deer,

# SPLINTERS

I'd been in constant fear of being killed by some monster. It never entered my mind that this might all end with me breaking my neck in Kevin Brundle's backyard.

The rain gutter saved my life. I grabbed it by my fingertips at the last second, hanging off the edge of the roof. If I didn't think it would make me fall, I'd have laughed at that moment.

The Bluetooth rang to life in my ear. Mina's voice.

"Ben? Are you all right?"

"I'm fine," I lied, looking down at the twenty feet of air beneath me. "Just took a tumble."

"And the cameras?" This girl didn't miss anything. Pulling myself up in a chin-up, I could still see the bag where I'd left it on the roof.

"Thanks for your concern," I muttered.

"Did I, or did I not ask if you were all right?" she asked with a hint of true confusion. "First, even," she added.

"They're fine," I said.

"Good. Our time's running out. Get the cameras above his bedroom window and the back door. I need to plant the rest of the bugs before the mission is complete," Mina continued.

Nope. She didn't miss a thing.

It was just as I was pulling myself back up onto the roof of the house that the question hit me.

I tapped the Bluetooth in my ear, "Hey guys, just how many laws are we breaking right now?"

"A lot," Mina said.

"It's best not to think too much about it," Aldo added quickly.

"That's what I thought," I said. Yeah, it was just another average afternoon of hanging out with Mina Todd. Breaking the law, indulging in conspiracy theories, nearly getting killed. It should have gotten to me. It should have made me feel wrong. Instead, I felt strangely exhilarated. At first I didn't know why, but, as I placed the camera over the Brundles' back door, it hit me. Ever since I had come to Prospero, I'd felt like I was being watched. There were eyes on me at all times, some human, some Splinter. For once, it felt great to be the one doing the watching. I knew it wasn't foolproof, I knew we might find nothing that would implicate Kevin, but to do something, *anything* felt better than doing nothing.

The second camera placed, I began to climb up the slope of the roof to what Mina claimed was Kevin's bedroom window. I didn't know how she knew which room was Kevin's, and enough of me knew better than to ask. What I did know was that the window was now open.

It hadn't been when I first passed by.

I climbed up the roof slowly, carefully, keeping an ear out for any movement inside. There was nothing. No movement, no voices, no sign that Kevin had come home early. I wanted to tap my Bluetooth to check in with the others, but if he had somehow made it home without us noticing, I didn't want to give us away by talking. Instead, I crept up the roof and peeked inside.

I didn't see Kevin. I did see Mina looking at me rather intently.

"Hi," I said, confused.

"Have you placed the other cameras yet?" she asked.

"One more to go. I saw the window was open. I wanted to make sure everything was all right before I tried for this one," I said.

"Next time, call in before you do anything unplanned. You were lucky. I was checking if outside noise would interfere with the bugs. If he had come home early and opened his window, you might have just revealed our presence. We would have failed," she said bluntly.

"I'm sorry," I said.

"Don't be sorry. Just understand the stakes of what we're doing here," she said, heading back inside. I sat on the roof, catching my breath and taking in what had happened over the past few minutes.

Then the Bluetooth rang to life in my ear, "Don't take it personal. She's like that with all of us when she's on a mission."

I laughed. "Thank you, Aldo. I'll take that under advisement."

I placed the third camera as quickly as I could above Kevin's window before climbing inside after Mina. Much like Kevin himself, his room was an orderly mess. His walls were plastered with posters from dozens of rock bands I'd never heard of, mostly advertising benefit concerts for various charities. The potted herbs he kept just beneath his window were vibrant and well maintained, filling the room with an earthy, almost spicy smell. His bed was a simple futon rolled into the corner (skipping the bed frame so he could save half a tree, I'm sure), and I didn't need to look too close to know the sheets had to be made of all-natural fibers.

Mina stood by his desk, hastily screwing the base of a lamp back together.

"What's that?" I asked.

Mina pointed to the laptop he'd left closed on his desk. "I expected him to still have a desktop that I could hide the bug in, but he must have upgraded recently. So . . . I had to improvise."

I didn't need her to explain twice. She'd taught me earlier that despite what movies would make you think, bugs and other surveillance devices will need a steady flow of power if you want a steady flow of information, which is why it's usually best to hide them in something that needs to be plugged in near where you expect important conversations to occur.

"Do you have the others placed yet?" I asked, tossing her the empty grocery bag.

She shook her head. "We've had some setbacks. Nothing devastating, but inconvenient. Kevin's bicycle wasn't in the garage. He must have taken it with them when they left. That will cut down on much of what we'll be capable of. I was still able to hide a bug in the kitchen and a camera in their garage door opener."

"Okay, what about his dad's office?" I asked.

Mina paused. She got that look on her face like she was holding back again.

"I hadn't gotten to it yet," she said.

"This one's finished?" I asked.

"Yes."

"Then let's get to it," I said. I didn't want to add that

actually breaking into another person's house without their knowledge made me a little uncomfortable (the roof was one thing, actually being inside . . .). Thankfully, I didn't have to. Packing up her bag, she led me purposefully through the house, out of Kevin's room, along the hallway, and down the stairs without the slightest hesitation.

"Have you been here before?" I asked.

Mina didn't look at me when she answered, "A long time ago."

"Am I going to get any more than that?"

Still, she didn't look. She pinched the bridge of her nose, squinting as if fighting off a headache. "Not yet."

I sighed, adding this to the rather long list of things I wanted to ask Mina about in the future.

If there was a future for us, at least.

She paused at the entrance to Mr. Brundle's office, taking in the room with wondrous, almost sad eyes. It was as if she had been expecting something else and was let down to find it just an ordinary, suburban home office. I was about to ask another question I was sure she wouldn't answer when the buzzing in my pocket stole my attention. Mina shot me a harsh look. I raised a hand apologetically. She had told me to shut off my cell phone before we began setting up surveillance. I hadn't forgotten, but apparently I had set my phone on vibrate instead of silent.

I pulled the phone from my pocket, meaning to silence it. When I saw the name in the window, I winced.

"I'm sorry, I have to take this, I'll make it quick," I said. Mina's gaze could have cut through diamonds. Luckily she was too busy disassembling the phone on Irwin Brundle's desk to stop me. I walked back into the hallway, pulling the Bluetooth from my ear as I took the call.

"Hi, Haley," I said. I'd been almost completely dodging her ever since Mina had brought me into the fold. I hated lying to her, constantly coming up with excuses why we couldn't spend time together. It was the only way I could protect her, and maybe if I could clear her name with Mina, I wouldn't have to lie anymore.

"Hey, Ben," she said. She was trying to sound perky, but she could not hide the sadness in her voice. No, sadness and something more. Fear.

"Is everything all right?" I asked.

There was a long moment of silence on the other end of the line. I expected her to hang up, to tell me that there was nothing to worry about and that she'd dialed me by accident even though she really just meant to see if I would take her calls.

Maybe that would have been better.

"You told me a while ago that if I ever wanted to talk to you . . . about what happened, that you would listen?"

That was unexpected.

"Yes," I said. I looked back to Mina, who couldn't have looked more irritated.

"I think I'm remembering. I've only seen it in dreams, but it feels real, it feels more like a memory than a dream. I can remember the forest. I can remember a cave. . . ."

Mina came at me quickly, eyes wide, "Hang up."

My eyes asked for an explanation.

"Haley, look, I'll be over in a couple hours, maybe we can talk this out—"

She cut me off, "I can remember people from the town being there with me! People who've been watching me! Ben, there's something scary going on—"

Mina reached up, grabbed the phone from my hand and hung it up.

"What the hell?" I asked.

"We have to go, now!" she said as she stormed back into the office and began to quickly pack up her gear.

"What's going on?" I asked.

She tapped the Bluetooth in her ear. "How soon?" She waited for a response, nodded and hastily set about putting the rest of the surveillance equipment in her bag.

"What is it?" I asked.

Mina looked at me, irritated, "If you'd kept your Bluetooth in, you'd have heard Aldo telling us that Kevin and his parents are coming home, right now. They are about to enter the garage, *right now.* We have to get out of here, *right now!*"

We should have run right then and there, but the look of defeat on Mina's face gave me what was almost certainly a terrible idea.

Plugging the Bluetooth back into my ear, I asked, "Do they have Kevin's bicycle with them?"

"Camera doesn't have a good angle on them but . . . yes, it's on the back of the car," Aldo answered me.

"Good," I looked to Mina. "Do you still have that GPS unit you wanted to put in his bike?"

She didn't need my plan explained. "That's too dangerous."

"So is living in this town, and we do it anyway," I said.

She looked at me, anxious. We could hear the low drone and thud of the garage door opening near us.

"I can do this," I said.

Mina nodded. She tossed the small black cylinder, barely bigger than my thumb, to me. Then, as if a better plan had just hit her, she unslung the bag from her shoulder and gave it to me, pausing long enough to grab a battered yearbook from it.

"What's this?" I asked.

"Backup plan," she said, "Come on!"

She pulled me into a closet just off of the kitchen, closing the door just as we heard the Brundles coming in. To say the least, it was a tight squeeze.

"I'm sorry," she whispered as she tried to shift into a more comfortable position.

"It's okay," I said.

"It's a small closet," she whispered again.

"I know," I said.

Under normal circumstances, the fact that I was pressed uncomfortably close to her in a closet would have held my attention; these were hardly normal circumstances. My heart was pounding. We could hear them putting away groceries, talking, laughing. They sounded so normal, so human, that it was hard to believe that Kevin was very likely a monster.

I just hoped there was nothing important in here they had to get in the immediate future because if they did, we were in trouble.

Soon enough, though, they left the kitchen. We heard them walk down the hall, splitting up. We only had to wait a moment longer before Aldo's voice rang in our ears.

"Okay, I think you're clear. Mr. Brundle's in his office, Mrs. Brundle's in the backyard taking some sheets down from the clothesline. Kevin's gone out back, too. Looks like he's dropping some garbage in their compost heap. The garage door's still open, I think you can make it out that way pretty quick," he said.

I opened the closet door and peered outside. The coast was clear. Crouching low, I hurried across the kitchen with Mina right behind me. Her heavy bag slung over my shoulder made this maneuver awkward, and I wondered how it was so easy for her to carry all the time.

We made it to the garage unseen. Kevin had taken his bike off the back of the car and leaned it up against the wall. It looked like he'd be using it pretty soon. I scanned the bicycle, trying to find a good spot to hide the tracker. I had no doubt that Kevin knew every inch of his bike, he would certainly be able to figure out if something new was attached to it, which only meant that I had to find some way to hide it inside.

The seat.

I grabbed the seat of the bicycle and twisted. With some effort, it came loose, and I found the base to be just wide enough to fit the tracker inside the hollow frame. It might rattle around a little, but maybe with some of the duct tape we—

"Get out of there now!" Aldo hollered over the line. "Kevin just told his dad he was heading out for a ride. He's coming for you. You've got twenty seconds tops to get out!"

I looked at Mina. She looked at me. Though she looked worried for a fraction of a second, the resolve on her face was clear. She pulled the Bluetooth from her ear and pocketed it, clutching the yearbook tightly to her chest.

"Finish the job. Finish it right. Then run. Run away as fast as you can. We can't afford you being caught. I will likely be in trouble for a while," she said. Then, looking at me with what could have passed for a smile, she added, "You've done well."

Swiftly, she opened the door to the house and darted inside. I quickly tore a strip of duct tape from one of the rolls in Mina's bag and used it to wedge the tracker inside the frame of Kevin's bike. I could hear voices inside, surprised, yelling. Mina sounded defensive, Kevin upset. I screwed the bicycle seat back on, made sure it was locked tight. I shook the bike, the tracker didn't rattle. It was perfect.

The fight sounded more heated. I made for the door, went to rescue her. I didn't know how, I didn't know what I would say to make this right, but I had to get her out.

*Finish the job. Finish it right. Then run.*

I cursed Mina Todd for putting me in this position. I cursed her for making me fight against every instinct I had.

Even more, though, I cursed myself for listening to her.

I ran like mad from the garage, then down the street.

Once I was out of sight and out of breath, I slowed to a stroll, trying to look normal. The kids at the Slip 'n Slide smiled and waved at me as I passed. I waved back casually.

I was clear. I'd made it. I'd finished the job, I finished it right, and I'd run away.

The mission was complete. But at what cost?

# 15.

## SO THIS IS A SOCIAL VISIT
### Mina

Sometimes I wondered if my mother knew the vague, erratic, uncomfortable way my mind cycled through events, favoring the most recent, when I was unable to work. If she did, she also knew she'd found a rare method of enforcing the order to "go to your room and think about what you've done."

The equipment was in place, and Ben was in the clear. Those were the two cycling thoughts that gave me hope whenever they came around, the ones I tried to hold onto the longest. They made time pass a lot more quickly than the thought that the equipment might not last long enough to be useful now that the Brundles had reason to be suspicious of me. Ordinary, uninformed people would just check that none of their valuables were missing and continue about their business with a lower opinion of me.

Kevin knew me better than that. The real Kevin knew enough to do a rudimentary bug sweep if he felt the inclination, and if he had been replaced . . . I'd heard Splinters regurgitate memories that could only have been made by the human. A Splinter Kevin might do the same thing. In fact, if Kevin had been taken, the Splinters might know a whole lot more about me than I wanted them to. I hadn't known about the memory transfer when I'd promised not to watch Kevin, and afterward, I hadn't really wanted to acknowledge the problem, not with the promise already made. Maybe I'd even liked having that security risk, taking the information the Splinters *weren't* acting on against me as evidence that Kevin was still safe, although that seemed like an absurd arrangement in retrospect.

I could have planted the essentials myself and come back with the rest later. Instead I'd brought Ben in, outside his area of expertise because cutting him out of his own plan had felt . . . what? Rude? Cold? Because I'd been sheltering his ego, or trying to impress him with my capacity for trust, or something else as ridiculous as that? And as a result, Kevin had the old yearbook back, the last of my stockpiled excuses to visit him, my computer power cord and my two best cell phones were locked in my mother's briefcase, and Dad was dropping in to call down the stairs to me at least once every two hours, making it impossible for me to download the feeds from any of my equipment or to call or find Ben to apologize. And those things would continue to be impossible for the next two weeks, or until Aldo could get his hands on the right obsolete replacement cord, whichever came first.

Two weeks.

*A few weeks, a few hours.*

I might not even get to talk to Ben again before he'd be reading my messages from his own desk, five hundred miles to the south, or from a new one in whatever town struck his mother's fancy next. I wondered if Mom would let him drop off my bag on his way out of town. I already felt naked from being without it.

I'd known it would be this way when I'd selected him, of course. The kind of hands-on work we'd been doing together was never going to be permanent, certainly not until he was old enough to go where he chose, probably not until after college, and maybe not even then. That had been part of the appeal, to have someone I'd personally trained in the basics too far away for them to take; someone I could turn my back on for two hours at a time and still trust; someone to talk to on the outside, to remind me of a whole world to protect beyond the borders of my festering little town; someone who would remember to fear and fight the Splinters even if they someday took me and all the other local human minds away. But it was getting more and more difficult to remind myself what a beneficial arrangement this would be.

I wasn't experiencing this difficulty for *dangerous* reasons, I was sure of that. I was finished with those. What the sensible reasons were, I hadn't been able to identify yet.

My one remaining phone was a prepaid with no minutes and only one text message left on it. I needed that to tell Aldo to watch my spare emergency tracker, which I attached to my bra to reduce the risk of being separated from it. Aldo responded only with assurance that he would watch both Ben's tracker and mine and keep himself in safety contact with Billy, followed with sympathies made brief by the prepaid's ruthless character limit.

After that, there was nothing to do but toss a new experimental stimulus in the specimen containment chamber with the half-rat Splinter every hour or so and wait for something to happen. Waiting meant hours of aimless brain exercises, which brought the thoughts into focus, both the good ones and the bad ones. Since there was nothing I could actually accomplish with them, I switched back and forth a few times, turning my keyboard on and off, opening and closing my newest Sudoku book, letting events cycle past, blurry, sharp, blurry, sharp, trying to decide which was better.

"Trespassing." My mother had repeated the word several times over, calmly, deliberately, as if that would change its meaning. "Trespassing. Twice in one day?"

I'd had no answer for that. There was never a useful one when she was reiterating the facts.

"How do you think this makes me look?"

There was rarely an answer for that either.

"How many times will I have to tell you to leave that family alone? Don't you think you've done enough damage yet?"

That one I answered, sort of.

"What damage would that be?"

She didn't answer me back, but she didn't break her calm, deliberate composure either, her lawyer's method of expressing rage. We both knew what damage she meant. It was on the long list of things we didn't speak about. She'd already reminded me, and that hurt enough.

"What were you doing?" she asked instead.

I'd tried to mention the yearbook again, my admittedly cheap excuse, but she'd waved it away.

"In the forest. With that *boy?*"

The edge to her voice when she mentioned Ben had stunned me for a moment.

"I thought you *wanted* me to meet a nice boy my own age." The way I'd pointed this out sounded very reasonable in my head, but I couldn't be sure how much my memory had altered it.

"Not if this is what you're going to do with him. Did the police scare him away, or was he just hiding better the second time?"

I didn't answer that one, didn't blink or look away.

"Honey . . ." Even in replay it made me shudder when she called me that. It was even worse than a term of endearment from Dad, like being patronized by a cold, digital smartphone personal assistant. "You know you don't have the best judgment around boys your age." That made me shudder harder. "And that's okay. You're young. But it does mean I have to be concerned about the ones who might be dangerous."

It was at around this point in the argument when I'd given up all hope of getting out of any trouble. There was only one reason I could think of that she wouldn't be overjoyed at the prospect of having me seen in public with someone as normal as Ben, and I couldn't even debate it with her without crossing our unspoken line.

"Dangerous because he's living with *her?*" I'd asked this very ferociously. "Or are you just afraid he'll stab me with one of his merit badges?" At the time I hadn't cared how much my rhetorical style of spite took after hers, but the resemblance sickened me afterward. "How long do you expect to have it both ways? I know *exactly* how much you care about what happens to the Brundles! Why won't you just *say* this is all about keeping me away from Ben? And how can you tell me he's dangerous if you won't admit *what she is?*"

Mom had stopped pretending to reason with me then. I tried to make my brain fast forward over her exhaustive inventory of all the things I was not to do for the next two weeks, but it skipped around and repeated that part in even more excessive detail than the rest. When it had finally temporarily tired of those few minutes and skipped further back to the debacle at the Brundle house itself, I spent a while trying to figure out when, exactly, in those critical, disastrous seconds, had something been tapping on the window . . . before I realized that the tapping wasn't in my memory, and it wasn't on one of Kevin's windows, it was on mine.

First there was a rush of that mad, unfocused, gut-deep sort of fear I still sometimes felt, the fear of all the inhuman things that window left me partially exposed to, the fear that made me want to set up the barricade and never touch it again.

Then it faded into the ordinary fear of a more probable human caller being spotted from the outside by one of my parents, which made me slide the window wide open so the visitor could roll down onto the couch inside.

It wasn't Aldo, and he wasn't carrying a power cord or a phone.

It was Ben, with my bag slung securely over his shoulder. He carried a six-pack of Monster and a round leather case about the size of a small birthday cake, which rattled with a very non-electronic resonance when he moved.

Mysteriously, I wasn't at all disappointed.

At least I'd get the chance to apologize, but I wasn't even quick enough to be the first one to do it.

"I saw him leave," Ben said, presumably about Dad after his last check-in. "I'm so sorry."

"It wasn't your fault."

"Yes, it was."

I could have contradicted him again, though I decided he might learn faster for the next time if I refrained.

"I'm sorry, too," I said instead. "I should have explained the plan better."

He handed me my bag, and I put it on, even though I knew I wouldn't be going anywhere anytime soon. I needed the weight of it.

He held out the six-pack, and I broke open the cardboard and the nearest can and took a sip, less for the fuel than for something to do with my mouth since I couldn't think of anything useful to say.

Ben waited silently for me to finish, as if drinking and listening were an uncommon set of activities to combine.

"Sorry," I said again, for a new reason. "I don't have

anything to tell you." I pointed at the darkened computer monitor. "I don't have access to anything here. We can't even do background research."

"I didn't come to work," Ben said as he put the rest of the six-pack on the arm of the couch, and opened the leather case.

Inside was a deck of cards, surrounded by carefully arranged stacks of plastic, colored chips.

"No one should have to risk joining the Borg without getting to play a few rounds of poker first."

"What's the Borg?"

He stopped halfway through taking the cards out of the pack to think about that for a few seconds. "Okay, we'll tackle that one next time."

With the cards all the way in hand, he looked from my cluttered floor to my more cluttered desk uncertainly, leaving me a final few seconds to back out.

I had that terrible knot of nerves I get in my stomach whenever someone expects me to do something that normal people find easy. The simple, compulsive multiplication it took to calculate the number of chips in the case and raise it to the number of cards in the deck didn't do much to loosen it. I could already imagine myself trying to remember and make sense of a handful of cards, the simple markings on them fluttering around the empty cavern in my head with nothing to hold them down, as obscured and inaccessible as if I hadn't put them in there at all.

It wasn't exactly as if I had anything better to do.

I scooped some clothes and instruction manuals off

the floor so I could sit with the Monster propped securely in the carpet at my side and leave Ben enough room to sit across from me.

"I'm not taking my clothes off," I warned him.

Ben froze for just as long as he had after the Borg question and got a lot paler. "Uh . . . okay."

"That does happen in poker, right?" I hoped I'd remembered correctly what little I'd heard.

"Well, yeah, but you only have to do it if you run out of chips."

I took stock of the few small stacks of chips he set in front of me. "Seriously?"

"No."

It took me a couple of seconds, but when my diaphragm did seize up to laugh, I had to struggle to make myself do it at a safe volume.

The reel of events Mom had left me with skipped off its track entirely, taking with it the crushing effort of keeping it all straight and orderly. Ben grinned, and something about that movement, even though it didn't increase the complexity of his appearance, made him spread out into a lot of my head, the way he had when I'd stitched him up.

There was no reason it should have been, but just watching him write up a list of terminology for me was enough to make me able to read the two cards in my hand easily. Jack of hearts, ten of spades. I remembered enough of childhood "Go Fish," "Snap," and "War" to know that they were consecutive and that this was likely to be significant.

"Okay, this version is called 'Texas Hold'em,' but the hands are the same in every variation. You can only count five cards as your hand at a time, and you have to include the two that are actually *in* your hand."

He went on to explain how and when which cards were revealed and what the different hand configurations were called and spent quite a bit more time than seemed necessary on the list he'd made of the hands' hierarchy of desirability. Other than the arbitrary order of individual card and suit values, the value of any hand on the list simply correlated inversely with its probability. That was easy enough to remember.

"So, how's the tongue?" he asked when he'd apparently run out of rules to explain. It took me a couple of seconds to figure out that he was talking about our last specimen.

"Still alive," I said, pointing to the containment chamber in the corner of the room. The tongue limply scrabbled against the glass wall, trying to fight its way out.

"Find anything about a weakness yet?" Ben asked.

"Not yet," I replied. "So far no individual item in this room has affected it in any way, so I need to start working on combinations. There are likely more permutations than it has hours to live."

"Yeah, looks like he's on his last legs," Ben said. "Too bad. I was almost getting attached to that ugly little bastard."

I was almost certain he wasn't serious. "It certainly attached itself to you," I reminded him, and the way he smiled before picking up his cards made me wish I had another joke ready to make him do it again.

Between that smile and predicting all the possible combinations the next three cards might give me, I couldn't pretend it was lack of mental packing peanuts that made me ask, after my first bet, what was probably a very stupid question.

"Why are you here?"

Ben didn't move his chips or set his cards aside even though, as he'd explained it, it was his turn to do one or the other.

"I'm . . . teaching you poker?" he explained again with less certainty.

"You don't like breaking rules," I noted. "Teaching me poker is urgently important enough to you to visit while I'm not supposed to have visitors?" I tried to sum things up. I didn't mention the other problem with his presence, the one whose call he'd had to cut short to plant cameras with me.

Without my equipment, I didn't know if she'd still been waiting for him when he'd gotten back to the Perkins's house or what new, urgent bit of intrigue she might have fed him to keep him believing she was human.

Finally, he looked down to flip over the first three cards.

Jack of spades. Queen of clubs. Six of hearts.

A pair.

"My dad taught me poker," he blurted out.

"That means yes?" I tried to guess. He hadn't answered my question, and normally I would simply have pointed this out, but, for once, I actually knew part of what he was thinking without being told. A whole, specific thought, not just the general lines of thinking, I could guess at based on the micro-expressions in the facial muscles that I'd worked so hard to learn to recognize.

He remembered what it was like to have two loving parents to trust unconditionally.

So did I.

I wanted an answer, but I was having some sentimental difficulty bringing myself to interrupt that kind of memory.

"I guess . . . yes. No, not exactly."

"Why then?"

He bet again. I did the same. Three of clubs.

"Because you're in here because of me. *My* plans, *my* bad timing—"

"So this is . . . what, penance?"

"No! Jeez, you make it sound like I shouldn't *want* to see you."

I calculated a 4.3 percent chance left of a third Jack, a 26.1 percent chance of two pair, and still I couldn't think of anything to say.

Well, I could think of one thing. That was the problem. It was crowding out all the more sensible ideas of things to say.

*Why* would *you want to?*

I wanted to know the answer, and I didn't want him to know I wanted to know—not on top of all the other normal things he knew I didn't know.

The contradiction rolled around the securely packed workspace of my head, and the desire to know had almost won when the opportunity passed.

"Look." He threw another chip onto the carpet between us. "I came up with the Miracle Mine idea, and the Kevin idea, and you didn't even like them, but that didn't stop you from breaking, and I quote, 'a lot of laws' to get them done without even thinking about it."

"I think about everything I do," I corrected him.

"Okay, fine, but you did it anyway. And when I was going to get in trouble for going for the bike, even though we should have run, even though I was the one who didn't think far enough ahead—"

"You will next time."

"What I'm *trying* to say is that I'm prepared to do the same things you'd do. Or I'm trying to be."

"Oh." I threw in a chip. Ace of clubs. No help, just a pair. "So, this is practice?"

Ben pushed his hair back the way he always seemed to when he was at a loss, so I thought at first I'd gotten it wrong again.

"Sure. Yeah," he finally said.

"Oh. Well, good. You could use some."

The resolution of confusion into order in my head usually felt a lot better than it did that time.

Ben dropped an extra three chips into the pot. With the cards on the floor, there was an 18.8 percent chance he'd been able to construct a better hand than mine. That probability was made immeasurably higher, I assumed, by this action.

I folded my cards, and Ben dropped his in favor of the modest pile of chips between us.

Two of hearts, seven of diamonds.

I looked back at the list to check that I hadn't forgotten a combination.

"You knew three betting rounds ago that you could only

form one of the bottom three hands, and you had less than a thirty-two percent chance of *that!*"

Ben stared at me for a moment, then caught himself. "How do you do that?" he asked.

That's easily the kindest way anyone's ever found to call me a freak.

I shrugged. "How do you know how to bet without doing that?"

He shrugged back. "Hey, I'm teaching here. I wanted to let you play a round all the way through."

"You spent three more chips than you had to for that."

He turned a little pink when he smiled.

"That's why I won."

He was right, of course. I would have put the cards against each other directly and won if it weren't for those three chips, but how he could have known that escaped me. He didn't seem to be preparing to explain, so I reminded him.

"Hey, you're teaching here."

He smiled a little wider. "Yeah," he conceded. "Whatever you have in your hand, pretend it's worth something, even when it's not."

That helped a little. I'm a fair liar. Not a great one, but performing my work in my home always demanded it, and I won a few hands once I realized Ben was more interested in predicting my cards than his own.

The next time I glanced at the clock, my guess at the time fell outside my usual six minute margin of error.

Well outside of it.

Somehow, in what should have been an hour, I'd

managed to spend nearly two and a half hours playing cards and doing nothing else. And what was more, my head was as crystal clear as it had been when we'd started. It occurred to me that this might be the reason I was dreading Ben's departure. I was definitely going to miss that still, calm, uncomplicated feeling.

# 16.

## WHAT'S PIE GOT TO DO WITH THIS?

### Ben

I yawned as I walked downstairs the next morning. It had been a late night, later than I was used to, but a lot of fun. I wasn't entirely sure yet whether or not Mina and I could be called friends, but now I had evidence of why I liked her as a person, rather than just vague suspicions. There were moments when you could get her to let her guard down, maybe even trust you, that she seemed almost normal. She would smile. Get close to laughing even.

The rich smell of a fresh pot of coffee filled the kitchen. It wasn't one of my favorites, but when you needed to open your eyes in the morning, there was nothing better.

My mom sat at the kitchen table, sipping a cup and reading the local paper.

"Good morning, Ben," she said with a smile.

"Morning. Where's everybody else?" I asked as I searched for a mug.

"Christine had to work today. She dropped Haley off at a dress rehearsal down at the park. She said she'd really appreciate it if you could come by later, talk to her during their lunch break?" she said, nudging me without nudging me. There was that knowing smile that no amount of my eye-rolling could ever get rid of.

"Yeah, I'll probably do that," I said. I poured myself a cup and sat down across from Mom. She looked at me, her smile strained, almost nervous. I was pretty sure I knew what was coming up.

"I hardly ever see you these days. You're either out with Haley or . . . what's her name?"

"Mina," I said.

"Right, with Mina so much, I barely see you for more than a few minutes a day anymore. How are you doing?" she asked.

*I'm fighting against a sinister plot by shape-shifting monsters to take over this town.*

"I'm all right, I guess," I lied. "Just hanging out, wandering mostly."

"Do you like it up here?" she asked.

There it was. There was her pitch. She was ready for a fight, and not long ago I would have offered her at least a token one, but this town, everything I had gone through . . . I was just exhausted.

"So you want to move up here?" I asked.

"Would that be so terrible?" she asked back. "You've got friends here, it's a really nice neighborhood, and your Aunt Christine said she had some friends who could likely hook me up with a nice job. Home prices are really low. We could get a house with a yard, and I hear they've got really good schools here, too!"

I didn't know what to say. It wasn't that this was unexpected. I'd known it was coming after our first week here. It didn't mean I had to like it. We would be uprooting ourselves, again. I'd have to start life over, again. I'd be in a town full of monsters who were very likely out to get me and destroy everything we held dear (at least I didn't have to add an "again" after *that* problem).

But then there was Mina. If we did move up here, she wouldn't be so alone in this fight of hers.

And there was Haley, even more alone in a way, unknowingly surrounded by monsters that had attacked her once already with the only people who knew enough to protect her convinced that she was a monster, too. I was the only defense she had.

And even selfishly, I didn't know if I could bear to leave this town with what I knew. I would spend the rest of my life wondering, looking over my shoulder, trying to figure out who was human and who wasn't. At least here, with Mina, I might have a fighting chance.

I put my head in my hands, wiping the sleep away and trying to remember how I'd answer this question if I didn't know about Splinters.

"I don't know. I do kinda like it up here, I guess," I said.

Mom smiled, put her hands on mine, "I won't make this change without you. I know . . . I know things haven't always been easy, and I maybe haven't handled things as well as

I could. If you want to stay down in San Diego, we can do that. But really . . . this would be a phenomenal opportunity for a new start. In a big city, we would be nobodies, but out here, we could be something. This is the kind of town where we could have a future."

Ordinarily, she might have been right about that, but with the way the Splinters worked, I had my doubts about our future.

Still, I smiled and took her hands in mine.

"Let me think about it?"

I borrowed Mom's SUV to drive down to the park. After Haley's call about her memories, I'd been planning to try to talk to her when I got back from Kevin's, but she'd been out with our mothers when I got there and asleep when I snuck back from trying to make things right on the Mina front. I wasn't sure how mad Haley might be or whether she still felt like talking. She had never shown any anger over how unavailable I'd been since discovering the Splinters, but I knew I couldn't claim to have been the greatest friend recently.

This wasn't a conversation I was looking forward to.

I sat down on the grass by the park's amphitheater, watching as they finished up play practice before lunch. I didn't know much about the play *Titus Andronicus*. From what I could tell, it wasn't entirely pleasant. Alexei's constant interruptions and baffling suggestions at scene direction seemed to do more harm than good, but enough of the young actors nodded and smiled that I had to assume he knew what he was doing. Still, the way he moved and spoke made it hard to believe anyone thought he was human.

Along with the few other friends, parents, and passersby who sat on the grass, I clapped appropriately as the dress rehearsal broke down for lunch. Haley stood by for a few moments, taking notes from Alexei. She looked to me briefly and smiled. I smiled back.

*So far so good.*

The medieval gown she was wearing was hideous, but made up and with her hair tied back in an ornate braid, she was quite beautiful.

She came down to me, smiling and waving back at one of her castmates.

"How's it going?" I asked.

Haley rolled her eyes dramatically, "If Robbie York can stop making jokes about his codpiece for two seconds and actually learn his lines, I think we might have a show by the end of summer."

Her smile faltered briefly as she looked around the crowd.

"You want to go for a walk?" she asked.

"Sure."

We strolled away from the amphitheater, almost to the adjacent playground. Aside from a few kids playing on the equipment and their mothers watching over them, we were basically alone. The cheerful façade Haley kept while on stage was gone; now she looked fearful and hesitant, her eyes darting from side to side as if she were worried about being watched. How quickly she could drop that cover made me realize how good an actress she really was.

"I've been wanting to talk to you for a while now. I just didn't know where to start," she said. "You've been out so much these days. I haven't really had anyone I could talk to about this. Nobody who would understand, at least."

*I barely understand.* That's what I wanted to say, but didn't for fear of revealing too much.

She bit her lip, looking away as if she were about to cry.

"I thought they were bad dreams at first," she said. "I thought that I must have been imagining things that might have happened while I was gone. But the dreams kept coming back, more of them, more clear . . ."

I put my arm around her shoulders protectively. She didn't push me away.

"What kind of dreams?" I asked.

"I remember running. Running through darkness. Out of a cave, into the forest. I feel like I'm being chased. I *am* being chased. By people I know, all calling for me, angry, but I can't understand them. Friends, neighbors . . . Mrs. Morgan from the dentist's office, Mr. Delgado from down the street, Britney who sits behind me in algebra. Alexei . . ."

She shuddered against me, drawing closer as if freezing even though it was hot as can be outside.

"Do you have any idea how hard it is to pretend things are normal around them when you feel something very wrong has happened and that they're a part of it? I remember them all looking down at me when I was in the dark. In a large, dark room that seems to go on for miles. Them and others I can't see, like they were waiting for something to happen to me, something that wasn't working," she said.

I held her closer, wanting to protect her from this nightmare.

"I didn't think too much of this at first. I thought, maybe this was my way of coping, maybe my mind is just piecing together memories from when I was out and when I was not and throwing them together with old nightmares," she said.

"That sounds . . . likely," I said.

She pulled away from me, looking at me defensively. "But these aren't just dreams, Ben," she said, shuddering softly. "There's nothing wrong with me. I'm not crazy. These aren't dreams; these are memories! I know it! Ever since I've gotten back, I've seen these people watching me! I thought it was like all the other attention at first, but whenever I walk through town, or drive to the store with Mom, or rehearse the play up here, I can see them watching and talking about me! They smile, they laugh, they pretend everything is normal, but it isn't! They look like people I know, but I know—I just *know*—that they aren't," she said.

Haley looked at me for support. I didn't know what I could tell her, I didn't know if I should say anything. We were treading into dangerous waters, and I didn't have Mina's help to know what information was safe to give out.

"You think I'm crazy," she said. "You do, don't you?"

"I don't."

"Yes, you do. My mom thought I was reading too much into this, she thought it was 'Post-Traumatic Stress.' She hasn't seen them looking through my window at night, she hasn't heard them talking about me when they're setting up their secret meetings!" she exclaimed.

This raised a flag.

"They talk about secret meetings?" I asked.

She shook her head, started to walk away. "Forget I said anything."

I grabbed her by the wrist. "Wait. I believe you, I do. I can't say why, yet, but I do. I just need to know more. What were you saying about that meeting?"

Haley darted her eyes back and forth again, trying to make sure we were alone.

She sighed. "Every day after rehearsal, Alexei goes into his office behind the amphitheater and is on the phone for about five to twenty minutes. One day last week I followed him, and I listened to his call. He was talking to someone about meeting up for a barbeque in the middle of the night. They talked about 'The Perkins Girl's Initiation.' It creeped the hell out of me."

She shuddered, coming back to me for comfort. Again, I wrapped my arm around her shoulders.

"It's going to be all right," I said.

"How do you know that?" she asked, looking up into my eyes.

"I don't know. I'll think of something," I said.

"Hey, Haley!" a boy called from behind us. A handsome boy in a medieval costume and a backwards baseball cap waved his arms to get her attention. "Alexei's got some more notes for you, said something about what to do with your hands when they're no longer attached!"

She sighed, calling back, "I'll be there in a second, Robbie!"

To me, she muttered, "I hate this play. Will we have more time to talk, soon?"

"Of course," I said. "All the time you need."

"Tonight?" she asked, hopefully.

"Maybe. Soon, I promise. I know someone who might be able to help you out with this. I just need to work some things out with them first," I said.

Her eyes brightened at that, and she smiled, stepping up on her toes so she could kiss me on the cheek. "Thank you," she said as she ran back to the stage.

I rubbed my cheek. I'm sure there was a stupid smile on my face (it's not often a pretty girl kisses you on the cheek), but she didn't seem to mind as she looked back at me one last time.

While Haley was immersed in conversation with Alexei, I ran back to the parking lot and pulled out my cell phone. Mina wouldn't be able to help out, not while stuck under house arrest like this, but there was one number I could try.

"What is it, Ben?" Aldo asked when he picked up. After a pause, he added, "Is Mina okay?"

"She's fine, Aldo. Listen, I need your help."


Alexei's bungalow behind the amphitheater looked like it was meant to be more temporary than it turned out to be. A construction trailer that might have been new when *Back to the Future* topped the box office, it had been made permanent by virtue of a cinderblock foundation and a sign that said "Park Office for Rent—Check City Hall for Availability." There were two doors, one with a permanent plaque on it that said "Park Maintenance," the other crudely printed up and taped to the door reading, "Shakespeare Summer Extravaganza!"

Something told me that was Alexei's office.

I looked over my shoulder toward the amphitheater. It sounded like play practice would be wrapping up soon. We would have had more time, but when I'd called, Aldo was doing chores and couldn't get out of them for nearly forty-five minutes. By the time he could get the necessary equipment and I could pick him up, the rehearsal had nearly finished. We were going to have to cut this close.

I tapped the Bluetooth in my ear, "You hearing me, Aldo?"

"Loud and clear. Alexei's got them working on proper pie-eating technique, but most of the actors have already started to clean up," Aldo said.

"Just keep an eye out," I said.

"For you, Ben, I'll keep two eyes out," he said. His voice was dripping with sarcasm, but I had no doubt he would do what he said. Aldo may have been a kid, and may have been protective of Mina in an annoying kind of way, but you could not doubt his competence or professionalism. He was smart, and he would have my back if Mina wanted him to.

Alexei's door was unlocked, which was helpful. The rest of his office, on the other hand, was much less helpful.

To call the place a mess would have been generous. In one corner was a couch, I think. In the opposite corner was a desk, I think. I think there might have even been some bookcases and filing cabinets lining the wall. I only say "I think" here because it was nearly impossible to see anything in this room through all the mess. The floor was covered with racks of costumes, cardboard boxes and stacks upon stacks of books so high they appeared to have transformed into pieces of furniture over time. A stack of cookbooks in the middle of the room, mostly about baking pies, stretched high enough to hold up a sagging section of the trailer's hanging ceiling. The walls were decorated with ancient woodcuttings of people in Elizabethan costumes and graphic depictions of what people used to think the inside of human bodies looked like.

"What's it like in there?" Aldo asked.

"It's like Hannibal Lecter's college dorm room," I said as I tapped a hanging mobile of obscure Shakespeare quotations. A faint skittering sound above set me on edge, but the squeaking sound soon after relaxed me. Just a rat stuck in the hanging ceiling, probably made it in through one of its many, many holes.

"Yeah, Alexei's always gotten into his plays; he *lives* for authenticity, if not age-appropriateness. Have you found his telephone?" Aldo asked.

Winding my way through the perilous obstacle course of books and boxes, I found his desk, cluttered with photocopied scripts, more ancient texts on vivisection, and pictures of himself in clown makeup. Beneath all this, there was indeed a telephone.

"Yeah, I got it," I said.

Between my lack of experience and Aldo having to look

up instructions on how to plant the bug he'd given me in the ancient landline, I spent about ten minutes longer in Alexei Smith's office than I would have liked, but they were minutes well-spent. I had the phone disassembled, the bug placed, then reassembled, then tested by Aldo, and I hadn't even made a mess of things. All in all, I was proud of my work.

"Uh oh," Aldo said in my ear.

"Uh oh?" I asked. My heart began to race. I knew what "Uh oh" meant.

"You gotta get out of there. Alexei's coming your way. Can you get out of one of the back windows? He can see the door perfectly."

I looked around quickly, panicking. The door was my only real consideration for an exit. All of the windows were blocked with heavy piles of books. I could probably knock them over and get out, but that would blow any cover we had. That didn't leave many options.

"You got maybe thirty seconds," Aldo said urgently. "Whatever you're gonna do, you gotta hurry!"

I looked up. An idea formed. It wasn't a very good one, but it would have to do.

"Thanks," I said, quickly turning the Bluetooth off as I began to climb the nearest bookcase. The hanging ceiling panel above me gave way easily, and as I looked into the musty, dingy space it hid, I found it was large enough to hide in. Hoisting myself up by the ceiling's metal frame-work, I scrambled into the dark crawlspace and set the loose panel back where it was supposed to be. Assuming Alexei didn't sleep in here (something that soon hit me as frighteningly possible), I'd be able to make my escape eventually.

Also, assuming that the ceiling's metal framework could hold my weight. Considering the age of this trailer, I chose not to think too much about it.

I looked down through a small hole in the ceiling panel that gave me a perfect view of the desk. Alexei entered the office, tripping slightly and laughing. After pushing aside some of the mess, he picked up the phone and began to dial. *Right on schedule.*

"Oh, hello, Henrietta!" Alexei said cheerfully. "So good to call you as always. Listen, I was wondering if you had heard the place is changing? Glen said he wants to throw tonight's party in his backyard; he has a new fire pit for cooking he wants to try with his new body!"

He laughed hoarsely. What I would have given to hear the other side of the conversation that Aldo was recording. That squeaking noise again beside me, something walking, crawling across my hand. When I looked over and saw the very large, very fat rat, I gasped, startled.

Alexei turned his head around with a start. Though normally smooth and almost sedate in his movement, here he moved like a cornered animal.

"Please hold that thought, my sweetheart, okey dokey?" Alexei said into the phone as he set it down. He knew the noise had come from up here, he just didn't know where. If only I could—

With the sound of snapping wood, his head jerked sharply to the side as if his neck no longer had any meaning. The crackling, popping sound of a stubborn tree branch being twisted off filled the air as his face contorted. Gill-like protrusions from his cheek formed wide, bat-like ears that rotated jerkily, looking for the source of the sound. A few black, dull eyes broke out on his forehead like a bad rash just as his bottom jaw unhinged and contorted. Three stalks, each about a foot long, topped with segmented, insectoid eyes, burst from his cheek and neck like fleshy flowers to join in on the hunt.

It took everything I had not to scream.

He stood up from his desk, listening, looking, even smelling with a nose that flattened into his face. He would find me. Soon. Then it would all be over.

The fat little rat trundled away from my hand. I reached out, grabbed the squealing rodent by the tail and tossed it through the nearest hole in the ceiling panels I could find. It fell with a dull thud on Alexei's desk. He looked at it quizzically, then laughed a throaty, inhuman laugh as he grabbed the squealing, frightened rodent in one of his hands. I half-expected him to toss it into that gaping hole of a mouth.

What happened next was infinitely worse.

There was that snapping, popping sound again, and the hand that held the rat contorted horribly. His fingers lengthened and multiplied, looking like bony, white spider's legs as they ensnared it. A toothy split, *a new mouth,* opened in the palm of his hand, pulling the squeaking, fighting rodent in with several tendril-like tongues. I could see it trying to claw its way free, looking up with confused, frightened eyes as it disappeared into the toothy palm of Alexei's hand. Soon, the mouth disappeared and the fingers retracted, the only sign of the rat's existence the misshapen bulge that moved slowly down Alexei's wrist.

He went back to the phone and picked it up, shifting his lolling neck to better hear. "Sorry, sorry, just finding a fresh morsel. Not as tasty as some, but meat is meat. You know how I have a hard time resisting? So anyway, I shall see you tonight at nine? That's the idea!"

I will never know how I kept my terror in check as I watched Alexei finish the call, slowly transforming back into a human. I remember him leaving the office some time later, I remember waiting, I even remember my escape and meeting up with Aldo, but only through a thick haze.

The only thing I remember clearly from that moment was fear.

Fear for having seen one of *them* for the first time.

Fear that I wouldn't be able to fight them if it came down to it.

Fear of becoming one of them.

# 17.

## THIS IS ALL SPLINTER
### Mina

"I'd rather not do this alone, but if I have to, I'll understand."

I wasn't sure if this was a serious offer, scribbled at the end of the note jammed through my window, or if Ben was doing that thing where people try to speed up other people's decisions by illustrating the absurdity of the incorrect options. Either way, there was really only one answer, the one I scribbled and jammed back into the frame in case he came back to check.

"I'll figure something out."

If Ben was right about what he had heard, we were potentially looking at more usable information than I could get from years of standard surveillance. List corrections, more people to be effectively certain about, maybe even new details on the nature of Splinters—their plans, their weaknesses. I couldn't leave the task of documenting all of that to anyone else.

And in the equally likely event that this almost-too-good-to-be-true stroke of luck, bestowed upon us, however indirectly, by the thing that looked like Haley, turned out to be a trap, I couldn't leave Ben to handle it alone.

Mom didn't often interfere directly with my work anymore, but when she did, she was always serious. And at the hour Ben had named, she would almost certainly be at home. She would be expecting me to serve my time peacefully, especially after I'd practically volunteered for it, but that didn't mean she wouldn't be aware of all the alternatives.

I was trying to think of some pretext to get her out of the house before the meeting when she called me to dinner. Even if I'd found one, it still would have left me with Dad to deal with. That was much less likely to be a problem, but it scared me more. At least with Mom, I already knew the worst that might happen.

If I got caught, and I almost certainly would, I could probably kiss my hard drive goodbye.

Again.

And it would be at least a month before I saw any of my equipment again, or anything else other than the walls of my room. There was no point dwelling on the cost. I *had* to go to the meeting. That much had been established. The only remaining question was how to get there with a long enough head start to watch it properly before someone was sent to find me.

It was past eight by the time we started eating, late even for a night when Mom was cooking, and I wanted badly to gulp down my entire plate of spaghetti as soon as I got it in front of me, but I was careful not to eat as if *I* were planning to be somewhere. Mom raised her eyebrows at the sheer quantity I had served myself, but as usual, she didn't say anything.

She probably never would until I got at least curvy enough to fill out a B cup, and I didn't mind if that never happened. What my mother referred to as her "assets" looked like almost as much of a liability in a fight or a chase as her taste in shoes.

At least the shoes could be used to stab something.

I like spaghetti. It requires concentration.

Once we were all eating, Dad asked his usual, unjustifiably optimistic, "How was everyone's day?"

My day had, of course, been pointless, so Mom answered, complaining about some act of sabotage against her current case without looking at him, as if I had been the one inquiring about the paperwork errors and political subtleties that plagued, as she would have put it, "people with lives."

I listened, and somewhere between the sound of her voice and the two strands of spaghetti that kept unraveling from the end of my fork, I was finally forming the beginnings of an idea.

"Yeah, I think I read something about that," I said in one of her brief pauses.

"About what?"

"That new witness they're letting in?" I hoped I'd interpreted her ramblings correctly. "It was in the local news." I hoped it was. It sounded like the sort of thing that might have been.

Mom narrowed her eyes at me, but that didn't give me much of a clue. Whether she thought I was lying or telling the truth, she would be annoyed with me.

"Have you taken up reading the paper again, Mina?"

It was working. I snorted a little louder than I normally would have over the amount of actual paper that was wasted on information people had perfectly good access to without it. "No. Why?"

"I can't think how else you'd be so abreast of current events."

As I've said, I'm not much of an actress, but I flicked my eyes toward Dad and away again within the correct window of time.

"What?" Dad asked when Mom glared at him.

"I wasn't online, Mom!"

She ignored me completely, and I took advantage of her distraction to eat as much as I possibly could before dinner officially came to an early end.

"If she has been, it's news to me!" Dad protested, and Mom scoffed.

"You have to stop doing this to me, dear."

She never called him "dear" when she was in a good mood, but when she was angry, it was her favorite way of *not* calling him "Sam" without directly saying why.

"I didn't do anything!"

"You have to stop treating me like an obstacle! I do my best to take you seriously, dear, I really do. You could at least show me the same courtesy!"

Right around then, when the argument stopped being about me, she remembered I was still there.

"We'll have a talk later, Mina," she said without looking back at me.

I stuffed one last meatball into my mouth to chew on the way downstairs, threw my bag over my shoulder, climbed up onto the grass outside my window, and lifted my bike from its rack while the voices were still loud in the dining room. I didn't know exactly how long I had before Mom's "talk," but by the sound of the one she was already having, with any luck, I'd at least get as far as the start of the meeting before she missed me.

The sun had fully set after the thirty-three minutes it took me to pedal up to Dr. Westlake's, and when the sporadic excuses for streetlights along his one-and-a-half-lane road finally illuminated, all they did was cast reflections on the insides of my glasses, indistinguishable from obstacles in the darkness ahead. I'd just gotten used to riding right through them when one of the tall, person-sized obstacles turned out to be solid.

Ben didn't make a sound when I hit him. Well, no sound other than "thud," and he caught me before I could scrape my bike and my elbow along the ground.

"Shh," he greeted me even though I hadn't made a sound yet. He was still holding me up. At least he was off to a nice, cautious start this time. "It's already started," he whispered.

He guided me forward to another lump of darkness that turned out to have substance—his mother's little blue SUV. He opened the rear door and hoisted my bike very carefully inside. I thought about pointing out that if he was killed or taken with the keys in his pocket, I'd be stranded, but I couldn't quite assemble the right words to say it without making it sound as if I expected him to screw up even worse than last time. And that scenario was only marginally more probable than someone in Prospero stealing a bike off the side of the road anyway.

I could already hear laughter, voices, the crackling of a fire pit, and a low techno beat coming from Dr. Westlake's backyard. No matter how distracted everyone was, there was no way we wouldn't be noticed creeping up that drive- way again. Our only chance of seeing anything was to circle around the back of the yard.

In the woods, in the dark.

Ben walked alongside me, up the drive of the next, darkened house over, toward the trees, not leading or fol- lowing, not looking back, but not overflowing with the certainty he'd had when we'd last been there, either, when he'd declared that we were going to find the Miracle Mine. A few paces from the first gap between the trunks, I saw one of his hands shake just a little before disappearing into his pocket.

He was being more than cautious. He was terrified. That's not a terrible thing. *I'm* scared of the woods at night and proud to say so. It's not the irrational child's fear that makes people do stupid things. It's the rational kind that *stops* people from doing stupid things, the kind that comes from knowing, based on hard evidence, that the farther I go into those trees, the less likely I am to come out again.

Ben didn't have that, at least, he hadn't at last report when the only Splinter he'd seen for what it was had been a creature in the middle of the street, our side of the tree line. Something had changed.

"Did I miss much?" I whispered.

Ben shrugged. "They haven't been there long. I was waiting for you."

He hadn't gone into the trees alone, ready to fix all the world's problems just by being *right* at them hard enough. Something was definitely different.

"What happened?" I asked.

He waited long enough that I wasn't sure he was going to answer.

"I saw a human one transform," he explained shortly.

That was all the detail I needed just then.

We stopped in a small clearing, a good distance back from the tree line, but with a wide enough gap to let us see into the yard, crouching down behind one of the ferns. We were close enough to make out the fire and the figures standing around it, which instantly killed any worries I'd had that I might be wasting my time.

None of them looked entirely human. They weren't trying to. Most of their human forms were partially intact, enough so that I could recognize the ones I knew with their faces turned our way. Alexei was in plain view, along with one of the theatrical society girls and that history teacher who'd only been very, very Probable before. Their extra parts were all wrong.

Arms were stretched out too far to reach the fire, some of them flattened out like giant tongue depressors to feel the heat on more skin surface. Most of them were at least half naked, with a blanket or jacket thrown over the side that faced away from the flames. Alexei's head was thrown back as though he'd never felt anything so wonderful before. Along with the bones from whatever they'd been barbequing, there were liquor bottles and half-empty food packages everywhere, mostly candy. One woman toward the back was gulping down Skittles with one hand and bacon bits with the other two, but I couldn't be sure of her identity due to the second mouth she'd also deemed necessary for this purpose.

There was a rapidly undulating mass, thankfully a good distance into the dark on the fire's other side, which seemed to have parts enough for four people, but I could only hear two distinct voices coming from it.

For the sake of the small dinner still newly in my stomach, I would have preferred to hear fewer.

Even worse, every so often, one of the ones around the fire would take another one's hand and press the skin together in the plain, clumsy, functional way I'd seen a few times before.

*Felt* once before.

It made me sick just watching, thinking about the thoughts *they* shared being pushed into *me* where they didn't belong, much sicker than the sounds coming from that writhing tangle of an uncertain number of Splinters.

Still, distasteful details aside, this was a gold mine. One more thing was effectively certain: there were no humans here. This was not a diplomatic or strategic meeting for the benefit of collaborators. This was all Splinter.

I could distinguish six separate threads of conversation, if not all the words of the furthest ones. Two were about the quality of the food. One was about which of the company would have to leave in the near future to acquire more alcohol. One was about the aesthetics of gender-neutral skinny jeans, and one was a small squabble about standard breakfast-eating protocol.

The sixth caught my attention simply because I couldn't hear it at all.

Two figures, all the way on the opposite side of the yard from the fire, were whispering to each other, as if they were actually afraid of being overheard.

I was pretty sure Splinters didn't keep secrets from each other. They were all pieces of the same big plague, after all, and specially designed to share information as easily as a touch, so whispers could only mean one of two things that I could think of.

One: Those two were discussing something they meant to keep even more carefully secret than the rest of this mess from any human who might happen by.

Two: They were so good and experienced at playing human themselves that notions like privacy had become habit for them, even among their own kind.

Either way, I needed to get closer. I wanted words, and I wanted faces.

Maneuvering there with Ben turned out to be a lot easier than I anticipated. I looked at him, then at them, then at the way forward through the trees, closer to their end of the yard. He nodded and followed my footsteps as quietly and quickly as I left them, as if we'd been doing this together all our lives. Whatever he had seen before getting there, I was glad it had happened when it did because the scene in that yard hardly seemed to faze him now.

The closer we got to the pair, the more I realized that faces were going to be a long shot.

One of the Splinters was fully dressed in jeans and an oversized hoodie. A bony, scythe-shaped appendage protruded from the left sleeve, and its owner kept running it absentmindedly over a hole in the knee of its jeans, producing a scraping sound like a whetstone.

"He's like the Grim Reaper," Ben whispered.

The other one was wrapped head-to-toe in a blue, king-sized comforter, its discolored, yellowish eyes just barely exposed.

Words were still possible, if not voices, exactly. The whispers were so soft and breathy that I couldn't even determine gender, much less identity, but I could catch the consonants.

"Trust me," said the one with the scythe, which seemed to me a very odd thing for one Splinter to say to another. They had to be *really* fine-tuned. "Everything's right on track."

"How long are you going to keep saying that?"

"Until it's time to start saying 'I told you so' instead."

The non-scythe arm stretched a few feet out of the sleeve of the hoodie toward the one in the blanket, but it backed away.

"Why are you even here?" asked the scythe Splinter.

"Better here than walking up to you in broad daylight to tell you that she's got every chance, every possible form of access—"

"Give it time. In a couple days, we'll get to take our biggest liability and make it our best tool."

"*Two* biggest liabilities," the blanket Splinter corrected. "And I told you, she's too young. You're not going to be able to control her that easily."

Ben gave me an awkward sideways glance, and I knew he was guessing at the subject of the conversation along the same lines I was.

"A couple of days," the scythe Splinter repeated. "A couple of days, and she'll do exactly what she's told."

It should have frightened me. If they *were* talking about me, I had some rough days ahead. Nothing any Splinter could do to me would ever make me cooperate; of course that didn't mean I wanted to see them really try.

But all I felt was a rush of hope. If I *was* counted as one of the Splinters' two biggest liabilities, if I actually had them worried, it meant there was a real chance, however small, that I could actually stop them.

Then again, it was more likely that they were talking about some other "she," and I had nothing to do with it at all.

That was the only thing that was able to draw my attention away from trying to catch a few more words to make sure: a shout from closer to the fire that definitely *was* about me.

" . . . What if it had been someone who knows what to

look for? Diana, or that revenge-happy bastard kid of hers with all the 'theories?'"

The breakfast food squabble had escalated. Jess, from the theatrical society, was talking to a man with graying hair the way people talk to hyperactive toddlers. Jess usually reminded me a bit of a hyperactive toddler herself—she was one of the society's younger members, just thirteen—but this evening she had her body elongated to be even more unnaturally tall than Jess was supposed to be. She had stopped shifting her weight back and forth and playing endlessly with her hair, and she was speaking with a calm firmness that would have made my mother proud. With hardly a signal between us, Ben and I inched closer to listen.

"That kid wouldn't think twice about it!" the man protested. "Lots of people wouldn't! It's not that strange! *They* do it all the time!"

"Not like that, they don't."

"I enjoy it. That's normal. They all think so."

"That's different. You know that. They were born enjoying things. You can't expect to be able to handle it the way they can."

He grabbed her hand, forcing me to swallow a fresh wave of bile, but Jess just looked annoyed and pulled away.

"At least *talk* like a human when you're telling me you can act like one."

"I've been out here for four hundred years!" the Splinter man tried for indignation, but there was a hint of petulance around the edges. "And I know what *he* knew after forty-seven more!"

"Talk to me when you've been out for four thousand." Still so poised, Jess drew herself up a little taller. "But you're right. You've had a good share of practice. Enough that I honestly thought you'd be better at it by now."

The Splinter man tried to do the same, but ended up a much less graceful, more lopsided pillar. "Four hundred years, and I made one little mistake that no one even noticed! It's not a problem!"

"One problem would be too many," said Jess. "We're counting on you. I said we should have used someone more experienced, but no, Sam vouched for you, and far be it from me to argue with what *Sam* wants. I knew I should have volunteered myself." She looked down at the distortion of Jess's body like it was a Christmas present she'd begged for but couldn't remember why.

"I'm doing fine. I'm doing exactly what they expect me to do!"

"It's not an expectation. It's a caricature."

"They're just donuts!"

Ben let slip a tiny, nervous laugh and then went back to looking painfully tense.

"Two dozen!" Jess went on. "In one sitting! In a public parking lot!"

"I'm sorry! They were *really* good! It won't happen again!"

"Mina," Ben whispered so softly that I almost thought it was a leaf rustling the syllables of my name by coincidence. "Is that . . . ?"

I started pleating and re-pleating the flap of my bag by feel, trying to see and hear everything just a little more sharply, trying to bring the slim, visible edge of the man's face into focus through the dimness and smoke, to filter out the Splintery, uninhibited whine in his voice and imagine what it would sound like, wholeheartedly imitating the more dignified mannerisms that would have come ingrained in that sort of body.

"For that matter, what were you doing, intercepting the Todd brat yourself when you could send someone? Just because she's contained for now doesn't mean you have to hand her reasons to suspect you!"

"I was in the nearest car when we got the call." His voice leveled out with confidence then, and I knew, even before he turned away from Jess in our direction, who he was.

Ben clapped a hand to his mouth, but it looked like he was less stifling sound and more trying to restrain himself from striding forward and ripping through Sheriff Diaz's jugular. Slowly, he pulled it away. "That . . . that . . ."

But either he couldn't think of a word strong enough to call him, or he could and couldn't bring himself to say it quietly enough.

"Yes," I agreed as quietly as I could while still making sure he'd hear me. "That's him."

Ben buried his face in his hands for a moment. "Stupid," he muttered. "Of *course,* they'd take the cops. Why would I think—"

"Shh," I reminded him. I couldn't blame him a bit for his reaction. The fear and anger were there and obvious, but they hadn't caused any errors yet. He was still in the shadows with me, thinking clearly, carefully avoiding twigs when he shifted his position to shake the nervous energy. Considering his greenness, I couldn't have hoped for a better ally.

Especially considering the fact that I wasn't feeling quite so rational myself.

Sheriff Diaz was on the Town Council, somewhere I'd never seen a hint of direct Splinter activity. That was my mother's domain, a place of secrets, of corruption and collaboration but *not* of infiltration, not a single sign of it in all the hours upon hours of audio I'd captured. By definition, all Council members had been Very, Very Probable Non-Splinters, until now.

She couldn't know.

Of course, she didn't. Jess had just admitted as much.

Badly missing my good phone, I dug through my bag for my old digital camera.

"I need proof of this one," I whispered, scanning the darkness for any other, less consequential faces, any more information lying around for the taking, before I'd have to risk forcing an early exit. "Be ready to run, just in case."

Ben adjusted himself on his feet, ready to spring out of his crouch, and looked at me warily.

I checked that the flash was turned off, centered as much as I could of Sheriff Diaz in the frame, with a little bit of Jess for good measure. He turned our way again, and I pressed down on the button.

Ben winced next to me at the sound, but none of the Splinters gave any indication of hearing it.

Sheriff Diaz certainly hadn't stopped to listen. The image was nothing but a dark blur of colors.

"I need a better angle. Wait here."

I did my best to make out the shape of the trees ahead, farther toward the driveway, the opposite side from the scythe Splinter, closer to the fire. I'd get a better look at the Sheriff's face while he and Jess argued, a better chance of catching something usable when he wasn't moving around. The way looked clear enough if I took it slowly. I'd be back next to Ben within a few seconds.

Just as I found another good space to peek between the trees, the Sheriff turned right in my direction for a good, lengthy sulk, his arms stretched long enough to drag on the ground even while they were knotted loosely together in imitation of how human arms fold.

I got the shot, and it stayed sharp enough on the view screen to be recognizable, but he turned farther, back toward Ben again, before I could take another.

I inched a little farther forward, hoping for another head-on shot if he turned back toward Jess. I was still a few feet shy when my shoe caught something that definitely wasn't a twig or a root, something of a texture I knew only too well.

I knew the chance I'd taken. It had been a worthy risk-to-benefit ratio, but I'd lost. I don't like to wonder what that tangled Splinter was doing in the trees alone, with all those boneless strings of itself draped all over my improvised path, before I interrupted it by tripping face-first into the row of glass bottles it had arranged around itself, releasing the aromas of chocolate and baby oil.

Even the Splinter's face was distorted, but it re-formed right next to mine, its eyes reflecting my camera's red light, and greeted me with something like a scream, a piercing, high-pitched sound like grinding metal, punctuated with chittering little pops.

The Splinters in the lot echoed it, and before I could find my shoe to free it, they were stampeding into the trees toward us.

# 18.

## WE NEED A TRAIL OF BREADCRUMBS

### Ben

Mina yanked her foot from the tangle of the hanging Splinter's body, pulling a stun gun from her bag and ramming it into the creature's screaming mouth in one smooth motion. It shuddered and jerked as it fell from the tree in a trembling mess. I ducked down quickly, helping Mina to her feet before I checked back on our pursuers. They would be on us in a matter of seconds.

We made a break for the forest, bolting into the pitch-blackness of the trees and hoping for the best. It wasn't easy. Even fifty feet away from the nearest yard, it was so dark that you could barely see your hands in front of your face, let alone the redwood trees the forest was thick with. I kept bouncing off of trees, stumbling over heavy roots, being goaded on by Mina as she kept tugging at my arm. How she managed at night with eyes as bad as hers, I'll never know. I just hoped she could see better at night than they could, that we would have some advantage, no matter how small, that would get us out of this alive.

For a few moments at least, I thought we had reason to hope. As frightening as their new forms were, they seemed large and cumbersome, ill-equipped to dodge between the trees with the ease we could manage. Several times I could hear them howling and cursing in their inhuman tongue, snapping tree limbs in frustration as they searched for us. I know I could hear Alexei's voice, clear and in English calling out, "Do not worry. They are ours soon. You will see!"

If he was confident, I could swear we had to be in the clear.

We were getting some distance, and their voices seemed farther away. They sounded confused. I was actually beginning to feel good about our chances of getting away.

Then Mina put her hand on my chest, forcing me to stop.

"Listen," she said.

I stopped. I could hear the faint sound of the wind rustling through the trees above us, the faint snapping of a pine cone falling not too far away, but other than that, dead silence.

"It's quiet," I said softly.

"No," she said, "Not that, it's almost like . . ."

Her eyes widened, and before I could ask her what was going on, she clapped a hand around my wrist and pulled me into a nearby thicket of bushes. I almost protested, then stopped myself. Mina's instincts had served us well so far. I was not about to argue with her.

Less than a second after we were completely concealed within the bush, I could hear them. The low, droning beat of wings. A faint beam of moonlight penetrated the trees near us, allowing me to see the horrors that had been sent after us. There were three of them that I could see, each about the size of a basketball, each with massive, dragonfly-like wings that fluttered and hummed as they weaved their way through the trees. It was only as they passed through the light that I could see what they really were.

Spare parts.

A hand, a foot, an extra head, parts that the bodies no longer needed, given wings and sent out into the forests as scouts to better track us down. They had probably sent dozens off in every direction. The head and the foot flew off, bobbing and weaving into the distance. The hand landed on a tree no more than ten feet away from us. It crawled up and down, its seven fingers making scrabbling, scratching noises as they fought for purchase on the bark. Two far-too-human eyes on stalks jutted from the severed wrist, looking around as if they sensed something. Its wings twitched. I tried not to breathe.

The hand shuddered, arching its back as a set of small holes broke through its carapace. At least five small, bright red snake tongues flitted through, tasting the air as it tried to find us out.

It must not have liked what it tasted. The tongues retracted, it flitted its wings heavily, and once more it was off buzzing into the forest.

"They're forming a perimeter," Mina whispered. "Next they'll pull inward, tighten the snare."

"We were able to dodge them there," I said, hopeful.

"Yes," she agreed, "but next time they'll try harder." We stepped silently out of the bush and continued through the forest. I could hear them in the distance, stalking, searching for us, but they had lost their fury. They were organized now, planning things out. We would have to wait for them to close the trap and then hide again, as close to its edge as possible, to let them pass right over us as their drones had. Then we could make a break for the town. Of course, that meant having to deal with those drones again.

On the plus side, I was pretty certain we would be home free if we could actually manage an escape here; none of them had really gotten a good look at us. If we could wait them out, if we could get out of here, and if we didn't run into any more Splinters in the town proper, we'd be in the clear.

Yeah, those were some pretty big ifs.

I had a pretty good internal compass, so I had a fair idea of where we were in relation to the town. If I always made sure to keep the town on my left, I figured we could hike a good mile or two into the forest if we really had to, but I hoped it wouldn't be necessary.

We had just made it to a crossing in a shallow river. With moonlight glimmering off the water, I was trying to figure out if it was shallow enough to walk across, or if we would have to use a nearby fallen tree that spanned the river as a bridge.

It was then that we heard the inhuman roar of rage and frustration in front of us. There was a sound of great violence as if trees were being ripped from the ground, and a few seconds later a boulder the size of a Volkswagen bug was hurled from the trees before us into the river. The thing was coming right for us. I looked at the boulder in the water, trying to gauge how deep it was. When I heard the creature's pace quicken, I decided the answer was "deep enough."

It was my turn to lead Mina by the wrist. I pulled her into the river, the icy mountain stream shocking me as it splashed around my knees. I pointed under the fallen tree. Mina understood. Quickly hiding her bag in a nearby thicket, she dove beneath the downed tree. There was a narrow gap, but she could keep enough of her head above water to breathe.

I dove in after, half-swimming, half-crawling as I squeezed in beside her. I could barely, just barely keep my nose above the water and stay concealed. The water was cold. Too cold. We couldn't last long here.

We couldn't see it, but we could hear it as it came out of the forest. Its growl was low and deep, mixed with that popping, clicking sound. As it searched the banks of the river, I could vaguely see it walking on four long, powerful legs ending in clawed hands. It soon came to our log, and for the briefest of moments I hoped it would walk on by.

There was a dull thud as it experimentally touched the log, pushing it a few inches to the side. We were still concealed beneath it, barely, but we had to shift positions. This difference was enough to push my nose completely underwater. I held my breath, hoping its inspection would be short enough to offer me the chance to breathe soon.

Another dull thud. Then another. A scratching sound

on the log. My heart started pounding heavily. It felt like it was trying to move the log, trying to pull us from our hiding spot. Any second now it would find us and—

Another thud. No, it wasn't trying to find us. It was trying to do something worse.

It was walking across the log.

Its heavy footsteps above us strained and splintered the wood. Its scrabbling, clawed feet fought for purchase as the log bowed slightly under its weight, pushing my head even more underwater. My lungs were burning, I wouldn't be able to do this much longer.

Then it stopped. Right above us. It had found us. I knew it. This was it.

One of its long, three-fingered claws came into view, dipped into the water in front of us. At any moment it would grab my shirt and pull me free. I hoped that Mina at least would be able to make a break for it as those claws dug into my chest. The claws came closer, closer . . .

And then they curled together as the hand cupped water and retreated above the log. We listened as the Splinter heavily slurped the water and then bounded across the log into the forest where we had come from.

I waited a few seconds, but the forest stayed silent. I pushed out from under the fallen log, taking coughing, painful breaths. Mina, shivering heavily, soon followed, grabbing her bag from the thicket.

"We gotta get out of here," I said through painful, chattery teeth, "Get warm, hypo—"

"I know," Mina said. Normally so tough, so strong despite

her frail frame, it was almost painful to see her like this. I pulled her closer to me as we both stumbled through the forest. Though I half expected her to push away, she didn't fight me. Under the circumstances, warmth was warmth.

I thought hard, trying to remember if we still had the emergency kit in the back of the SUV. There should have been some thermal blankets in there, thin, but capable of reflecting the body's heat back in, something which might help save—

One of them was leaning up against a tree in front of us. The man in the hoodie. The Reaper. His vaguely insectoid face stared at us curiously with four shimmering, black eyes. Glossy black quills poked through his sickly green scalp where he should have had hair, and where his mouth should have been was an ungainly mess of muted, worm-like tentacles. Horrible though his face was, it was that left arm that truly held my attention, that long, curving sickle of bone jutting out from the stump that used to be his hand. It was utterly lethal-looking, and if he decided to leap at us with his powerful, grasshopper-like legs, I'm sure he would have taken us.

Instead, he cocked his head slightly, and the corners of his face contorted into what could have been a smile.

"Go," he croaked deeply.

I looked to Mina for confirmation, expecting to see her reaching for a weapon, only to see a look of surprise and confusion on her face I didn't know was possible.

"Go now!" he croaked more urgently, waving his bone-sickle toward the town. As if to emphasize his point, he leaped through the air in the direction of our last pursuer. Mina looked like she wanted to fight, but with this chase and half-frozen, she didn't have the energy.

We didn't talk much as we walked back to my mother's SUV. We didn't have to. I'm sure Mina was running over everything we had just seen, probably tallying off names and faces against her various lists.

My train of thought was much more simplistic. Between reliving the various moments I'd cheated death that day and trying to raise my core body temperature while I drove her home, I had a hard time shaking one fact: a Splinter had saved our lives.

Something felt very wrong about that.

# 19.

## DEAL BREAKER

### Mina

I didn't try to be quiet when Ben dropped me at home. He stayed a few extra seconds after I'd gotten my bike out of the car, as if he were actually thinking about coming in with me, and I had to wave for him to get away while he could.

I wouldn't have bothered trying to get back in through the window even if my mother hadn't conspicuously pushed the living room curtain aside to look out at us. Bag over my shoulder in plain sight, camera within easy reach in the front pocket, still shivering and dripping river muck with every step, I walked straight inside the best way I could—through the front door.

Mom was sitting on the couch the way she always did, as if it were a throne and even stiffer and more uncomfortable than it was. She had spread paperwork all over the coffee table, and she was poring over it intently. For a moment I remembered much too vividly the long afternoon she had spent teaching me chess at that coffee table, back when the sight of her there had been something to look forward to. I did my best to forget it again quickly.

She waited just a few seconds longer than I expected her to before addressing me, the way she somehow always could.

"Good evening, Mina."

I didn't flinch, and I didn't lash out. I didn't think about what state my room was probably in after she'd searched it in an inevitable fury. I just stood there.

Finally, she looked up.

"Exactly what the *hell* is wrong with you?"

"We need to talk," I said.

"You're damn right we do."

"Just let me get a couple things."

She didn't get up, but she stopped me before I could start down the stairs to get my lists and anything else that might make it easier for us to share notes. "Unless you need a blanket or a toothbrush, you won't find any 'things' down there."

I backtracked to the spot across the table from her and the mud puddle I'd already started there. This was worse than I'd hoped but not worse than I'd anticipated. It wasn't time to fight her or worry about rebuilding. It was too important that she listen to me.

"Okay," I said. "Then we'll just talk."

"You first," said Mom, but she didn't wait to listen before telling me exactly *how* to go first. "What's gotten into you lately? How long have I been putting unwarranted trust in you? Where *were* you tonight?"

"You know where I was, Mom. I was spying on potential Splinters."

It had been years since I'd spoken that word out loud in front of her, and I saw it catch her off guard for half a second.

"There's no such thing as—"

"Yes, Mom," I said firmly, "there is. We both know there is. And you need to know what they're—"

"*Enough!* You're finished this time, Mina. I mean it." She looked at me steadily over the table, still without standing, and I knew she was telling the truth. She knew I would retaliate and there would be nothing more she could do to me in return, and she was prepared to rescind the deal anyway. "No more Splinters. No more cameras, no more bugs, no more Ben, no more Aldo, if that's what it takes. You're going to stop pretending to know what you're talking about and *leave it alone*. Or—"

"Or you'll hand me over?" I suggested, carefully, without raising my voice.

"To a shrink, maybe," Mom threatened, determined to misunderstand me. "See how far you can get in life as a documented paranoid schizophrenic."

I've never been to a psychiatrist, but I've been called crazy more than enough times to prompt me to do some research on the subject. I know if she ever decided to send me, I'd be branded with *something* and medicated to the hilt, but I'm confident I'd be able to lie well enough to dodge heavy antipsychotics.

"Okay, Mom," I said. "Hear me out, and you can take me wherever you want. You—"

"It's *over*, Mina!"

"I heard you. I just—"

"What part of 'no more Splinter talk' do you not—"

"Sheriff Diaz has been replaced, and I can prove it!" I shouted this at her so loudly and rapidly that I startled myself as much as her after the rest of our hushed argument. Then I shouted it again, even louder but more slowly, just in case I'd said it *too* rapidly to be understood the first time.

For several seconds, Mom didn't move. Her voice was hushed when she answered, but not nearly so calm.

"I asked you to stop pretending to know—"

"I *do* know!"

I scrambled to turn on my camera and scroll to the right picture before she could collect herself and block me again. When I'd found it, I pushed the view screen under her nose, not caring how much water I dripped over the papers in between us, not caring if she took the camera away along with everything else, as long as I could be sure she looked at it first.

She did look. Her eyes narrowed on the picture, and she raised a hand to the camera to steady it. I let her.

I lost count of the seconds she spent simply staring at it.

"Mina," she said finally and very, very softly, "you have to be absolutely certain about this."

I spared her my analysis of the nonexistence of absolute certainty and simply nodded.

"I can't play around with theories and speculation here," she said.

It should have terrified me, how scared and serious she looked. She was a collaborator, yes, but she was still human, an informed human, and if she was worried, that meant there was reason for me to worry, too. For a few moments, I was only ridiculously pleased that the two of us were finally talking about the same thing, at the same time, out loud, in plain, simple words.

"I saw him," I told her. "I heard his voice. It was *him*."

She handed the camera back to me, and in the fraction of a second it took me to get a grip on it, I was almost certain I felt her squeeze my fingertips.

Then she looked away and became the mother I was used to again, her cool, sarcastic, commanding voice already echoing across the room, perfectly familiar, even if its words were anything but.

"Dearest, darling, light of my life, get your counterfeit, two-faced, underhanded, interdimensional ass in the sitting room, *now!*"

Interdimensional. It was nice, in a way, finally knowing the correct term.

Dad came in from his studio the way he always did when he was interrupted unexpectedly, picking craft glue off his fingers and looking ridiculously, nervously hopeful that someone might be about to say, "It's okay. It's okay that you're here. No one's blaming you."

Mom finally stood up, as tall in her chosen set of heels as he was in his socks, and set her stance in front of him.

What she really said was, "I want a divorce."


It had seemed like such a fragile, delicate operation, getting my parents to fight over dinner. Three hours into their second fight of the evening, all I wanted them to do was stop.

Neither one of them had so much as glanced at me when I grabbed my power cord and phone out of Mom's open briefcase, pulled down the door to the attic, and started gathering the rest of my equipment. I had my room almost back to its normal setup, minus a few old notes Mom had torn beyond repair, and had adjusted all my lists based on the progress at the meeting, and they still weren't showing any signs of letting up.

Both were shouting at the tops of their lungs. Mom's usual self-control was fracturing noticeably, and Dad's usual charade of reasonableness was all but gone.

"We had a *deal!*" Mom's voice was perfectly audible from my room and probably from the street outside. "You have your Council, and we have ours! You take what we agreed on, and you leave us alone to make adequate lives out of what's left!"

"It was considered a necessary security measure," Dad said with no decent amount of regret.

"You *lied* to me!" Something glass or porcelain broke against the wall with Mom's words. "We're supposed to be partners! You told me we'd be peacemakers! And I *believed* you!"

"We *are* peacemakers! If this isn't peaceful enough for you, I promise you, it's only because you haven't seen enough of the alternative!"

"It was supposed to be a truce! But it's really an uncon-ditional surrender, isn't it? I let you take everything from me! I let you have Sam, and I couldn't even let the world see I'd lost him!"

I wanted to turn up the backlogged feeds in my ears to block out her voice, but just like I could never bring myself to delete old files with even the remotest chance of becoming useful again, I couldn't throw away the information reverberating freely through my ceiling.

"I gave you every little evidence adjustment you ever asked me to arrange! I signed away my family *and* my self-respect in that treaty, and I never asked for any of it back! But *your* people take back whatever you want, don't you? And you expect us to deal with it!"

"No!" There were a few echoing, wood-like cracks, and I could picture Dad transforming back and forth in agitation. "It was only Diaz, and only after the last fatality!"

"You lied!" Mom repeated. "And I'm finished making good! I can't trust you with Prospero, and I won't trust you with my daughter!"

There were a few seconds of silence, but there was no relief in them for me.

"She's my daughter, too."

If Mom hadn't answered for me with the ringing slap of her hand on his face, I might have shouted back myself, right from my desk chair.

*"No, she isn't!"* Mom snarled like a cat standing guard over newborn kittens. "You can wear my husband's face, and keep his shop, and sleep in his bed, and have people call you by his name, but you will never be him, and *she will never be yours!"*

The tight, wet heaving in my chest was reaching an alarming frequency, and I got up to lock the door, in case someone saw fit to wander in before I could make it stop. Something else hit the wall above. It sounded like Mom was piling things, probably Dad's things, next to the door.

"And neither will I!" she added. "Never again!"

"You know, you weren't exactly my favorite part of the arrangement either!"

"Oh, you poor thing!" Mom sneered. "Trapped for a few lousy years of immortality in a diplomatic marriage! Is that *all* you've had to put up with?"

"Diana, think for a moment. You don't want to do this."

"Get away from me!"

"Think about the cleanup. You'll spend the rest of your life in the Warehouse. We'll have to set up another human representative. And where do you think Mina will be then?"

I couldn't turn it off. My peripheral, packing peanut trains of thought wouldn't fade out and leave everything else in a harmless blur because none of it was truly peripheral. Above me was the confrontation I'd been waiting for for years, one I'd listened to and picked apart for countless hours before it had ever even happened. In front of me were the notes and equipment I'd been deprived of for days with hours of material to sift through.

And in fresh memory, there were new pieces to fit together. Some of them I didn't see how I ever would.

A Splinter had let us go. *A Splinter had let us go.*

There had to be a logical explanation, of course, but it made me realize just how low a spot I was in, the fact that a concept so uncomfortably contradictory to every other reliable detail I'd ever collected was the one thing on my mind that was contributing the least to the sore, clicking lump in my throat.

I'd wanted Mom to call Dad out for nine years. I'd expected to be happy when she finally did.

I'd been wrong.

Instead, I was just tired and sick and disappointed, disappointed in a tiny hope I hadn't even known I'd been holding out, that my real father's situation might somehow be less desperate than that of a very probably irretrievable Splinter hostage, or at least that it wasn't really all my collaborating mother's fault.

I had no expectations for how the mystery of The Reaper, Ben's fitting nickname for our rescuer, would resolve, on the other hand, so there was still the chance it would be in some tidy, satisfying, or even helpful way.

If only I could think of some place to start to get it there.

I was arranging my notes on every distinct Splinter ploy I'd ever documented, looking for the slightest connection, trying not to feel any more of Mom and Dad's circular screaming in my upper respiratory tract, when my newly reclaimed favorite phone vibrated in my pocket.

I cleaned some stray droplets off my glasses and tested the steadiness of my voice, in case I was about to need it, but it was only a text message waiting under Ben's name.

*Don't know when you'll get this, will try visiting tomorrow if I don't hear back. Haley's getting worse and remembering more. She NEEDS to talk to YOU, asap.*

The nervous twinge in my stomach was automatic, the worry that he was too close to her, physically and emotionally, that any day she would decide take him, and he would let her, out of some outdated feeling of trust.

But that evening, it felt like almost as sensible a lead as any other I'd been able to find.

I texted back.

*Off the hook for now, long story. Soda Fountain of Youth, tomorrow, 10 a.m., both of you.*

## 20.

Ben

I almost expected Mina not to show. I knew she believed Haley to have been compromised by the Splinters. I also knew that she hadn't seen Haley for more than a few minutes since she had appeared at the funeral. I was sure that if she could just talk to Haley for a few minutes, if she could just hear how afraid she was, that Mina would see that Haley was human.

Maybe.

Okay, I wasn't sure at all. But the idea of leaving Haley helpless and uninformed in the raving, panicked, trauma-flashback state I'd found her in when I got back from the Splinter barbeque was unthinkable. Without even changing out of my soaked clothes, I'd contacted Mina the moment it had been safe to take my arms from around Haley's shaking shoulders.

Haley looked at me nervously now, taking occasional sips off her root beer float, but without much conviction. She was lucid and reasonably collected this morning, but like any sane person in Prospero should, she kept darting her eyes around periodically, scanning the room for anyone watching her. Aside from us, Billy, the two tourists taking a picture of a stuffed Sasquatch in the corner, and the stuffed jackalope next to our table, we were alone in the Soda Fountain of Youth.

I didn't blame her for her paranoia. While we were waiting for Mina, she'd seemed as mentally prepared for the worst as someone could be, so I had given her a crash-course on Splinters as I knew them, fully admitting that Mina was the true authority on the subject and that she'd fill in all the gaps when she got here.

I had to admit, Haley took the news a lot better than I expected.

"I feel like I'm going to throw up," she said.

It looked like she was going to get teary. I made to grab a napkin to hand to her. Before I could, however, Billy slid smoothly by our table, a broad smile on his face and a napkin in hand.

"Feel free," he said, handing it to her. "But if you do, please don't make too much of a mess, since I'm the one they're gonna make clean it up, and lemme say, nothing makes me wanna blow chunks more than seeing someone else's, you know what I mean?"

Haley looked up at his broad smile, slightly confused.

"Thank you. I think I'll be fine," she said dubiously.

"Right on, right on," Billy said as he looked at Haley, then me. "You two together?"

"No," I said.

He turned to Haley. "You eighteen yet?"

Haley looked scandalized. "No!"

"Never hurts to ask." Billy laughed, looking up as the bell jingled above the front door. "Ah, Jailbait! Got an early parole?"

Mina stormed into the Soda Fountain of Youth looking like she was ready to go to war.

Briefly, I began to regret calling this meeting. By the look in his eyes, I could see Billy's thinking wasn't far from mine.

"Want your usual?" he asked.

"Sure," she said dismissively. She reached into her bag and pulled out three quarters, pressing them into Billy's hand. "'Kashmir' and 'Immigrant Song' should do it, but if this goes long, pop in some Butterfly."

Seeing how serious she was, Billy dropped his smile. "Gotcha. I'll get your malt coming right up."

Mina sat across the booth from us as Billy fed one of her quarters into the jukebox. After a few seconds of silence, the pre-programmed music that had already been playing gave way to a heavy beat of electric guitars and brass. When I recognized the song, I couldn't help but crack a smile.

"You like Led Zeppelin?" I asked.

"I neither like nor dislike them. What they are is long, loud, and on this jukebox, all of which work well toward our not being overheard here," she said, eying the tourists as they grabbed a booth.

We waited in silence for Billy to bring out Mina's drink. Once he did, she took a long, luxurious sip from the overpoweringly chocolate concoction, and let out a heavy sigh.

"All right, we should get started," she finally said. She pulled a taser from her bag and set it down on the table, casually but threateningly aimed at Haley's chest. Haley recoiled, but boxed in by me on our side of the booth, she could not escape.

"Mina!" I exclaimed. "What the hel—"

She raised her other hand. "Ben, be quiet. If you trust me, trust that I know what I am doing. She will get her chance to talk, but I must have mine first. Okay?"

It wasn't okay, but she left me little choice. I looked at Haley. Her eyes were wide, but she hadn't tried to run for it yet. Maybe she'd be able to get through this.

Mina addressed Haley, "If you are who you say you are, then I would like to apologize in advance for whatever inconvenience this may cause you, and I would like to assure you that this is a necessary precaution. If you are not, then you know as well as I do that if you force me to use this, it will hurt you tremendously and might even cause you to lose your composure in a public place, which I've been told is quite unwise. So, that out of the way, has Ben told you about them?"

"Yes," Haley said.

"That will save some time then. The situation is this: three months ago you went missing. Though the official story is that you wandered off in the middle of the night, got lost, and wound up surviving for two months off of whatever you could find in the woods before blundering back to town in time for your funeral, I can say that I am effectively certain that story is a lie. With the possible exception of some mild post-traumatic stress, you haven't displayed the kind of symptoms of psychosis necessary to have done that by sheer accident. I am also effectively certain that you were taken by Splinters for assimilation and replacement, and I also believe it probable that you are not the real Haley Perkins, but are rather a Splinter replacement of her. Ben, on the other hand, believes that you are not a Splinter. Since I have come to trust his judgment recently, this puts me in a quandary."

Mina paused, took a long sip from her malt, then asked, "Who are you?"

Haley looked taken aback, "What?"

"*Who* are you?" Mina asked again.

"I'm Haley Perkins," Haley replied, confused.

"*What* are you?" Mina asked.

"I'm . . . what?" Haley asked. She looked to me for some help. I couldn't offer any.

"Mina . . ." I said, trying to calm things down.

"Why are you here?" Mina demanded.

"Ben told me you could help," Haley said.

"*Why* are you *here?*" Mina demanded more firmly, tightening her grip on the taser.

"Because I want to help *you,*" Haley pleaded. "I mean, if you're trying to stop things like what happened to me . . ."

I raised my hands. "Listen, Mina, maybe you should—"

"I don't believe her," Mina shot back.

"Don't believe what?" Haley asked.

"That you're human, that you're here to help, that you—"

Haley slammed her hands on the table in frustration.

"If I knew this was the 'help' that Ben promised you could offer, I'd have never come here! I came because he said you knew how to fight them, because you could make them pay, because I wanted to make them pay for what they did to me!"

Mina was silent. Haley shook her head, laughing angrily.

"You want to know who I am? Fine. My name is Haley Perkins. My birthday is April fifteenth, my mother's maiden name is Kent. When I was five, I accidentally killed my goldfish when I knocked his bowl off the bookshelf, which until fairly recently was the saddest moment of my life. When I was seven, I had an unhealthy fixation on Orlando Bloom, which I thankfully got out of pretty quick. I've got a scar on my foot from when I stepped on a nail when I was ten. It went all the way through, and I had to get a tetanus shot. My dad left us four years ago when he refused to keep taking his meds because he thought they made him dull. He's schizophrenic, did you know? Not a lot of people do. I hated him for leaving us. I hated him more for potentially passing it down to me, and until recently the thing that scared me most in the world was the chance that I might wind up exactly like him! Is that human enough for you?"

Mina considered Haley. I could tell that she still didn't believe Haley, not by a long shot, but something she had said clearly got to Mina. She loosened her grip on the taser, slightly.

Haley sighed. "I don't need you to believe me. I don't need you to trust me. I just need to know what happened, what's *happening* to me. I don't know if I can trust anyone else around here, so I think . . . I think I have to put my trust in you. Ben says you know a lot about these Splinters. That you've been fighting them for a very long time. If anyone can tell me what's happening, it's you."

Mina cocked her head slightly, giving Haley another of her long, appraising looks.

"Will you at least hear her out?" I suggested. "She guided us to that party. She gave us a lot of names we didn't have before. Don't we at least owe her the benefit of the doubt?"

This further seemed to trouble Mina.

"Please, just hear what she has to say," I said.

Mina reached into her bag and pulled out a handheld digital recorder. Pushing it towards Haley, she pressed the record button.

"Talk," she said.

Haley smiled slightly, grateful, I'm sure, for anyone to give her a chance.

She started off slowly, recollecting what little she could remember with any certainty of her disappearance, her time away, and of her eventual return to town. At best, her information was spotty, recalling just vague, confused images that could easily have been mistaken for dreams. It was as she began to open up about her actual dreams that she gained more confidence. Though the images she spoke of terrified her, the fact that Mina neither stopped her nor laughed clearly gave her strength. After a while, I started watching Mina more than Haley. As usual when she was focusing intently on a subject, her face looked almost blank with eyes that stared at and through Haley all at once. It was a look I was still having a hard time getting used to.

The bell above the door rang. Instinctively I looked over, checking for any of the faces from Mina's ECS list, or someone I might recognize from our escape the previous night. I couldn't help but imagine The Reaper standing there, telling us to move on with that horrible bone sickle.

Instead I saw the very human silhouette of someone

looking our way before dodging outside and to the left. Something about the build, the hair . . . it was familiar.

I stood up, ready to pursue. The girls looked at me.

"I'll be right back, I just have to check something out," I said.

I walked to the door, went outside. Heading around the left side of the Soda Fountain, I could see no one on the sidewalk, but a bicycle speeding away. *Gotta be sure . . .*

Pulling the cell phone from my pocket, I made a call.

"What's up, Ben?" Aldo asked.

"Can you pull the tracking data from the GPS unit we put in Kevin's bike? See if he's anywhere near The Soda Fountain of Youth?" I asked.

"Two seconds . . ." Aldo said. I waited closer to ten. "All right, yeah, he's close by, riding away like a bat out of hell. That what you were looking for?"

"Yeah," I said, unsettled. "We might have to get out of here sooner than I thought. Keep an eye on him for us? Something might be going down soon."

"No problem," Aldo said. "Bad?"

"Maybe," I said as I hung up.

By the time I got back to our booth, Haley was finishing up recalling her nightmares, tying the faces she remembered seeing in the darkness with the people she'd seen watching her in town since she had returned. They both looked up at me, worried.

"Trouble?" Mina asked.

"Maybe," I said. "We might need to wrap this up sooner rather than later."

Mina nodded, subtly, then dropped back into one of her blank thoughtful looks. Haley looked at her, concerned.

I sat down next to her. "She does this a lot. It's a good thing, I swear."

Haley looked at Mina as she tried to collate the information. "Are you sure?"

"Not really," I admitted as the clock ticked on. I looked nervously over my shoulder, expecting a Splinter invasion at any moment. I had never seen Mina lost in thought for this long before. Did it mean she believed Haley, or was she getting ready to attack? I didn't think she'd dare attack Haley in the middle of a diner, but when it came to how Mina responded to Splinters, I chose not to rule anything out. She tightened her grip on the taser ever so slightly, but she did not raise it from the table.

Finally, she said, "Given everything you have described, I can state with effective certainty that you were taken by Splinters, in all probability so they could assimilate you."

Haley nodded softly, gripping my hand tightly. This was clearly news she expected, but it still wasn't easy to accept.

"I see two possibilities for what happened next," Mina said. "Well, there are actually many possibilities, but two that hold the highest level of likelihood. The first is that they tried to take you but were unsuccessful. There *have* been cases, extremely isolated and rare, but documented, where a person with some major mental defect or brain damage was taken for an extended period of time and ultimately rejected. If this is the case, if you have inherited some or all of your father's mental problem and just have yet to exhibit signs, then you are incredibly lucky."

The look on Haley's face was not one of gratitude. Mina didn't seem to notice that she had delivered potentially devastating news.

Of course, the fact that she was hesitating told me she was holding back something even worse.

"What's the second possibility?" I asked.

Mina hesitated, looking from Haley to me, then back to Haley.

"What's the second possibility?" Haley repeated, sounding scared.

"That this is all one big lie. That you're a Splinter who's been impersonating Haley ever since she supposedly stumbled out of the forest, and that you're trying to manipulate us toward whatever nefarious ends you might have."

I was about to speak up and try and offer some more defense for Haley, but Mina raised her free hand again.

"But since Ben seems to believe in you, and since much of the information you have provided would do more damage than good to the Splinter cause, it seems more likely at the moment that the first possibility is correct."

This should have been great news. I should have felt some great victory at getting Mina to bring Haley into the fold. I didn't. She was still holding something back.

"Why do I sense a 'but' coming along?" I asked.

There was another jangling over the door. A boy and a girl, each no more than ten, came in smiling, sidling up to the bar. Too young to be Splinters. Mina put the taser back into her bag.

She continued, "It seems *likely* that the first possibility is correct, but unfortunately, for our purposes, it doesn't make much difference. The memories Haley has are partial at best. If they're coming out as dreams, it's possible that there's more trapped somewhere in the subconscious, but unless she can unlock any more on command, I don't see what she can offer us."

A few weeks before, I would have focused on the fight that followed. I would have focused on Haley protesting that she could be of some help, and Mina saying that she meant no offense and was just telling the truth. Before, I would have, but this time I didn't. A memory from the first time I'd really talked to Mina suddenly hit me like a freight train. It fell into the category of *"so crazy it just might work,"* but if it did, I was fairly certain we'd know everything we needed to by the end of the night.

"Hey guys, quiet down," I said. "I got an idea."

Though they both looked at me like I might be a little crazy, they listened intently. With a smile, I craned my neck and called out.

"Hey, Billy! You doing anything tonight?"

# 21

# THIS IS TRYING EVERYTHING

## Mina

Schizophrenia.

I'd never expected that word to make me so hopeful, especially not so soon after Mom had invoked its perpetual threat.

Schizophrenia.

It's hereditary. That's the real reason Mom would never take me to a psychiatrist. If schizophrenia *did* turn out to be the term of choice for what I was, it would haunt her for life, just like me.

And if Haley was telling the truth about Mr. Perkins, there was every chance she was carrying the gene, which meant there was also a chance, small but significant, that I'd been wrong about her, that she was telling the truth about *everything*.

As far as I could tell, Haley was as normal and functional as people came, both before and after her disappearance, but if there *was* something wrong, something small and buried, waiting to manifest, maybe something mild enough that the Splinters had expected, for two months, possibly, to be able to work around it, then her story held water.

Haley could be human. Not just human but a human who had been to the mine, who knew, somewhere in deep, repressed memory, where it was and what was inside it.

Of course, if she *was* a Splinter reject, that would also make her an ECNS. Permanently. There would be no danger in Ben or anyone else spending time with her.

That thought didn't give me quite the hope and relief that it should have, but it didn't make me any less desperate to know.

I don't place *excessive* faith in the powers of hypnosis.

It seems a vague, imprecise, unreliable method of investigation to me, and I had no intention of accepting anything we might uncover with it without some solid verification.

But as much as I pretended otherwise to Billy, I still remembered the odd feelings and vivid, unfamiliar thoughts that had bubbled up in me the one and only time I'd allowed him to use me in his demonstrations.

There was some real, if unpredictable, power there, and if it could give us anything at all to *try* to verify, that would be something.

Splinters hiding from each other, appearing to help humans, disappearing a girl for two full months and *then* sending some version of her back. There was every possibility that some or all of these oddities were connected, and we might be very close to finding out how.

Billy pulled out all the theatrical stops for the occasion, enough that I really wanted to remind him that we were still investigating a Splinter abduction. We needed substance, not spectacle, but if the thrill of being asked to show off was what was going to make him give the task his best effort, it was worth sitting around in the dim candlelight with Ben fidgeting on one side of me and Aldo restlessly video recording nothing on the other, breathing incense far too sweet to contain any functional herbs I knew of, watching the smoke swirl in crushingly vast, empty silence.

The idea of all the stillness and quiet was supposedly to relax Haley as much as possible before we got started, but none of it really seemed to be working.

By the way she kept glancing at Billy, I wasn't sure if she was more worried, or pretending to be more worried, about what memories she might uncover, or about being asked to relax in his intimately lit living room not half an hour after he'd handed her one of his characteristically un-charming compliments.

Either way, she was almost as pale as she had been on her funeral day, and every couple of minutes she would drop her head onto her knees and hyperventilate for a few seconds.

After nearly half an hour of this, if my internal clock was working with so few reference points to set it to, Billy got up and moved toward the one tattered pleather arm chair where Haley was sitting. This triggered, or at least coincided with, another gasping fit, so Billy stopped and glanced over at Ben.

"Help us out over here?"

"Please," Aldo added, cleaning his video camera lens for

the fifth time. "People don't throw away decent camcorders. I have to have it back in Dad's closet before he misses it."

"I *know*," Haley snapped. "Sorry, sorry," she followed up right away. "I'm trying."

Billy raised his eyebrows at Ben again.

Ben looked uncertain but got up from the equally tattered pleather couch we'd been waiting on and knelt next to the chair.

"It's—"

"It's *not* okay," Haley stopped him. "They took two months from me. Two months, just gone! Two months of them doing God knows what with me! Nothing about this is okay!"

Ben didn't claim to know or understand. He didn't remind her how much might depend on what she could recall.

He just said, "You don't have to do this."

It took all the focus I could scrounge together to sit there without contradicting him and simply *hope* that this was one of his acts, the kind that could pry restricted maps out of historical society offices, even though it really didn't sound like one.

Haley shook her head firmly. "Yes, I do. Anything I can take back, I have to do it."

Ben looked at her hand, scratching absently at a hole in the armrest, and after another moment's hesitation, wrapped it in his.

I got the strong feeling that any input I might have the urge to offer at that moment would likely be counterproductive, so I looked away from his face and the intricate patterns of incense smoke to kill that little bit of clarity I'd been using.

I could still hear him.

"Everyone here wants to help you with that," he told her.

At least that was true.

Haley took a deep, shuddering breath followed by a deeper, steadier one, and her hair made a light tapping sound against the pleather as she nodded.

Ben stayed crouched next to the chair, holding her hand, and after a few more breaths that didn't break back into panicked gasping, Billy knelt down across from them, carefully took her other hand, and began to talk. His tone was already different, slower, smoother, mystical, and more formal.

"I'm going to talk you through some visualization. You will still be here, yourself, with your own free will. You will remember everything that happens. You have the power to reject any image or suggestion. If you want the images to stop, you have the power to wake up instantly, safe, with people who care about you."

It was just the introduction, but I knew it well enough to look up and gather myself. We were finally getting started.

"Watch the smoke," he told her. "Relax your feet, one toe at a time . . . you can feel your ankles relaxing, your knees relaxing, every bit of tension draining away with the sound of my voice . . ."

I drifted a little while he led her through the rest of her

joints in sequence, trying not to fall asleep to the sound myself.

" . . . Your eyelids are too heavy to keep them open anymore. You're leaning back and sinking deeper into the chair. The chair is becoming more comfortable, softer with every word . . . softer . . ."

Haley had stopped clutching Ben's hand, letting Ben and Billy each support one of hers as if they were sleeping kittens.

"You're at home, in bed, before all this happened."

Haley tensed a little but slowly relaxed as Billy went on.

"You feel perfectly safe and secure. You can feel your own sheets, your own pillow. You can smell your mother's favorite laundry soap. You roll onto your back, and you can see the same patterns on your ceiling that you see every night. Someone else is in the room with you now. It's someone from here in Prospero, someone you know."

Haley's left hand balled up for a moment in Ben's.

As calmly and smoothly as he had set the scene, Billy asked her, "Who is it?"

"I can't see him," Haley answered dreamily. "It's too dark."

Ben gave me a look at the word "him," as if that narrowed the suspects down to a manageable handful.

"He's coming closer to you," Billy went on. "He wants you to go somewhere with him. You're sitting up to look at him. Your eyes are adjusting to the light."

"He's behind me," said Haley. "No matter how I turn. He's behind me and . . . around me! All around me!"

I was tempted to look and think myself away again. If this had been any less important, I probably would have.

I didn't need any help with this part. I already knew better than I wanted to what it felt like when they took you, the part before they got you wherever they were going, at least.

"Where does he want you to go?" Billy asked.

"Away," Haley answered unhelpfully. "Somewhere else. Far. So *fast!*"

"What do you see on your way?"

"I don't see anything. My eyes are covered."

There was a choking sound in her throat, and oxygen suddenly felt very sparse in my lungs. If abduction procedure was at all standardized, he had covered much more than her eyes.

I don't know if Billy realized how pointless this part was or if he meant to offer her some sort of relief, but he finally hurried things forward a little.

"You've arrived somewhere. Your eyes come uncovered. You look around at your new surroundings. What do you see?"

Haley's eyes stayed closed, entranced, dead to the present real world, but the hyperventilation had started again.

"*Wrong,*" she moaned softly. "Everything wrong, dark, no light, not even the moon, but I can see . . . so many bodies!"

"What else can you see?" Billy coaxed more gently than I ever could have.

Haley shook her head just slightly.

"Are there walls?"

"No."

SPLINTERS

"Are you still outside?"

"No!"

Billy faltered a moment. His hands and Ben's and Haley's were all white-knuckled against each other. Ben's expression seemed to be asking Billy for some kind of help.

For the first time, I thought about the way Splinters swapped thoughts and found a shred of appeal in it. If Haley could have explained this to Ben and Billy through those clutching hands, if *I* could have reached out and touched the exposed skin of her arm myself, sitting there on the armrest, and let whatever it was she knew seep right into me without the trouble of making her understand or find words for it, I would have, whatever other sickening intrusions came with it.

Aldo toyed with the focus on the camera, as if a slightly sharper impression of the shadows on Haley's face would make it any clearer what was happening in her head.

This was where we had been trying to get her, this place with no walls that wasn't outside, where people went and Splinters came from. She was in it, so close to whatever secrets they went to such lengths to hide there, and she couldn't give us *anything*.

Billy looked at Ben and then at me, and I wanted him to push, to drag out any little scrap of a hint he could. It might snap her back to reality, and after that we'd probably never get her this far again, but it was better than missing the opportunity entirely.

If we'd been free to talk out loud, I was sure Ben and I could have argued that point for hours.

Billy found a compromise without our help.

"You have to leave there now," he told Haley. "You're leaving to go home now. Which way do you go?"

Haley relaxed just slightly. Escaping. That had to be a happy thought, in a way, and it was still a useful one.

"Up."

Not quite as useful as it could be, assuming we were talking about the Miracle Mine.

"Sideways-up. Climbing. Sticky."

"You're climbing closer to home, closer to the things you know," Billy narrated, back in his usual hypnotic stride. "You're going to make it. You're going to be fine. You're luckier than the others. Why?"

"They're tired of me."

"He's letting you go?" Billy asked.

"He isn't here," said Haley. "He left me here. Unfinished."

"You're almost out now," Billy encouraged. "You can see things ahead that aren't wrong, things that look familiar. What do you see first?"

"The sky!"

I wished I could share Haley's enthusiasm for a glimpse of the least localized feature on the planet.

"A tree!"

This *couldn't* be all we were going to get.

"A tree above me! Sticky-alive like what I'm climbing, like him when he's all around me. It's blocking the sky, the stars, won't let me out . . . And it's *moving!*"

"You have time to look at the tree," Billy told her. "Everything else will wait for you. You're stopping to look at its height, the color of its bark, the spread of its branches, the texture of its leaves. What kind of tree is it?"

"It's a . . . a giant redwood. A *giant* giant redwood. But it's not a tree!"

Ben shot me a look, and this time we were in total agreement. Finally, we were getting somewhere.

"How is it moving?"

"It's crawling to the side, away from me. It's letting in more sky in the front. *He's* making it move. He's here!"

"You're leaving," Billy repeated. "You know you will succeed. You're leaving now. He can't stop you. What does he do?"

"He doesn't see me," Haley whispered, as if she were afraid of somehow fixing his mistake through time. "He's climbing down next to me, but he doesn't see me because the place I'm in still isn't right."

Billy tried to prompt her again, but she spoke over him.

"The tree is crawling back! There's sky, but it's closing!"

"You're making it through. Nothing can stop you," Billy promised, but Haley kept gasping.

"It's closing!"

"You're on the other side," Billy tried. "You're out. You're on your way back home."

But Haley shook her head violently. "It's closing!"

Ben pried one of his hands away from hers to shake Billy's shoulder. "That's enough."

Billy seemed to agree, but he looked at me first.

"We have what we need," I confirmed.

"When I count to three," Billy concluded, "you will wake

up safe and happy and thrilled to have taken back the memories that are rightfully yours. One . . . two . . . three."

Haley snapped out of it right on cue, but she didn't look happy or thrilled. She jerked her hand away from Billy, threw both arms around Ben's neck, and started sobbing into the front of his shirt. Ben held her with a closeness that was difficult to watch and a shell-shocked expression that wasn't much easier.

Aldo looked at me and pointed at the camera, trying to decide whether to turn it off.

Billy hovered awkwardly over them. "Haley?"

She didn't acknowledge him. It looked like he was considering patting her on the shoulder or something but couldn't quite make up his mind. When he moved toward her, she shied away, further into Ben's arms.

"Haley . . . I'm sorry . . . I . . ." he glanced around at the rest of us, looking for some kind of absolution, but no one gave it. Not because we blamed him but because whatever absolution he needed, we needed it, too. "I'm . . . I'm going to go for a smoke."

I didn't want to be alone with Ben and Haley just then, or any more alone with them than I needed to be. I had nothing to offer her, not the way he did, and there was nothing more for me to gain by watching them.

I nodded to Aldo to stop recording, but when I tried to squeeze past the armchair to follow Billy out into the backyard, Haley grabbed for me and latched onto the edge of one of my front pockets.

"Stay, Mina." Her voice was ragged with crying, but

the words were clear and steady and serious. "Please stay. Please, tell me, *did it work?*"

I needed her to let go. I wasn't ready for this. I needed to turn on my music and reorganize my head and sort out all the new evidence before I could possibly know how to speak to her.

In my hurried, spur-of-the-moment guess, I answered her like a human.

"Yes." I squeezed her hand, hoping it was as real as it felt, and that I'd be able to pry it off of my pants soon without either tearing them or making her cry harder. "It worked. You did great."

She smiled up at me, so inexplicably brightly, so *gratefully,* that even with the inside of the mine still a frustrating blank, even with Billy unfairly exiled to the yard for trying to do a good thing, even with her not-quite-vindicated fingers digging into both Ben and me, I couldn't help thinking, just for a moment, about how much I might enjoy knowing an ECNS Haley Perkins.

And that's when something shattered the front window in Billy's kitchen from the outside.

Ben was on his feet before the glass had finished falling, pushing Haley and Aldo and me behind the couch at the far side of the living room. I wrenched Haley off of me to get my nearest flamethrower out of my bag, and so I could turn around to look at the Splinter, The Reaper, sidling easily through the fragments covering the kitchen sink, down onto the littered tiles, down the hall toward us, that scythe bone extended in front of it.

Aldo fumbled the camera into its cushioned case and shoved it under the nearest bean bag chair, out of sight.

I pressed the first flamethrower into Ben's hand.

Haley screamed and latched onto my arm while I was digging for another one, and I shook her off.

I regretted it the moment The Reaper reached us and, without a moment's indecision, wrapped its flexible right arm around *her*, tightened it like a python, and pulled.

Ben blasted it with a jet of flame near where its elbow should have been, and it scurried backward, dragging Haley headlong over the couch and along the floor, back toward the open window, its skin searing and bubbling and weeping where the flames had charred the hoodie away from it but maintaining its integrity.

I abandoned my search for another flamethrower and grabbed a cleaver instead, vaulted the couch, and swung. I would have cut the grasping arm clean off, but The Reaper struck out with its scythe, and I had to stop, jump sideways, and clear it like a jump rope to keep my feet attached.

Ben grabbed Haley's outstretched hands to try to anchor her, and when Aldo took aim with his taser, Ben waved him off.

"Not while he's touching her!"

Aldo and I both tried to catch Haley's legs to help Ben pry her free, but The Reaper scuttled too far out of reach, both Haley and Ben skidding along behind him, leaving a thickening trail of blood through the broken glass.

They put up a fight at the window, but not a long-enough one for us to join in. Ben wedged himself into the sink, holding Haley with one hand and the faucet with the other. Haley was screaming,

"Not again! Please, not again!"

I was amazed she hadn't gone back to sobbing yet. Splinter flashbacks were bad enough when they weren't real.

Finally, just before Aldo and I could catch up, The Reaper stuck the point of its scythe into the fabric and skin on Ben's chest and simply pushed him away, trusting his grip or his sternum to break.

Thankfully, his grip went first.

Ben would have climbed out after them, right through the shards left in the window frame even after they were out of sight. The only thing I could say to stop him was, "We know where they're going."

Once I was sure Ben wouldn't leave the moment my back was turned, I ran to throw the back door open.

"Billy, get the car started!"

He met me at the door, still stubbing out a half-finished joint, its sweet, focus-killing scent more overpowering on him than the incense had been.

"What happened? Is she okay?"

"They must have known she was onto them!" I explained as fast as I could. "They took her, but they're too late! She's already told us! The Miracle Mine is hidden under a Splinter replica of a giant redwood! It was *right there* the last time you drove us up there! I knew we were close! Start the car. We have to catch up before they can get her inside!"

Billy didn't ask any more questions just then, and he paused only a moment before digging for his keys.

"Aldo!" I stopped him before he could climb into the van after Ben. "You're on backup. Make sure we have at least a twenty minute head start, but then come pick us up with all the *human* help you can get."

Aldo didn't quite nod, not willingly, but he was far too smart to take the time to argue. "Twenty minutes," he repeated. "Be careful, Mina."

## 22.

### HONESTLY, I'D PREFER FOLLOWING A WHITE RABBIT

#### Ben

Billy's bolt cutters made short work of the chain that held the gate shut. The two of us pushed the wrought iron gate open with a roaring squeal that sounded like it would summon every monster within half a mile. We were lucky, though, for no monsters came running out of the darkness at us. We only had the faint sounds of the forest nightlife to keep us company.

I handed the cutters back to Billy as we made our way back to the van. My hands were shaking. I didn't know if it was more out of fear or anger.

He smiled at me, worried. "You okay?"

"No," I said. "We could have fought him . . . it off. We've done it before. This didn't have to happen."

"You could've, but you didn't," Billy said, clapping a hand on my back. "You can beat yourself up about it, or you can do something about it. You want my honest opinion?"

I didn't really, but I said, "Sure."

"These freaks, they've got this town. They've messed

with you since you got here. They've messed with Mina for longer than I've known her. If you guys find them, you save Haley first because that's what you gotta do, but if the chance comes up, and I'm pretty sure it will, you show them no mercy. You kill them. Don't think they won't do the same thing to you, you feel me?"

I looked him in the eyes, and for the first time, I could see Billy was completely serious. At the time, I had a hard time arguing with him. I could see their faces, distorted, monstrous, ready to kill us all. Mina's dad. Alexei. Kevin . . . Consequences be damned, I had a feeling that I might be able to kill that night if I had to.

"Yeah, I feel you," I said as we got in the van. Mina sat in the back, taking stock of the odd array of weapons that Billy had gathered together from his "secret stash." In addition to a fairly standard collection of knives, hatchets, and even a chainsaw, he had some more exotic choices. While Mina considered a cattle prod and a large flamethrower made out of an insecticide sprayer, I was more interested in trying out Billy's homemade bang sticks. Basically a set of foot-long, sawed-off lengths of broomstick with some modified shotgun shells duct-taped to the end, Billy had rigged them to go off when stabbed into something with enough force. I looked forward to trying one or two of them out on The Reaper.

Though, knowing Billy, there seemed an equal chance I'd wind up blowing off one of my hands just trying.

"Are we through?" Mina asked.

"Yeah," Billy said as he started up the engine and drove us up the bumpy dirt road.

As usual in the back of Billy's van, we held on for dear life and hoped for the best. At the same time, Mina did her best to show me the pictures from the old miner's journal on her phone.

"I've got what we know of the mine's layout memorized, but you should study it too in case anything happens to me," she said. She soon began babbling excitedly, "Of course, these diagrams are not very well drawn, and not by an expert, and the layout likely changed over time with cave-ins, and assuming the Splinters—"

I put my hand on her shoulder and squeezed reassuringly. "We'll be fine. Out of everyone here, I'd trust you to singlehandedly find Haley and get us all out of this alive."

Mina smiled up at me slightly, "You do know the odds of all that happening are incredibly low, right?"

I nodded. "We have to try."

A few moments later, Billy skidded to a stop. "If I'm not mistaken, guys, this is where you two were headed while I was busy almost getting arrested."

We left the van, taking along everything we thought could be of use. Tools, flashlights, bottled water. I slung the heavy, improvised flamethrower over my back while Mina filled her bag with as many bang sticks as she could. Billy took along a long spool of a couple thousand feet of clothesline, shoving his revolver down the front of his pants.

He gave me the chainsaw.

Geared up, we headed along the forest trail, following Mina's flashlight beam as she led the way.

"So you're sure this thing isn't going to blow up on

my back?" I asked Billy as we trudged, motioning to the flamethrower.

"Like, ninety-nine point nine percent sure, man," Billy said.

"You said a hundred percent earlier," I said.

"Well, I was a little more baked then," he shot back. "I mean, you should be grateful Jailbait had me make that in reserve anyway! Shouldn't you be worried more about fighting some giant Splinter tree and going into the 'mine of mystery' and saving Haley than little things like exploding?"

Mina had stopped in her tracks at the darkened edge of the clearing.

"I don't think we have to worry about the tree," she said.

Billy and I followed her into the clearing. It was alive with activity, the gnarled, viney bushes on the ground writhing and contracting. The massive tree that had blocked the mine entrance had moved to the side, rocking back and forth slightly on thick, tentacle-like roots. The dark entrance of the mine loomed before us like a gaping dragon's mouth, the faint green glow from within promising otherworldly terrors.

"Well, at least they were nice enough to leave the door open for you," Billy said.

Billy tied the end of the clothesline spool to a nearby, non-Splinter tree in a series of messy knots. It wouldn't win him any merit badges, but it looked like it would hold.

"Say it again," Mina said.

# SPLINTERS

Billy sighed dramatically, like a put-upon child. "Three tugs mean you found Haley and are coming up, four tugs mean you haven't found Haley and are coming up, three, then two tugs mean you're in trouble and need help, and one long pull means you're being carried off and probably eaten by some underground terror."

"I never said that one," Mina stated.

"You might as well have," Billy said, irritated. "Listen, I don't see why I can't come with you. You're going to need all the help—"

"We can't just stand around here arguing!" I snapped. "Every second we're here, they're dragging Haley farther into that mine. If we don't go in there now, we could lose her forever!"

Billy clearly wanted to keep arguing but shut up when Mina glared at him. He scowled but still handed Mina the spool of clothesline.

"Just be careful, you guys, all right? I've become kind of attached to you," Billy said, playfully punching Mina on the shoulder. She smiled faintly but quickly turned on her flashlight and made for the mine entrance, trailing clothesline behind her. I started to follow, but Billy put his hand on my shoulder.

"Take this. For the tree," Billy explained as he handed me the chainsaw I'd set down when we saw the tree had moved.

"The tree's out of the way," I said, not looking forward to carrying another awkward, heavy weapon in addition to the flamethrower.

"For now," Billy said simply. I hadn't considered the

possibility that it might move back while we were inside. I took the chainsaw gratefully and followed Mina into the darkness of the Miracle Mine.

It was cool and musty inside. That didn't surprise me. What did surprise me was how light it was. I'd been in caves before, and once inside of an abandoned mine on a school field trip. A certain distance away from the entrance, you find yourself in a darkness more pure than you'd think possible. In here, however, we could see even beyond the beams of our flashlights by the faint green glow that seemed to come from everywhere at once. Looking down, I could see why.

Nearly every surface of the mine was covered in a spongy, vein-like material that pulsed faintly with the green light. Tangles hung from the ceiling like grotesque, malformed roots or vines, occasionally leaning toward us, but for the most part hanging lazily in the air, dripping long, slow trails of slime. The disgusting, living carpet captured our footprints perfectly as we descended.

And the heavy, three-toed footprints of a Splinter.

"Looks like we're on the right track," I said. We had to be at least a hundred feet in at this point, the entrance long-since invisible in our downward hike.

"Possibly," Mina said without elaboration. She looked off at a crudely dug side-tunnel and mused, "That must be the escape tunnel."

"What?" I asked.

"The tunnel the miners dug to escape on their own. I'm surprised it hasn't caved in by now," she said.

"No, I was asking what you meant by 'possibly,'" I clarified.

She was quiet, thoughtful as we walked farther into the mine. "Has it occurred to you that maybe we're being led here? That maybe the tree being out of the way and the footprints here for us to follow are part of a trap rather than good fortune? That Haley is just bait that your Reaper is using to draw us here? What kind of sense does it make to free us one moment and attack us the next?"

I did my best not to be annoyed with Mina at this moment and failed. "I guess it depends on who The Reaper is. If it was Kevin, or even your dad, I could see him letting us go out of some sick sense of priority or honor, but going after Haley because that was what he was told to do. Honestly, I don't know if the Splinters have ever made sense to me. But what I want to know is, if you think this is a trap, why are you still here?"

She didn't look at me when she said, "Because this is the closest I've ever gotten to answers."

I turned, about to ask her what kind of answers she was looking for, when I saw it. It was simple, something I could have missed if I were any less on edge, but I caught it clear as day on one particularly slimy, root-covered wall.

The beam of my flashlight wasn't aiming straight.

I trained it on the wall at about chest-height, but the light nearly fell to the floor. I tested this, training the light farther up the wall, but it curved about four feet lower than it should have.

"That shouldn't be," Mina said as she tested her flashlight

beam against the same stretch. Anywhere else she aimed it, the beam was straight, but on this section of the wall it curved. Even more disconcerting, upon closer inspection of some of the vines, I could see slime on them, but it was dripping upward.

She set her flashlight on the ground and went to the wall, tearing at the forest of slimy, pulsing vines, forcing her hands further inward.

"There's a crevasse hiding here, maybe even a tunnel," she said as she struggled with the roots. "Hit it with the flamethrower. I think that should open it up!"

Though I feared it exploding in my hands, I gave the weapon a try. I set down the chainsaw and ignited the kitchen-lighter fused to the end of the sprayer. With one press of the trigger, a fine stream of flaming gasoline shot from the end of the weapon. Much like the light and the dripping slime, it did not quite go where I was aiming, but it found its mark on the wall all the same, rapidly burning away much of the slimy, creeping mess of vines. It did reveal a narrow fissure in the stone wall of the mine.

We checked the ground. The footprints led in.

Mina slipped into the crevasse first. It was a tighter squeeze for me, one I had to make by taking off the flamethrower and pushing it in ahead of me along with the chainsaw, but after twenty feet or so, the way opened into a wider, downward-sloping tunnel. It was almost too steep for us to walk down safely, but the fleshy carpet we walked along kept us from falling down, so long as we stayed close to the wall.

The farther we walked along that narrow, slanting

tunnel, the closer-in the walls seemed. The fact that it felt as if gravity had shifted slightly and was actively pulling us farther into the tunnel didn't help either. It felt as if the laws of physics from our world were slowly falling away with every step we took toward that eerie green darkness.

Mina stopped maybe ten feet from the end of the tunnel. She cocked her head, then looked at her hand as if she had never seen one before.

"What is it?" I asked. At least, that's what I think I asked. At that moment, I was transfixed as the sound of my voice seemed to solidify as a rippling wave in the air. It embraced Mina, wrapping around her before popping in a small, near-invisible explosion behind her.

She looked at me, eyes wide.

"You think that's strange, watch this," she said as she raised her arm above her head, making me stagger slightly as her voice hit me. At first it looked as if she had raised her arm and dropped it quickly to her side again, but then I saw it slowly arc through the air appearing to take a full minute, leaving a trail of darkness in its path.

"What is that?" I asked, raising my hand in front of my face and seeing the same frightening effect.

"It appears that time and space aren't working quite like we know them," she said. "I think what we're seeing is the past, present, and future simultaneously."

I raised my hand, fluttering it around like a bird, and, despite my anger, caught myself laughing at the sight.

"It's like being in *The Matrix*," I said.

She cocked her head. "Which matrix?"

"Another time," I said, checking that the rope trailed

behind us. It was still there, but going by the spool, we would be running out very soon.

"Come on," she said, leading me slowly into the opening ahead. I was so disoriented by the strange atmosphere of the tunnel and so eager to get out, I nearly started running as we got to the end. It was only Mina standing in the way that stopped me from spilling over the edge entirely.

At least, I think *edge* was the right word.

The vast chamber we had stumbled into was unlike anything I had ever seen before. It was perfectly square and at least a hundred feet across, though the way my depth perception was messing with me, it might have been a mile for all I knew. It had the shape of a massive, inverted stone step pyramid with tiers of decreasing size descending in front of us maybe a hundred feet down, ending in an opening that glowed brilliant green. Looking up, I could see that we were only about two thirds of the way up the structure, and greater tiers still ascended above us. It was like being in a great, ancient stadium.

Somewhere far away there was a heavy, mechanical sound at regular intervals, as if there were many great gears at work. Massive crystalline stalactites hung from the ceiling above us, pulsing and glowing iridescent purple hues, while most of the room itself was lit by thousands of small, glowing green blobs that floated through the air. A few floated by us casually, and for a moment, I wondered if they were alive or just a natural part of the environment down here. Mina reached out to push one away from her, only to see it sprout small, spider-like legs. The legs thrashed out, pushing away from Mina, before retreating back into the blob as it hovered away in its new direction.

I was running my hand over some ancient, inhuman writing that had been carved into the crumbling archway around us when Mina called for my attention. She was looking at a large brass sign bolted next to the archway that looked to be a fairly modern addition. On it was what looked like the same block of text written out in perhaps fifty different languages. About nine lines down, I read what it had to say in English.

PROSPERO
STATE OF CALIFORNIA
UNITED STATES OF AMERICA
NORTH AMERICA
EARTH

"What do you think that means?" I asked.

Mina was staring out at the other levels of the stadium, a crushed expression barely controlled on her face. Slowly, she pointed at another archway opposite us on the next level down, then another one farther off to the left. As I learned to adjust my eyes down here, I could see a few more gates on other levels.

It took her a few seconds to answer, and when she did, it was with a fragile imitation of her usual matter-of-fact confidence.

"It means that my hopes that Prospero might be an isolated outbreak were . . . unfounded. This is how they get from place to place. This place . . . it's a place between places. Not on Earth, but connected to it somehow. It seems that each of those gates connects to a different location somewhere else in the universe, and this is how they travel."

"The *universe?*" I asked, pointing to the sign. "You mean the world?"

She shook her head, decidedly, resignedly. "If they have to specify Earth on the sign, it means they're likely on other worlds, too."

The enormity of the thought made the hairs on the back of my neck stand on end. She waved me to the edge of our tier and pointed down. I looked at the spongy material on the floor about fifteen feet beneath us. I could see the tell-tale, three-toed footprints heavily embedded in it. What I couldn't see was a way down.

"Do you think there's a staircase somewhere?" I asked, not particularly hopeful. I doubted very much that Splinters needed to use stairs.

Mina moved her hand sharply through the air, staring at it as it moved slowly, then swiftly. She looked down at the tier beneath us, putting her toes up to the edge.

"Wait!" I called, too late. She jumped.

I expected to see her landing in a heap with a broken ankle or leg, screaming for help. Instead, she slowly fell to the level below us. She looked up at me, flashing what I could have sworn was a smile.

"How did you know *that* would work?" I asked.

Before she could answer, she crouched down and jumped up with all her might, landing right next to me with the grace, if not balance, of a ballerina.

"How did you know that would work?" I repeated.

This time she definitely smiled, whatever the sight of those signs had done to her already switched off and locked away somewhere in that eerily compartmentalized brain of hers.

"The floating lights," she explained. "Gravity doesn't seem to have any logical, constant effect on them, or on anything in here. But the one that landed on me had some sort of rudimentary consciousness." She pointed out into the void, and I watched the lights for a moment, drifting in that deliberate, self-preserving way, like insects, but without visible wings. "That's what gravity responds to for them. Thought. And it will respond for us, too. It goes in whatever direction you want it to, if you focus hard enough."

As if testing a theory, she walked up to the wall next to me, put her foot on it, and began walking up it, before jumping off and landing next to me.

"See?" she said, beaming proudly.

I suddenly began to feel very dizzy. I looked down at the level beneath us, gulped, and focused just as Mina had told me.

I jumped, fell for what felt like twenty seconds, and then landed as lightly as a feather. Mina landed next to me. I smiled at her, hopefully. She smiled back.

We jumped down a level at a time, occasionally having to dodge side to side to find more footprints or a better landing spot where certain portions of a tier had collapsed with age. The rope trailed out behind us like a lifeline.

Mina compulsively wrote out the city names from the archways we passed on her arm. It slowed us down a bit, but when—*if*—we made it out of here, this would be good information to have. They passed by almost in a blur.

ROME

CAPE TOWN

XI'AN

BUENOS AIRES

BAGHDAD

The signs all felt random, as if the Splinters had just chosen a handful of major cities to invade. And Prospero. It was a few tiers from the bottom, when we found a sign marked KARAKORUM, that everything made terrifying sense.

Right now, Karakorum isn't much more than ruins out in the middle of the desert, but centuries ago it was the capitol of the Mongol Empire. Like Rome, Xi'an, and Baghdad, it was a major imperial and cultural center. A center of influence and expansion. If the Splinters had chosen it, it seemed very likely that they had been with us from almost the very beginning. The magnitude of this scared me more than I could put into words.

We jumped down to the final tier. Below us, at the bottom of the stadium, was a brilliant, glowing pit that showed us nothing of the world beyond. The footprints appeared to be going in its direction, though.

Cautiously, Mina tossed in the spool of clothesline. It pulled taut after it disappeared into the green, having reached the end of the line.

"You can turn back, if you'd like," Mina said as she peered

down into the green. "I'll understand. And I promise, I *will* do everything I can to save Haley."

I looked down into the green abyss, and I gulped. I thought of Haley. I thought of Mina.

That did it.

I jumped.


I fell down for maybe one second. Then the direction that was supposed to be down changed, and I fell sideways, landing with a heavy thud on a stone walkway. I looked back at the glowing green portal and saw that I'd fallen maybe six feet. The spool of clothesline lay limply on the floor next to me. I couldn't help it. I laughed.

Seconds later, Mina flew through the portal and landed on top of me roughly. Our eyes met for one awkward moment before she climbed off and helped me to my feet.

Briefly, I considered making a joke to defuse the situation, but when I looked up (at least, I think it was up), my ability to make jokes completely disappeared.

We were in a vast chamber, greater than the stadium, so great that I could see neither ceiling nor walls. Stretching into the sky were stone pillars, walkways, and structures shifting in position mechanically across all three of their axes like a constantly moving, giant puzzle box. The sound of great gears far off made sense now since I could see several large gears bisecting the floor, ranging in size from just taller than me to at least a hundred feet high. Hanging from many of the structures were thousands of man-sized, egg-shaped pods, all glowing as faintly green as the millions of light blobs that floated through the air. Nothing about this room made sense. None of the angles should have worked, but there it was before our eyes, so wrong, so impossible that it took everything I had not to go mad just from looking at it.

Greeting us just in front of the entrance tunnel was a large, crumbling statue of an ancient monster. It was improbable and lumpy with long, lethal-looking claws and folded wings. I wondered if he was supposed to be a warning or a representation of one of some ancient society's gods. Neither would have surprised me.

"So, this is the Warehouse," Mina said in awe. I looked at her, questioning. "It's what I've heard Dad call the place where humans are taken after they're captured, where they're taken over and made into Splinters."

Upon further consideration of the large green pods hooked into the structure, I said, "So those are . . ."

"Only one way to be sure," Mina said as she looked down, found the trail of footprints, and began to track them along a narrow stone walkway. Following the trail turned out to be a task easier said than done. With the next mechanical groaning of gears, our walkway shifted horizontally, pointing us in a new direction, in a new part of the expanse. The way we had come from shifted away as well, and the floor began to spin and connect with new adjacent pieces. One of them allowed us to skip across to the base of part of the pod structure, giving us some semblance of stability, but the realization that this Warehouse shifted its orientation every few minutes was not particularly comforting.

Up close, each pod was maybe eight feet in height and covered in purplish veins that met at the top in a large bundle suspending it from the structure above. Within the nearest translucent pod, I could see a person floating in a viscous fluid, vague and shriveled in the gloom, barely even a person anymore, as if his body—or her body; it had become difficult to tell—had been drained. At once I felt a fresh surge of pity and anger for this person, for Haley, for every single person who had ever been taken by the Splinters. They had to pay. We had to make them pay for what they were doing.

Idly, Mina walked up to the pod and rapped upon it with her knuckles. Though the pod appeared soft, its surface sounded hard, even hollow. As she touched it, it lit up like a television.

It was almost as if we were in someone's head. A man, middle-aged judging by his reflection in the glass, waiting in line for a café to open. His eyes drifted off to the side, looking up as the rising sun backlit a massive, gothic cathedral. Faintly, we could just hear him chuckling.

After a few seconds of that, the picture disappeared.

"What was that?" I asked.

"I think . . . I think we just saw inside the Splinter's mind. I think we just saw where it is right now. Could you identify the location?" Mina asked back.

The cathedral looked familiar. I racked my brain before I could find a name that matched up with its impressive architecture. "That was Cologne Cathedral. In Germany."

Mina nodded, writing that name down on her arm with

a question mark. She looked at the next nearest pod and proceeded to touch it, but I grabbed her hand before she could.

"We're here to find Haley, remember? I don't think we'll be able to just by trying each of these pods one at a time. Let's try to find those footprints while they're fresh."

She nodded, a bit dejected, but all the same helped me search for any part of the structure that contained fresh Splinter footprints. Still, it was hard to stop her from touching the occasional pod, seeing flashes through some monster's eyes as they pretended to be human.

An elderly woman carrying groceries on the Tokyo subway.

A medic with a group of Canadian soldiers fighting some skirmish in the middle of a desert.

A young woman drunkenly stumbling down the Las Vegas Strip.

Seeing the number of pods, considering how many lives were stolen so these Splinters could take over . . . it made me sick.

After maybe five minutes of searching and dodging the structure's constant shifts (though sometimes we were forced to ride up or down a few stories), we finally picked up the trail again. It was fainter, the veiny carpet slowly healing back to its intended shape. We followed the path with greater urgency, dodging more shifts and often nearly being knocked over by more pods as they swung around on their glowing tethers, climbing various curling staircases and pillars.

More of the tethers connected to each other the farther

we went, some joining into large, pulsating tubes, all of them leading in the same direction, toward something. We reached it after about fifteen minutes. The center of the Warehouse, a clear, circular area where all the tubes attached to the pods coalesced and merged, feeding into . . .

Honestly, I'm not quite sure what it was they fed into. I don't know if there's a word in any language capable of describing it.

Floating maybe a foot off the ground was what looked like a window, maybe twenty feet high and sixty feet wide. All of the purple tubes fed into the top of it, pulsing as if this window were their very source of life. Looking through this window, I could see what appeared to be a dark sky, and a landscape that stretched on forever in an endless sea of gray. This ocean roiled and moved as if it were alive, the nearest portion seeming to rise in our direction as we approached before crashing back in on itself. Mina was transfixed by the sight, touching the window, even taking away a glob of the night sky before it splashed through her fingers and back toward the window.

I was about to tell her not to touch it again when I heard a faint, childlike voice behind us.

*"Help me."*

I turned around, so certain the voice was nearby, and padded down the nearest row of pods.

Finally, I found it. A lone pod with empty tubes on either side of it where two more pods should have been. Mina caught up with me just as I saw the face beneath the swirling green mire was Haley's.

This was it. It was over. They had her. Everything we

had done, everything we had fought for, it was pointless. They had won.

I dropped the chainsaw and collapsed to my knees, pounding the ground with my fist.

"Damn it, damn it, DAMN IT!" I yelled, my voice bouncing off the ground and nearly flinging me back to my feet. "THEY GOT HALEY!"

Mina approached the pod cautiously and put her hand upon its surface. The image that appeared on it was dark and confused, but after the shapes began to make sense, a sick feeling of dread hit me in the stomach.

It was an image of both of us from behind, staring at this exact same image on the pod's surface.

"Got me?" Haley's voice purred from behind us. "Oh, Ben, they never lost me!"

## 23.

### Mina

Ben didn't pause nearly as long as I would have expected him to before revving up his chainsaw.

Its vibrations made deep, shimmering ripples in the too-thick air that stung when they broke over me. Haley winced at the first wave of them, but she was still smiling when she leapt out of the way, as lightly as if she were on wires, and landed on the side of one of the pods, standing at perfect ease, parallel to the floor.

Those massive gears gave another crunch, and the pods began another of their grinding shuffles.

Ben silenced the saw and cursed, his voice muffled by that air. He lunged to grab the pod with the real Haley in it, missed it by inches, and locked his arms around the stem of the next one. He reached out for me as it swung away, but I only saw this in the reflection on the shimmering pods in front of me.

At the same moment he'd jumped for the real Haley, I'd jumped for the fake one.

The moment Ben was out of sight, already shuffled away

from me in some un-trackable set of moves, I knew I'd picked the wrong target.

But at least I didn't miss.

I crash-landed right on top of the Splinter Haley, pinning her to the vertical wall of a pod as if it were the floor. And I was going to make the most of it.

She coughed when my elbow collided with her throat, but then she laughed, Haley Perkins's laugh, contaminated with a sort of baby-giggle, the kind that comes from someone who hasn't quite gotten the hang of lungs yet.

"Can't kill me," she sang at me. "Can't kill me without killing her."

I could feel her shifting and changing under me, preparing some sort of attack, probably deciding whether to grow spikes out of her chest or force some debilitating, nauseating image into my head. I had to subdue her quickly, and I couldn't let go of her to do it. The moment I did, I was sure she'd be gone. There was just one awful option.

I pulled the switch to electrify the cattle prod Billy had given me, glad for the moment that if this was how I was going to have to do things, at least Ben wouldn't have to watch. I held the prod up, or down, or sideways, next to where Haley's face met mine.

"I'd prefer to avoid that," I agreed. "But I won't leave her buried in here alive. Feel free to present me with a third option."

Haley screamed when I touched the prod to her shoulder, not like a girl or a baby, more like a beetle hiding in firewood when it's lit, a squeal of pressurized air between wooden cracks of breaking and re-forming joints.

I may have screamed a little too when the current ran from her body through mine, but I held myself together. Just barely, and only by knowing that every bit of it was that much worse for her, for a *Splinter*.

I wasn't in full command of my muscles just then, never mind my spatial comprehension, but I was able to jerk the prod away after just a few seconds, and I waited until my jaw had stopped seizing before asking again.

It took Haley that long to regrow her ears anyway.

"How do we get her back?!"

Haley was cracking and twitching under me, bits of her bulging and sinking into and out of unnatural shapes, but that baby laugh was back.

"You just disconnect her at the source. And then you *take* her!"

She nodded over my shoulder at the unfathomable, boundless space of endlessly shuffling pods, inviting me to leave her and join Ben in searching that effective infinity.

The fact that she was still breathing almost certainly meant that he'd already been hopelessly separated from her host's pod.

I didn't stop to think about how I'd find him again, or how we could possibly find someone who couldn't even call for help. I just pretended to think about it for long enough to brace myself before giving us another jolt.

"Take me to her!"

My whole body buzzed with the charge, each cell trying to rip itself in half with its spastic little dance, but there was no time to brace for the next shock. Haley grabbed me by the shoulders, her arms shaking but strong, growing themselves thicker and longer for extra leverage, ready to throw me off, and I jabbed the prod into her neck in the vital few seconds before she could.

The surge stopped her controlled transformation, but with my grip still weak from the last one, even her involuntary spasms were enough to send me pinballing away, bouncing hard off of four different pods before I could remind myself to call one of them "floor," the cattle prod clattering off in another direction.

The pods shuffled again.

Mine shifted backward four spaces and up another three by my present orientation, and for one panicked moment, I couldn't see Haley.

She was going to get away. She was going to leave me alone in this endless, labyrinthine hell, catch up with Ben before he could take back the real Haley, and then she would take him, too, just like they had wanted all along.

Then, with the next crunch of gears, she swung lightly back into view, hanging in a handstand on the bottom of a pod.

She wasn't trying to lose me.

She didn't have to. This was her territory. The Reaper probably hadn't gone far after "kidnapping" her, and there could be any number of other Splinters waiting in any shadow for Ben.

There was even the chance that she was trying to distract me from trying to help him, but even if that was the case, she was still my best chance of finding him before something else did, of finding the real Haley, of finding *anything.* She was all I had, my only reference point in the sea of identical pods.

I tightened my mental hold on my imaginary gravity, drew the first bang stick from my bag, and launched myself at her again, burying the shell in her shoulder, which splattered across the pod behind her.

She cried out and lengthened her other arm at me with more velocity than the real Haley could have thrown behind her best punch, knocking me back three pods while she rebuilt.

"Take me to her!" I repeated.

"No!" she watched me reproachfully as I gained on her, drawing another stick.

She ran a hand over her newly repaired shoulder, her imitation of Haley Perkins's. "This one's mine!" She giggled again triumphantly and leapt off in a new direction, staying just one pod ahead of me, choosing each step with care. "And when I've done my job, they're going to let me keep it!"

"Your job? You mean bringing Ben down h—"

I jumped and stabbed another shell into her forehead without finishing my sentence. She wasn't ready for it. I grabbed an air freshener flamethrower while I waited, kneeling on her chest, for her head to regain a recognizable shape. Underneath us, the sun glinted brightly off of Sydney Harbor for some other Splinter's stolen enjoyment.

Blood, bone chips, and gray matter melted back into generic Splinter goo and then hardened into new parts of the same humanoid illusion.

Ben's distant voice called out my name after the shot,

then again a few seconds later, a few shades closer. Maybe he had given up searching for Haley without clues and started searching for me by the sound. Or maybe The Reaper had caught up with him, and he was screaming for help. The Warehouse's stifling acoustics made it impossible to guess just where or how far away he was.

As soon as Haley's hair found its normal, thick, silky texture, human enough to make that horrible, acrid burning smell, I ran a long, purple jet of flame through it. I missed at first and had to compensate for a warp in the space between us.

"If anything happens to Ben," I explained when I was sure she could hear me, "I will incinerate you, hostage or no."

*I'm sorry, Haley.*

That thought arose very clearly in my mind, but didn't change what I was willing to do.

The Splinter Haley jerked her head to the side to minimize the space near her hairline where the skin kept bubbling off of the bone and re-growing. "I don't give a damn about Ben!" she screeched.

"Then take me to him, and Haley, point us to the door, and go back where you came from."

"No!"

"Why him?" I grabbed her one-handed by the hair and knocked her head against the pod, hoping to keep her too dazed to fight. "Of everyone in . . ." I was going to say Prospero, but the scene glimmering under us changed my mind, " . . . everyone in the world, what do you want with him? What's happening to him *right now?*"

"Nothing!"

"Is it Kevin? Is *he* going to take him? The one with the scythe? Are you using Kevin?"

"Kevin?" Haley didn't seem to expect that guess. "No! I *said* we should take Kevin, but no one would listen to me! He knew Haley Perkins, and he knows about us! If Ben had let him hang around us, he could have ruined everything!"

Kevin was still clean. Probably. I tried to hang on to that relief, let it calm me a little, but there were too many other details, losses for me, wins for her, for *them,* reasons I wanted to rip her into tiny pieces and watch them burn whether it would do anyone any good or not.

I needed to stay on task. I needed to learn, to understand, to find Ben, find Haley if I could, see if I could find anyone else who could be saved, and escape knowing better how to fight another day. That was the only possible positive outcome, and I couldn't lose it to the swelling feeling in my chest, in my skin, as if my blood were heating and thickening like jelly on a stove, ready to boil over and split me open along every vein in my body if I didn't do something very violent to keep it stirring.

It was a feeling as strong and almost as dangerous as the one I couldn't have for Ben, and just like that one, I'd felt this only once before, to catastrophic effect.

That didn't mean I had to ease up on Haley. She was durable. But I couldn't finish her while there was a chance she could be made to help.

"Your people attacked us with that deer! It went straight for us!" I recalled, willing her to tell me something about their claim on Ben, something about Creature Splinters I didn't already know, *anything* that would make me accept her continued existence for a few more seconds. "Ben needed stitches!" I rammed the wrong end of the bang stick into her chest until I heard two separate snaps. "It could have killed him!"

Haley looked pained and confused from the shifting of her ribs as they knitted back together, but she smiled at me. "You needed him to believe you, right?"

"Oh, of course!" I knocked her against the surface again and saw a fresh smear of blood there for a moment before it healed away. "It was all for *my* benefit! You called me to say, 'stay away from Ben Pastor, Ben Pastor is ours,' just to make *my* life easier!"

"No." Haley shook her head and winced when her hair reached the end of its slack. "I told you to stay away to make sure that you *wouldn't*, even if he told you to!"

"You've done everything you could to make him trust you! To get him alone with you! You made him think you were *her!*" This was what I screamed at her. It was easier than screaming, *You made* me *trust you! You made* me *think you were her! With only three lousy months of practice, you made* me *think you were human! You made me think you were a survivor. You made me think you were someone like me. And then you made me take Ben down here myself, right into your "Warehouse" when all I've been trying to do is keep him from ending up in it.*

"You've been after him since you got here!" I shouted out loud.

"This is not about your boyfriend!" Haley shouted back.

"Ben is *not* my boyfriend!" I lit the aerosol again and touched the jet to side of her neck. "I *killed* my boyfriend!"

I moved the flame up her face, wanting to see it leave a deeper impression. "*Your* people made me do it!"

The fire wasn't nearly enough to hold in the feeling, so I switched it off and hit her with the can instead, bringing the corner of it down on her skull four, five, six times with my full strength.

Haley was crying out, raising her hand to try to cushion her face, but when I stopped, she was giggling again before the blood had even receded from around her left eye socket.

"*Really?*" she snorted, so amused and interested that I was sure she didn't know. "Wow, I mean, they told me you had issues, but I thought they just meant your parents and stuff!"

"I have three more bang sticks!" I informed her, grabbing one of them and holding it over her throat. "And the last time I can take your head off your shoulders, I won't risk letting it grow back!" I lit the flamethrower in my other hand. "That's how long you have to start making sense!"

"Okay, okay!" She raised both hands over her head.

"Why Ben?" I asked one more time.

I hadn't heard Ben's voice for over a minute, but I was sure I heard it then, responding to his name. He was still incalculably far away, but so far he seemed to be alive.

"Because he was *there!*" Haley answered me. The pods began another set of moves beneath us, and I had to adjust my mental gravity to keep my position. Haley didn't take advantage. She was all back in one piece, but she'd stopped struggling. "I was just supposed to be gone long enough to be a mystery too good to resist solving," she explained. "But I knew from the way he looked at me at the funeral. I knew by the way *you* looked at *him*. Haley Perkins's brain seems to be very good at noticing things like that."

I raised the stick a little. "What way?"

"You know what way."

Arguing that point was going nowhere. "What does that have to do with bringing him here?"

She rolled her eyes at me. "Not him, *you.*"

The pods ground to a temporary halt, and I realized zero point two seconds too late why she'd stopped fighting me. She had been waiting for just this arrangement, and as soon as it was perfect, Haley punched me hard in the stomach with a fist newly grown out of hers, knocking me backwards into the next pod. I spread my feet and would have landed on the front of it, perfectly poised to attack, if there had actually been a pod there to land on.

There was nothing but an empty space.

Before I could collide with anything and make it a floor, Haley had jumped up and touched the tube above me. Glimmering, translucent petals sprouted down on all sides of me and hardened within seconds into a fresh pod.

"I did it!" Haley jumped up and down on the pod next to mine like a child who's just learned to spell her name. "Oh, my God, I did it! I caught Mina Todd!"

I didn't ask questions after that. I was too busy kicking every sticky, unyielding wall of my newly grown cage, shoving a bang stick where the seam between its petals should have been, trying not to let the ricocheting shrapnel that lodged itself in my left side and shoulder slow down my subsequent efforts, but Haley kept leaping about and babbling.

"*Ben* isn't the one who *exists* to destroy us! *Ben* isn't the one who sleeps with a taser under his pillow and armed guards waiting at his call to make it *impossible* to deal with him the normal way! Ben's just the one I knew would listen to me, and I knew you'd listen to him! I knew it! They thought it was a stupid idea! They thought it would make the Council too mad at me for spending time with him, like I was going to steal his body and run away to San Diego just to get away from their stupid rules! They didn't think I could do it, but I was right!"

She was still going on this way when the lining of the pod began creeping up my legs with that horrible, sticky, suffocating texture. I aimed the flamethrower down at it, but it was like trying to boil away a river with a kitchen match.

The Splinter substance worked its way up to my waist, attached itself to my elbows, and sucked me backward into the inner wall. Haley's squeals of celebration were the last thing I heard before the lining grew over my ears.

There was an instant of blinding pain when the sharp points emerged from the sticky mass around me, razor-tipped threads of Splinter, finer than a blood vessel, burrowing under my skin, under my muscles, wrapping around my heart, my lungs, tunneling under my glasses, in through my tear ducts and the soft spot at the nape of my neck.

The process took just long enough for me to think one thought with the entire cavern of my mind, every remote corner of it focused to a single point. *I will not be one of you. I refuse. You cannot make me.*

And then I was somewhere else. Some*one* else. Myself,

but reset to the very beginning with everything I had ever been wiped utterly blank.

For a moment, there was nothing at all. Then things started to come back in a stream of chaotic, disjointed images that were barely familiar, as if someone else were watching a highlights reel of the life I could no longer remember through my eyes.

The real me would have understood that I was being read.

But for the moment, I was two years old, hitting the back of a rocking chair against the wall of my parents' sitting room.

I was five and playing chess with Mom, making her laugh when I accidently moved my rook diagonally.

I was seven and sitting on my dad's lap in his workshop, my *real* dad's lap, sobbing into his jacket while we waited for the glue to dry on my favorite porcelain doll's face.

And then I was nine, and I kept being nine, and I couldn't stop being nine when I heard the crash of breaking wood in the middle of the night and knew that something terrible was about to happen.

I was nine and in my big sleep t-shirt and bare feet, tiptoeing across the dark living room where the sound had come from, surprised to see all the wooden furniture still intact, closing in on my first glimpse of the monster.

It had my father's face, but everything else about it was wrong. The limbs were too long with far too many joints. Other stumps with sharp, bony points sprouted asymmetrically from its torso.

Its right arm lifted and bent, almost where the elbow

should have been but backward, and came swinging down like a morning star flail, knocking something, someone, hard against the floor.

I recognized my uncle's voice when it cried out in response. It had read me too many stories to mistake.

I felt the gasp slip through my lips. The monster froze to the spot to listen.

Without turning, without moving at all except to shed a patch of hair that was in the way, the back of its head blinked open a pair of freshly grown eyes, exactly the shade of my father's, and looked back at me.

"Mina."

The only word I could find was the one I didn't believe anymore.

"Dad?"

And then I was suddenly ten, hunting Creature Splinters in the forest with a borrowed rifle that was much too big for me.

I was eleven, stretched out on the floor of my room with a nine-year-old Aldo, my overly complicated early list system spread out around us, trying to explain my latest deductions to him and marveling at how easily he understood.

I was twelve, hanging from the Prospero Middle School bleachers by a fast-fraying sweater, one of my more vile nicknames scrawled across my face in itchy permanent ink, while Patrick Keamy and his assorted goons practiced chucking dirt clods at me, and Haley Perkins, the real Haley Perkins, stood in front of them, intercepting the lazier throws with a ruler and yelling at them to get a life.

And then I was fourteen, the flood of images slowing back to a clear, ambling stream again, and I was crying for the last time in the presence of another being, human or otherwise.

His name was Shaun Brundle, and I was happy to see him, happy after the replacement of five classmates in a single week to curl up for a moment in his arms, to let him watch over me and kiss away my exhausted tears and examine for me the surveillance footage I had already poured over for so many hours that I could no longer see it.

I thought he'd spotted a clue I'd somehow missed when he directed my attention to the monitor, until I caught his reflection in its glass surface, raising the keyboard over my head and bringing it crashing down.

To my small credit, I didn't stop to mourn, not then. I just grabbed my paring knife off the desk, stabbed, and twisted.

He gasped and shuddered, eyes wide and hurt and confused, ordinary-looking blood gushing out over my hand, and for a moment I dared to hope it would be just that simple.

Then, in one quick wave of a chain reaction, the blood hardened to the consistency of stale gummy worms.

I pulled back instinctively, and the blood gave a squelching, sucking sound against my skin. I could feel fresh, liquid blood joining it when I twisted the blade, and Shaun winced with its movements but didn't loosen his hold. The thickened blood crept along my arm, almost dripping upward, in sticky, rubbery tendrils, pulling me in further until my fist, with the knife still clutched in it, was pressed against his imitation of a spine.

The bones of my arm snapped somewhere inside of him, Splintery sharp edges cutting gashes into the flesh that even *my* body's excellent self-healing capacity would never erase. Then he was around me, *all* around me like inch-thick shrink wrap, carrying me out the window, I didn't know where.

I was fourteen and seven more minutes, cutting my way free just before the tree line, pouring lighter fluid over the Splinter even while it twisted itself back into Shaun's shape and told me with his stolen voice, "If you kill me, you kill us both."

To make his point, he put a hand on the bare skin of my ankle and forced in his threat, the cold, hard, crystal clear image of *my* Shaun, locked away in the greenish dark somewhere, pale and slouched limply to one side with half-open dead eyes.

I knew that "both" meant the real Shaun, not me.

And I knew he was telling the truth.

It was not ignorance that made me touch the flame to his dripping skin.

I did it because of that hot, thick-blooded *killing* feeling that couldn't let him get away with what he had done to my Shaun and to me, that couldn't let him *win*.

I was fourteen and ten minutes more, lying on the grass where Kevin found me, broken and bleeding and reeling with imposed thoughts that weren't my own, explaining to him why the fast disintegrating, charred mess on the ground had both inhuman parts and remnants of his brother's clothes. Still fourteen and telling him every bit of what I knew, more to stave off shock than for any sensible reason. Fourteen and teaching him how to make me a secure tourniquet, holding him in my one good arm while we waited for the ambulance I knew I had to risk, as if it were for him instead of me, soothing him as best I could while he sobbed and gibbered but never once called me crazy.

And then I was fourteen and two more months, standing with Kevin in front of the headshot that took the place of Shaun's missing body at his funeral, where he told me he was finished. No revenge, no answers required, just moving on, hoping I would join him, knowing that I wouldn't.

And finally I was sixteen, spotting Ben for the first time in person, across another colorless funeral crowd, at the same time hearing faint, frantic words in his newly recognizable voice.

"Mina! Mina, can you hear me?"

Words that he wasn't speaking yet.

I was sixteen, sixteen and myself just minutes ago, beating the aerosol can against Haley's skull and being flung backward into the open pod space.

Then there was nothing again, nothing at all but a faceless shape forming itself with tremendous effort out of a sticky, clinging ocean, all the way across the immeasurable room from me but at the same time so close that it might as well have been inside me, sucking everything else in me away.

Except for one thought, one thought hanging there after all the images had finished washing over it.

*I refuse.*

I grabbed that thought and held it. I clutched it with all of me and felt a shudder, a shockwave, run through my pod and out through the ones surrounding it.

I used that thought to wrench my eyes open and stood there in the Splinter sludge with its hooks still lodged deep in each of my organs, fully conscious and gladder than I had ever been in my life to possess my fractured and possibly not-quite-sound mind.

I could see the inside of my pod and the distorted image of the Warehouse outside, but that wasn't all. I could *feel* the inside of *every* pod, hundreds of thousands of bodies with Splinter pressed against the skin, hundreds of thousands of sleeping minds.

Most of them were empty, silent, vacant, nothing but a blurred impression of one of the distant scenes playing on the pods' surfaces, but others were sharper, more human, more alive. And in that ungainly cavern of my head, I had room for them *all*.

I expected my own pod to keep fighting me the way it had at the start, but one more thought, *I refuse,* made the gelatinous goo around my right leg shudder and melt away. This time when I kicked the wall that had withstood a shotgun blast, it gave way like cheap window glass.

Ben had caught up to the sound of the struggle, and I caught a momentary glimpse of him standing on the pod opposite me with Haley in a headlock, the motionless blade of the chainsaw pressed to her throat, before they both saw my pod shatter.

Haley's look of unconcern dissolved into terror.

"Mina!"

Ben let her go and leapt across to me, still calling my name. He tried to grab my hand, but I waved him back and looked over his shoulder at Haley's face, trying to absorb her every detail of imitation until I could feel without a doubt which sleeping consciousness was a perfect match.

"The real Haley is fifty-six pods to your right, fifteen forward from there, and forty-two straight down. You can catch her if you freefall. Cut her out at the connection and she'll live. I'll be right here."

Ben hesitated, letting the next shuffle draw that much closer.

"Go!" I shouted, and even in the muffling, shimmering, echoless air, he listened and fell sideways out of sight.

Haley looked back and forth for a moment in abject panic between me, prone and defenseless in front of her in the broken pod, and Ben, plummeting toward her life-line to sever it. Then she sprang after him, leaving a time-displaced streak of blonde behind her.

## 24.

TWO DAMSELS, THE REAPER,
AND A GUY WITH A FLAMETHROWER
WALK INTO A WAREHOUSE

Ben

I tried to remember everything Mina had said, everything she had showed me, about how gravity worked down there. I tried to let that comfort me as I plummeted through the shifting, shuddering structure of the Warehouse, bouncing the light blobs off of me and hoping they, and not some other moving piece of stone, were the only things I would hit before I landed.

It didn't help much.

I focused. I focused as hard as I could on a safe landing on the platform beneath me. I pushed out all thoughts of splattering on the ground like some old cartoon and imagined a soft landing that I would barely feel.

I closed my eyes.

*Soft landing.*

*Soft landing.*

*Soft landing.*

I don't think I could have been more surprised when I

actually did land softly on the platform below, light as a feather. If I hadn't been busy laughing like a loon out of pure relief, I'm sure I would've tried to come up with some witty, action movie-esque thing to say.

The platform I landed on was narrow, maybe ten feet wide and about fifty feet long with three pods on either side of it. The pod on the far left side was Haley's. I had no idea how I was going to get her out. The chainsaw might do it, but I might cut into her just as easily. The flamethrower was worth considering, maybe melting her out, but that was just as risky. The tools in my belt all seemed so pitiful compared to the hard shell of the pod.

And to make matters worse, I also had to contend with the padded footfalls of the Haley-Splinter landing behind me.

"Son of a . . ." I muttered.

I dropped the chainsaw, whirling to face her with the flamethrower.

She was faster, more used to moving down here. I didn't stand a chance. She ripped off one of her own hands and threw it at my left foot. Its freshly grown claws lashed out and dug into the ground, bolting my foot in place. Her other hand soon followed, locking my other foot to the floor. Tendrils of bone and tendon stretched from their severed stumps, wrapping around me, binding my legs, chest, and arms. I tried to flex my wrist, to aim the flamethrower at her.

The Haley-Splinter shook her head, smiling an all-too-Haley smile. "Let's aim that somewhere . . . a little less dangerous."

Impossibly strong and sharp tendrils wrapped around my wrist, aiming the flamethrower at my legs. This would be a problem.

She looked at me curiously, a childlike smile on her face as she walked towards me slowly. The snapping, popping sound of her further transforming made looking at her like staring at a pond in a rainstorm. When the sound waves had subsided, parts of the creature that stood before me more or less looked like the Haley I knew. Her sundress was in shreds around her ankles, and long, floor-length tentacles mixed with her shimmering blonde hair, spilling around her shoulders and wrapping around her nude frame like a madman's vision of the *Birth of Venus*.

"Like what you see?" she purred, running a regrown finger up my chin. I remained silent. I would not dignify her taunts with a response. The Haley-Splinter laughed at me. "I never thought I would like it. Back home, we don't think much of these bodies. They're a way to fulfill our never-ending desire for sensation, but at the same time ugly, imperfect machines. A lot like you would look at an old, rusting car. Everything in you screams, *Don't get in, it's not safe,* but you get in anyway because you need it to get where you want. But when I got this body, I knew it was beautiful. It's nothing like back *home.*"

She stretched the last word out like it was an insult. "You don't know how good you have it. Back home all we do is exist. There is no feeling, no identity, barely any indepen-dent thought. We don't get any of what you would consider simple pleasures—sight, taste, sound, touch . . ."

She ran her hands up and down her body, her

Medusa-like tentacles moving with them suggestively. ". . . You can touch me, if you want. Anywhere you want, any *way* you want," she suggested, flashing me her innocent eyes. "I've tried many, many things since I got this body, but there are a few I need help with. I did always think you were cute, you know."

"You're damaged goods," I spat back.

"Maybe," she said sweetly, too sweetly. "But then that's what you like, isn't it, Ben? The girls with the sad eyes, the ones with the tempers and vendettas, the ones with the night terrors and the absentee fathers and the—"

"You're not Haley!" I cut off the list of her acts.

"No, I'm *better* than Haley!" she roared at me, her eyes flashing red. "Haley was like all of you, squandering the gifts life in your world allowed her, ignoring every opportunity she had to *enjoy* sensation because of your pitiful human ideals of restraint and morality. If she knew how bad things could be, she would have enjoyed this more."

She exposed herself to me lewdly. I looked away, closing my eyes tight, trying not to think about how the real Haley would feel if she could see this. I could feel her sliding behind me, wrapping more of her tentacles around me, caressing me, trailing sticky mucous up my arms. It took everything I had not to vomit.

"When you're one of us, you'll enjoy this more. Trust me," she laughed. I opened my eyes long enough to see a vacant pod slot rotate into place next to me. I looked back at her, watched her rubbing herself closer, more insistently against me, her tentacles starting to undo the clasps of my flamethrower. I looked down at those monstrous claws holding my feet in place.

A plan formed. It was going to be unpleasant, to say the least.

I pinched my eyes shut, and gritted my teeth against the pain to come.

"Not likely," I said as I pressed the trigger on the flame-thrower. A ball of fire erupted around my legs and feet, nearly engulfing my lower body. Haley leaped back, shrieking madly, chittering and popping in that alien tongue. My pants, my shoes were on fire. More importantly, the claws holding me down let go, running away like wounded animals. I jumped forward, preparing to do the good-old stop, drop, and roll, when I heard her begin to transform behind me.

Before she could, I turned to face her with the flame-thrower ready, seeing her fierce and pitiful eyes boring into mine.

I let her have it. She became a living fireball, thrashing and rolling around on the platform as she screamed and screamed and screamed her alien scream. This bought me enough time to drop to the ground, shed the flamethrower, kick off my burning shoes and pants (glad for having worn boxers that day), and toss them away. My legs were pretty thoroughly burned. Nothing permanent, I wagered, but there'd be pretty extensive blistering for a while. Seeing flames licking around the base of the flamethrower, I instinctively kicked it over the edge of the platform.

I only realized how stupid that was when I heard the

charred Haley-Splinter let out a loud, painful moan behind me. She was between me, the chainsaw, and the real Haley. I had to free the real one before her Splinter died, and I had no way of doing it.

"HEY!"

The voice calling behind me was the most welcome sound in the world. I turned to see Billy Crane at the end of the platform, standing firm in his jeans and sweatshirt and holding his ancient revolver. I didn't know how he'd gotten down here, and I was sure there was one hell of a story to go with it, but I couldn't have been more grateful.

I made to call out to him. She beat me to it.

"Billy!" the Haley-Splinter croaked dryly. I turned to her, watching her try to reform as she shed away burnt flesh and reached out to him. "I did it! I got Mina Todd in, she'll be one of us soon, and Ben, I got him too! I did it!"

I looked back at Billy with dawning horror. He smirked at us as he tossed his gun into the abyss, casually pulling the hood of his sweatshirt over his head. His eyes glowed red as his body began to contort, his legs lengthening and snapping backwards, his face becoming horrifically insec-toid as one arm became a thick, bony sickle.

He was The Reaper.

"A new era is dawning. Your death will mean many great things to come," he said as he bounded toward us.

I ducked in time for him to leap over me. The Haley-Splinter screamed as he landed upon her, cutting her neatly in half with his sickle-arm. He bounded away from her, leaping to another nearby platform.

I had my chance.

I ran between the two struggling, reforming halves of the Haley-Splinter and picked up the chainsaw. The pod was hard, Mina rapping her knuckles on it proved that, but looking at the purple veins that suspended it, I bet they were pretty soft. I revved the chainsaw, dodging the hard wave of sound that shot from its blade, and leapt through the air toward Haley's pod.

"NO!" the Haley-Splinter cried out, too late.

The chainsaw messily cut through the veins that held the pod suspended, snapping the chain in a spray of sparks when it finally cut through. The pod slowly dropped to the platform. The two halves of the Haley-Splinter thrashed and screamed in agony, still confusedly trying to rejoin as they slowly melted into a puddle of the same non-descript gray ooze we had seen in the great window. Soon enough, there was nothing left of that either.

As the Splinter disintegrated, the pod around Haley melted into a thick slurry of green and purple slime. Haley lay limply in the middle, face-down in the muck. I tossed the ruined chainsaw aside and ran to her, rolling her onto her back. It was Haley, all right. A little malnourished, a little drained, but definitely her, dressed in a tattered, almost completely deteriorated nightgown.

"Haley?" I asked, shaking her by the shoulders. She wasn't breathing. I panicked, wiping the muck from her mouth and nose, checking her airway. I was running through the steps from my CPR certification when she coughed. First weakly, then raggedly, expelling a large amount of the thick green slime.

Haley Perkins blinked weakly up at me.

"Ben?" she mouthed, barely a whisper, looking at me like she hadn't seen me in five years. With a sad, guilty twinge, I realized she hadn't.

I nodded silently, smiling down at her. "Yeah."

She smiled faintly before she passed out.

I considered trying to rouse her before I went off to search for Mina, but decided against it when I realized the Warehouse was falling apart.

The entire structure shuddered around us as if it were in pain. The regular, mechanical clockwork sounds of the great gears sounded strained. The regular movements of the shifts were jerky and less predictable, if that were even possible. The pods around us throbbed, their occupants writhing about in agony. The swirling, floating lights looked confused as they merged and split apart from each other, moving like frightened schools of fish.

Whatever we had done . . . it was bad.

Climbing the structure while carrying an unconscious Haley in my arms wasn't easy. The strange gravity certainly helped, but it was an exhausting ordeal made all the more difficult by the constant shifts. If it weren't for the directions Mina shouted, I wouldn't have been able to find her. As time passed and the Warehouse began to shake more violently, her directions became more infrequent. I feared that when I got to her, I would not find the Mina Todd I knew.

By the time I found her, she was nearly unrecogniz-able. She'd been half absorbed into the pod. Fibrous, slimy tendrils wrapped around her body, some of them appearing to puncture her skin. The pod writhed and thrashed around on its own painfully. Thick, wormlike shapes moved beneath Mina's vacant-looking face, her eyes rolling back into her head. It was trying to take her, but she was fighting it. Hard.

I set Haley down and went to Mina, thrusting my hands into the pod and trying to sever its link to her. Mina grabbed at me, trying to push me away.

"Wait, just another second," she protested.

"There's no time!" I pleaded as I ripped at her bonds.

"I've almost found him!" she shouted, unmindful of the tentacles that tried to force their way into her mouth.

I didn't know who she was talking about. I didn't care. Wrapping my arms around her, I ripped her from the squealing, shivering pod. It retracted away quickly like a deflated balloon, and the last remnants of the tubes that invaded her skin melted away in trickles of green and purple muck.

She lashed out at me in my arms, kicking and struggling to get her feet on the ground. With a look of pure rage, she punched me in the eye, knocking me flat on my back. In spite of her size and the blood oozing freely from her hundreds of puncture wounds and a deep gash in her side, she was incredibly strong.

"I had him, I had him . . ." Mina repeated as she looked back at the shriveling remains of her pod, shortly before it shifted away with the rest of the Warehouse.

"We have to get out of here!" I yelled, "This place is falling apart!"

"But . . ." she looked back down at the retreating pod. She then looked at me, confused.

"Where's Billy? I heard him down here with you," she said.

"He's one of them. He's The Reaper," I said. I didn't need to say any more. Within the space of three seconds, Mina looked uncomprehending, devastated, and enraged before falling back to her thoughtful standby.

"Are you okay?" I asked.

"No," she said simply, looking off into nothingness. "No, I'm not."

"How do we get out of here?" I asked, trying to get her to focus. Though her attention came back slowly, eventually her face dropped into its blank, thoughtful mode. She watched the various malfunctioning shifts of the Warehouse, then grabbed me by the arm.

"This way!" she said, running off down a nearby staircase that had shifted our way. Scooping Haley back up into my arms, I ran after her. She traced an odd, twisting path across various shifting platforms and stairwells, taking us up a few pillars, even forcing us onto one of the great, spinning gears as we made our way to the entrance.

The glowing green portal taunted us in the distance, a shimmering beacon in a sea of darkness. I could see the stone altar built around it, the shadow of that great, terrible statue in front of it. It was at least a hundred yards away, probably even more given the way light was distorted around here.

The sounds of many wet collisions behind us stole my attention. Patches of the fleshy carpeting started to rip themselves off the ground, colliding with the floating lights and forming a massive, cell-like organism that began to float toward us.

"What is that?" I asked.

"A defense system. Like white blood cells fighting off an invading organism," she said with absolute certainty. I didn't want to ask how she knew that.

"And we're the invading organisms," I said.

"Yes," Mina replied, looking back at the portal in the distance and the impossibly long gap before it. Beneath us there was nothing but blackness that could very well have gone on forever.

"Do you trust me?" Mina asked.

"Of course," I said. Then I figured out what she meant. "Wait . . ." I said as I stared down into the abyss.

"We have to," she said simply.

The defense system lurched through the air towards us. She was right. At that moment, I wished she wasn't. I wanted to hold her hand as we took that leap of faith, and I could tell she wanted to as well, but with Haley in my arms, that would be impossible.

We took as many steps back as we could without getting too close to the defense system, got a running head start, and leapt through the air toward the portal. The shrieking mass behind us followed, but I could not focus on that. No, I had to focus on a safe landing, on staying in flight, on not dying. The portal got closer to us. The inky blackness beneath us was not going to take us. We would make it. The shrieking came closer. I looked back. It was almost upon us.

*It can't beat us.*
*We're going to make it.*
*We're going to make it.*
*We're going to—*

We landed on hard stone at the base of the great statue. Mina was off faster than me, running into the portal. I was right behind her.

The world shifted sideways again as I went through, flung to the ground in a heap in the great stadium. Mina helped me to my feet, goading me along as we saw the defense system begin to pull itself through the portal behind us. We began to jump up the levels of the stadium one at a time, passing by several archways.

ISTANBUL
ULURU
BOSTON

I stopped after the third city I didn't recognize.

"We're going the wrong way," I said, pointing to the signs. "We didn't pass by any of these!"

Mina hazarded a glance back at the growling, thrashing beast behind us. We'd gained some ground on it, but it was catching up quickly.

"Let's keep going along this level, see if we can find something we recognize, then head up from there!" she yelled over the din of the beast's roars.

I nodded, following her as we ran along the level of the stadium, passing by archways that seemed too far apart.

# SPLINTERS

THEBES
ST. PETERSBURG
JERUSALEM
XI'AN

That name was familiar. I shouted, "Xi'an! Start going up!"

Again, we ascended the steps, counting down the familiar archways as the defense system grew louder and larger behind us. It whipped out a heavy, barbed tendril that smashed a section of landing next to us, sending boulder-sized pieces of stone flying in every direction. We were able to dodge them, just barely, just as we reached the archway for PROSPERO.

It was strange, running up that narrow crevasse of a passageway again, getting used to how things like gravity and sound were meant to work. The exhaustion of our voyage into the Warehouse began to wear on me. Mina, too, for that matter, looked heavily winded and ready to fall over at any moment. The defense system roared behind us, but pursued no further. It seemed it could only exist in its own world. That much, at least, was a comfort.

It was difficult getting Haley through the narrowest section of the crevasse, but after some careful pushing, we got her back into the real world.

I went out last, struggling in the darkness to see Haley and Mina and figure out just how we were supposed to get out of here. Then I really looked at Mina, noticing something that made me smile.

"I see you held onto your bag, at least," I said, pointing to the tattered satchel she had somehow kept through the attempted assimilation process.

She smiled at me, vaguely, before reaching into the bag and pulling out a flashlight, "It has its uses."

Mina kept a quick pace in front of me in the mine, and though my burns were screaming for me to slow down, I kept up with her. We'd gotten Haley, and we'd escaped from the Warehouse, but this was not a place we wanted to be caught. Especially if Billy was still lurking around us somewhere. I tried to wrap my head around what he had done. He had hidden in front of us all this time, but he helped us. I didn't know what to make of it. I don't think Mina did either, not just then. She was angry, I knew that, but beyond that I could not tell. At the time, I didn't feel like fighting her. I was tired, I was in agony from the burns on my legs, and I was dreading walking all the way back to town barefoot, and—

"Wait," Mina said, stopping dead in her tracks. We should have been able to see the mine entrance, open and bright with the night sky.

Instead, we saw the pulsing hulk of a Splinter redwood tree blocking the mine entrance, its roots reaching out for us like the arms of the damned.

"Oh, come on!" I exclaimed. "Can't we catch just one break?"

"We just invaded the Splinters' Warehouse and escaped with our lives. I'd say we've caught an anomalous number of breaks so far. Statistically speaking, we were due for some bad breaks by now," Mina explained, looking at the tree, then at me.

"You don't have the chainsaw," she said.

"Neither do you," I said a bit too angrily. She looked at me sympathetically, then turned about on her heel and started running into the mine.

"Where are you going?" I asked.

"I'm getting us out of here!" she exclaimed.

Burns be damned, I was willing to follow her if she could make good on that. She led us down about a hundred feet back into the mine, into the crudely dug side tunnel we had passed by earlier.

The escape tunnel.

If it hadn't meant dropping Haley, I think I would have hugged Mina then and there.

We climbed through the awkward, narrowing tunnel that had clearly been dug by desperate men (or Splinters, as it may be) with no particular focus on comfort and every focus on getting out. Soon the tunnel narrowed to a point where we were crouching, then crawling. I had to set Haley down and let Mina inch her slowly forward while I crawled painfully ahead, pushing the flashlight out in front. After maybe fifty or sixty feet of this, the tunnel narrowed to a point where it felt like it had caved in, but I was sure, so sure that we were close, that if we just pushed and kept digging . . .

I scooped handfuls of dirt and threw them behind me, clawing for freedom, not caring that it might all cave in around us at any moment. I was so sure, so certain . . .

Finally, I broke through. My hand met cool air, gripping

a thick patch of dry grass and weeds. I cheered, and I could make out Mina smiling in the near darkness behind me. I grabbed at the edges of the hole, trying to widen it.

Then I felt powerful hands wrap around my wrist and pull. Every nightmare image possible hit me all at once. An army of Splinters waiting to take us back down into the nightmare, ready for our blood. Billy standing by to tell us that his aid was nothing but one great, big cosmic joke.

When I emerged from the ground, I saw my savior was none other than Kevin Brundle. His presence didn't exactly instill me with feelings of warmth and confidence.

"Hang tight, brother. I have you," he said as he pulled me from the earth. I looked around wildly, trying to find something, anything to use as a weapon, when he looked over his shoulder and called out, "Aldo! I got them over here! Get the blankets out of the trunk!"

Looking at my state of dress, he smiled and added, "There should be some sweatpants and spare sandals in there, too. Grab those!"

"Got it!" Aldo cried out somewhere far away.

I still didn't trust Kevin, but if Aldo had brought him . . . maybe it was time to take a chance on him.

"Mina and Haley?" he asked.

"Right behind me," I explained.

"Are they . . . them?" he asked, hesitantly.

"Yeah," I said. Without hesitation, he dove headfirst into the small tunnel opening. My respect for Kevin was growing by the minute.

He came out seconds later, gently dragging Haley into the cool night air. By this point Aldo had joined us, carrying a pile of fresh blankets and the clothes Kevin had called for. He looked at me, and though he clearly wanted to laugh at my lack of pants, the burns shut him up.

"It's that bad in there?" he asked as he handed me the sweats and sandals.

"Worse," I said as I gingerly pulled on the sweats.

Mina was the last out of the mine. She silently nodded at Kevin. He returned the gesture.

"We need to get out of here quickly," she said, instantly authoritative. "After what we did, this area should soon be swarming with Splinters. Haley needs someplace to recuperate. My house is not an option, nor do I think hers is."

"My parents are out of town for the next couple days," Kevin offered.

"Perfect," Mina said. "We'll need to debrief her, find out what she knows and fill in the gaps on what she doesn't. We'll need to tend to our wounds, and find out what happens next."

"This isn't over, is it?" I asked.

"No," Mina said without elaboration.

## 25.

### Mina

"No one can see her until she's ready to play along."

It took me the better part of an hour to communicate the importance of this to Ben.

"You expect her to pretend, after all of this, that she's been herself the whole time and everything's okay?"

"Yes."

I didn't have to say so alone. Kevin and Aldo tripled my voice.

Haley was half-unconscious, half-delirious, tossing and turning on the couch in Kevin's pool house, the four of us kneeling around her, trying to guess how long ago she had known the names she kept calling out, how close she might be to putting her ransacked mind back in order.

"Whatever they chose her for, it's over," I explained.

"What do you mean, 'whatever they chose her for?'" Ben repeated. "That thing tried to make Splinters out of us! If it hadn't been for Billy—"

"The *point*," I said, stopping him, "is that now that we

know about her, she can't be used the same way as before."
I wasn't prepared for another round of debating Billy's
actions while I still couldn't come up with a single explanation that fit. "And the Splinter who had her body isn't
coming back for it. So, there's a chance, a *tiny* chance, but a
chance, that they might decide she's not worth the trouble
and leave her alone. But if she starts drawing attention to
herself, talking about what happened, acting like she might
remember where the mine is and maybe even go looking
for it, that chance becomes zero. She'll spend the rest of a
very short human life fighting to keep the next minute of it."

Ben looked like he wanted to argue, but I could tell in
the way he swallowed that he was starting to understand.

"They know *we* know where it is," he pointed out.

"We *chose* to go looking for it. She didn't. And it's too
late to do anything about it for us."

"Yeah," said Kevin. "Everyone remember to thank Mina
for the short, violent, paranoid life."

But there were no signs of regret in the small, sad smile
he gave me, or the way he tucked the afghan closer around
Haley's shoulders when she rolled over again. It was the
same look of acceptance he'd worn when Aldo had admitted to gambling on his help, partly due to how likely he
was to agree to any plan involving the words "Haley" and
"rescue," but mostly due to his access to cars and how easy
the bike tracker (and its thoroughly un-incriminating
archives) made him to find.

Ben looked Haley over again, too.

"She needs medical attention." He picked a few flecks

of dried blood out of Kevin's carpet (where I'd accidently let my shoulder drip on it) to make his point. "We all do. We should at least—"

"Medical center's not an option," Aldo said before I could. "If they could replace us all quietly right now, that'd be a cleanup job well done. The three of you check into that place at the same time, and you might as well jump back down the mineshaft and hook yourselves in."

"Okay, fine," Ben conceded, "but this isn't going to cut it." He closed the lid of Kevin's parents' first aid kit over its useless supply of Band-Aids, sanitary resuscitation masks, and dried-out tubes of calendula ointment.

"You're right," I said. "I'll have to go get *my* kit."

The blister fluid soaking into Ben's borrowed sweat pants was turning an unsettling color, and I was in no mood to gamble with any part of my future dexterity when there were perfectly good sutures, tweezers, and antiseptics under my bed. "I think I even have some feverfew tea. If we can chill it and get her to swallow any, it might help. I don't know."

"No one's going anywhere alone."

I thought Ben was hinting at Aldo to put down his diagram of Haley's pod wounds and come watch my back. Aldo must have thought so, too, judging by the newly hurried rate of his sketching, but by the time I was finished double-checking every phone and tracker in my bag and clothes and arranging my tasers and flashlight in easy reach, Ben was the one who'd left his spot by the couch.

I've never really liked being helped to my feet. A hand doesn't make as steady an anchor as the ground, even if it is more conveniently placed, but I didn't object, especially not when I was gripping Ben's elbow with my currently preferred right arm for several extra seconds of support while the muscles all down my left side cramped, tensed, and spasmed against the sharp edges that didn't belong in them. Without the aid of fresh adrenaline, they had become all but unusable.

Ben glanced back once at Haley, dozing under Kevin and Aldo's riveted observation. Aldo looked up from the diagram at us.

"Don't stop now," Ben advised him. "We'll need to bandage her up when we get back."


My mind wasn't at its sharpest, but I know Ben and I spoke on the walk to my house. At least, Ben spoke. He recalled every detail he could of Billy's "help" and then told me what felt like every word the Splinter Haley had ever said to him, as if he felt the need to confess.

I listened and answered mainly with, "Yes," and occasionally, "No," doing my best to stand up straight enough that he wouldn't try to hold me up again, all my new unanswered questions skipping and rotating around my head, which was oversized, unsecured, and largely empty again.

Most of them were about Billy. Like exactly how long ago the real one had slipped out of my sight. Or whether I'd ever really known the real one. Or exactly where the hell the Splinter one had disappeared to after we'd escaped the mine. Or how long it might be before I made some other fatal error on the ECNS list.

If I ever needed to add a new adult again, I wouldn't just let him kill a Creature Splinter in front of me and call it proof. That was certain. But if my mistake had been somewhere else, I'd learned nothing to prevent the next one. And even if I *could* pin down how I'd missed that he was a Splinter, it didn't get me any closer to reconciling that fact with the way he'd let us go in the woods behind Dr. Westlake's, armed us to the teeth before sending us down into the mine, and, according to Ben, helped him fight off the Splinter Haley.

I didn't doubt Ben's honesty, or his judgment under normal circumstances, but I was seriously wondering if the odd little reality distortions in the Warehouse had somehow temporarily done something to his perception.

I thought about all those minds in the pods, too, now missing from mine. For several full minutes, I had known them all, and for the first time in my life, there had been more information in my senses than my memory could record all at once. It wasn't just disorganized and lost in my head now. It wasn't there at all. No matter how tightly I packed my consciousness, whenever I tried to remember who they all were, all I found were vague impressions without shape or sound.

I couldn't distinguish my father's mind.

I didn't know if that was because there were too many, because I had been separated from his for so long, or because his was one of the blank, drained, old ones. I wasn't sure which was worse.

There was a part of me that was absolutely sure that

if I'd stayed hooked in for another half a second, I could have found him.

Another part wondered if that same half second would have killed me.

Splinter reject. I wondered about that, too. ECNS for life. Too strange and broken and somehow wrong in the head to be replicated. It wasn't that I'd ever had any illusions of total normality. The past cases of Splinter rejection had been a small, unspoken source of hope to me for exactly that reason, but for the most part, I'd always assumed that I couldn't be quite *that* different, quite *that* wrong. I'd certainly never planned to find out.

I tried to focus on being relieved, proud even, that my brain could break a Warehouse pod, but unpleasant questions about that worked their way into the cycle, too—how deep my defect might go, how it might change with age, whether it might lessen my competence to perform my work in some way I wasn't even capable of understanding, whether everyone who had ever called me crazy might technically be right.

I kept doing long division in my head, going over dreams and memories to check that they were still easy to tell apart, testing every cognitive function I could think of to make sure they were working the way I remembered them.

Everything seemed to be the same, including the way it all changed when I looked at Ben, whether closer to or further from how it was supposed to be, I wasn't sure. That's why I had my eyes to the ground while I let us in the door at the bottom of the stairs into my room. I was double-checking my ability to find A above middle C without visual packing peanuts, and it wasn't until I heard the door slam behind us and Ben breathe in very sharply that I realized I hadn't checked around the corners the way I usually did.

The thing that had been waiting for us was in full human form—at least, it was after the extended leg that had kicked the door closed had receded to a natural length—yet it looked less like my father than it ever had before.

He was sitting on my bed, surrounded by my utterly useless amulet and herb collection, arms folded and resting on my closed medical kit, all tentative, hopeful imitation of my father's warmth drained from his face.

Ben took a step in front of me, his grip tightening on the flashlight, ready for another fight, and cautiously extended one hand, summoning that easy, charming smile that was always at his disposal.

"Good evening, Mr. Todd. I'm really sorry to drop by so late, but—"

"This will be a great deal easier without the pretense, Mr. Pastor," Dad cut him off.

Ben returned his right hand to the base of the flashlight, and I reached for the flap of my bag.

"I'm not here to hurt you," said Dad. "Not tonight," he added. My hand was on the half-empty can of air freshener, but I didn't pull it out. "I'm here to let you two know how close you came."

"To what?" I asked. Wanting to sound strong and composed, combined with seven years of wanting to scream terrible and very unpretentious things at him, made my voice sound a lot like my mother's again, but I didn't mind so much this time. "To finding out how to stop you?"

"To ending the peace your mother and I have devoted our lives to preserving," he said very calmly.

I sidestepped out from behind Ben so I could see him properly. There were plenty of problems I wanted to point out in that sentence. I started with, "Where *is* Mom?"

"She's safe."

I had to fight back a horribly vivid image of Mom "safely" encased in one of those pods before Dad clarified.

"She's staying with a friend tonight. Don't worry. She won't leave your surveillance range." He smiled grimly when he said this, and I tried not to let any surprise show on my face. "We've agreed to give this one more try. I believe she's already selected a marriage counselor."

I didn't respond to that, just stood there trying to decide if I was glad Mom was coming home or disappointed that she'd given in again, imagining some poor therapist trying to scratch the surface of my parents' differences.

"All we ever wanted for you was a normal life," Dad told me. "That might be the one thing we never disagreed on. Relations between humans and my people . . . you could say it's a family business. But we did everything we could to keep you out of it. I hope you'll remember that. Of course, that clearly isn't going to happen now, so you need to know what it is you're playing with."

This sounded sickeningly like an initiation speech, so I stopped him there.

"My 'business,'" I said, "is *humanity*, not Splinter-human 'relations.'"

Dad smiled, almost laughed, and then stopped himself. "Sorry. It's just been quite a few years since your mother's said those words to me. I'd almost started to miss the sound."

*"Mom* may be able to forget what you are for long enough to have *relations,"* the word summoned images that brought the beginnings of the killing feeling, and I fought it down, "but *I* never will. I know what you do to people. I know—"

"I'm well aware of what you know, Mina, and of the much longer list of things you don't know. For example, you don't know about the meeting currently in progress where I presented my argument not twenty minutes ago against your execution." He held my gaze for a moment to let the words sink in before turning to Ben. "And *your* replacement. My associates came to see my point of view. Barely."

I didn't bother hiding my skepticism. "Why would you do that?"

Dad looked back at me. "You're welcome. Your mother and I have been able to extend you a great deal of diplomatic immunity, Mina, but there is a limit. If my people get word of your involvement in *one more* fatality, I will not be able to protect you."

"I never asked you—"

"And before you start planning out ways to martyr yourself, you should know—"

"I don't want y—"

"I wouldn't even have been able to do it this time! Not if you'd done the killing yourself again! You have no idea how lucky you are that Ben beat you to it!" He looked at Ben. "Of course, that's not so lucky for *you.*"

"Do you expect me to be *grateful?*" I was shouting louder than I like to, having to fight too hard to keep the aerosol can in my bag. "For being allowed to get away with taking back one little piece of what your people have taken from—"

*"Do you want your answers or not?"* Dad shouted over me. "Or are all those bugs and cameras just an idle exercise of Aldo's technical prowess? You want to know how things are? Then for once in your life, Mina, *shut up and listen to me!"*

I shut up, and I listened, and after waiting an infuriating length of time to make sure I would stay that way, Dad explained.

"Prospero has always been . . . something of an embarrassment to my people. It's a small backwater burg with nothing to offer in terms of entertainment, power, or culture, but in spite of its inconsequentiality, our rate of permanent death here is astronomical, to say nothing of the rate of emergency replacements for security purposes."

I didn't blink even though it was clear he already knew enough to blame me.

"I'm . . . what you might call a lawman, to my people, the unfortunate lawman tasked with supervising this problematic little colony since its inception, and I've seen it through times you can't possibly imagine. Yes, we butt heads with the humans here. Yes, we've found it necessary to come to a formal arrangement with some of your respected representatives, and yes, we offer them and their families consideration in the donor selection process. The latest revision of the Treaty of Prospero was signed just under two years ago, after your most extreme transgression, and most of the new verbiage was intended to deal with our . . . vigilante problem. The next time a human acts against us in a *pattern,* two kills or more, the treaty is void. There are many of the opinion that what happened tonight came close enough to qualify, given your obvious influence over the situation. I was able to convince enough of them to sign a new draft. After the debacle with Sheriff Diaz, you two are to be kept alive and aboveground, for now, as a sign of good faith. But neither of you can set foot outside Prospero again."

Ben opened his mouth to object, and Dad held up a hand.

"We're already making the arrangements with your mother. It's a *wonderful* job opportunity. And as long as you cooperate, she'll be left to pursue it in peace. But make no mistake, either of you." He leaned forward over the kit, looking back and forth between us, his fingers elongating just slightly beyond their human shape along the catch. "If you try to leave, or if you kill again, you forfeit the deal for yourselves *and* your kind, and within a day, there won't be a single human left in Prospero over the age of twelve."

Two kills or more and the treaty is void. No more rules, open season on humans. Finally, Billy's angle was coming into focus, and I didn't like the look of it.

Dad looked between us once more before holding the

kit out to us. "Go on," he said. "Take care of your friend. No one else is better qualified."

Ben took the kit. "Will she—"

"She'll be fine," Dad told him. "Unlike the three-month-old you slaughtered over her."

Ben didn't flinch at the accusation. He turned to go. I wasn't quite ready.

"I won't apologize for rescuing a human being," I said. "If what we did tonight was a crime, you might want to have a stern talk with some of you own people, too."

"The matter with Billy Crane is an ongoing investigation," Dad replied shortly. "But thank you for reminding me. If either of you happen to have any information about his possible next move that you'd be willing to share, it might make the lenience you're receiving sit better with some of your more vocal detractors."

"You mean you don't know where he is?" I asked. I hadn't imagined it possible for Splinters to hide from each other, especially not now that I knew how all those minds looked and felt and sounded hooked together like that, funneled into that one central pool, but of course I couldn't remember it all. There could have been gaps anywhere.

Ben looked at me with a flicker of hope that meant he didn't understand what Billy had done yet. He *wanted* Billy to get away.

"I mean exactly what I said," Dad answered, watching us both expectantly.

"If I had the slightest idea where to start," I said, "to find and destroy the Splinter who set us up, even *you* wouldn't have to bribe me to tell."

Dad nodded.

"Just making sure."

The walk back to Kevin's I remember better. My thoughts were clearer, one thought especially.

"We were used," I explained.

Ben looked at me blankly. "Used how?"

"Billy meant for us to kill the Splinter who had Haley. Maybe I was supposed to do it, or maybe he thought you'd be enough to breach the peace as long as I was with you. That was his plan."

Ben was silent for so long that I thought he must be formulating an argument, but when he finally reacted, he kicked the nearest tree with a cry of frustration so deep that it had to be fueled by every horrible bit of sudden understanding, along with what must have been a great deal of pain from disturbing his singed skin.

"I trusted him!"

"So did I," I reminded him.

"He was helping us find the mine!" Ben shouted. "All along, he was doing it for this!"

"Probably called Sheriff Diaz himself," I realized out loud. "Just to make sure we'd know exactly where to go but wouldn't do it until Haley had us all ready to follow her."

It took a few more blocks of walking, a few more stretches of silence and sounds of self-reproach before Ben was coherent again.

When he'd stopped looking angry and settled into looking dejected, I said, "I'm so sorry." I might have gone on to repeat this a few more times than was helpful. "About trapping you here, I mean. That was never my intention. I'm sorry."

Ben shrugged at the ground. "Hey, I've always wanted to be able to say for sure where I'll be living next week and the week after."

I was sure this wasn't quite what he'd been hoping for, but pointing that out didn't seem likely to make it any better.

"I'm sorry about your father," Ben said suddenly after a few silent steps. "I'm sorry I haven't said that before. I'm sorry about what happened to him."

I shrugged back. "He's down there somewhere. We could still find him. I'm sorry about your eye." I could already see that it was going to blacken. Then something else occurred to me that I couldn't believe I hadn't said long ago. "And I'm sorry about what happened to your father, too."

Ben shrugged and changed the subject again. "So, you've killed a Splinter before? One hooked into a human?"

"I told you that."

"Yeah. Sort of. And that's *all* you told me."

For the first time since Kevin, I considered repeating the story, sure somehow that Ben would understand, but I was already worn out with the recent hours of thinking about it.

"Not tonight," I said.

Ben nodded, and we continued in silence past a few more driveways before he asked, "So, what do we do now?"

I stopped walking so I could whisper and be heard even though there was no one in sight on the street. "There's dissension among the Splinters," I summed up quickly. "They're not all of one mind, and tonight one of them dragged us in blind, unprepared, and way over our heads. Billy tried to use us to start a war between Splinters and humans, a real, open war, and we're lucky it didn't work because we weren't ready, and we would have lost. But that treaty is a joke. Even my mother realizes that. And if someone's trying to get it broken, it's only a matter of time before they succeed, with or without us. I won't play by those rules, not forever. There will be a war, and when it comes, I know what side I'm fighting on."

"What side *we're* fighting on," Ben corrected me.

I hadn't wanted to assume, after what helping me had already cost him, but I'd been hoping he'd say exactly that.

Ben shifted the first aid kit to his right arm and held out his left hand, the one closer to my side of the sidewalk, offering, not to shake mine, but to hold it.

And, in spite of Dad's best efforts, it wasn't until that moment that I truly realized how much danger I was in.

This was my last chance. If I didn't find a way to stop, right then, run away or say something awful enough to make Ben withdraw the offer, I was, without a shred of doubt, going to find myself feeling entirely too much again, caring entirely too much about things other than the fate of humanity, too much for it to be possible to make every

# SPLINTERS

choice correctly. I was going to fall irrevocably, the way I'd known I might from the moment I saw Ben face-to-face.

I would stop the Splinters if it killed me. That had not changed.

But if it killed Ben . . .

Every passing second made it harder to answer that question.

Possibly, I was already too far gone, because Ben's hand waited only a few short awkward seconds before I laced my fingers through it.

## Acknowledgements

Thanks go to our amazing agent, Jennifer Mishler, for all her support and expertise, and especially in this case for helping us polish (and sand, and saw large bits off of) the first act of this book, so we could start *The Prospero Chronicles* off with a bang.

Thanks to our publicists, D. Kirk Cunningham and Marissa Shields, to executive editor Christopher Loke, and everyone else at Jolly Fish Press for all the work you put into making each book a success.

Thank you to Scott Carter for teaching Matt everything he knows about the importance of storytelling and character development.

Thanks to Denis, Katinka, and Heather Titchenell for all the support and many a night of brain-mending comedy games.

Thanks to all the wonderful readers, bloggers, and authors who frequent our blogs and pages.

Thanks to everyone who's ever produced a work of art we've come in contact with, because you've all shaped our work in some way or other.

Finally, special thanks to everyone who attended our wedding back in 2011, because this book is what we were working on instead of writing thank you notes like civilized people. We hope you understand!

MATT CARTER is an author of horror, sci-fi, and yes, even a little bit of young adult fiction. He earned his degree in history from Cal State University Los Angeles, and lives in the usually sunny town of San Gabriel, California, with his wife, best friend, and awesome co-writer, F.J.R. Titchenell. *Splinters* is his first published novel.

F.J.R. TITCHENELL is an author of young adult, sci-fi, and horror fiction, including *Confessions of the Very First Zombie Slayer (That I Know of)*. She graduated from Cal State University Los Angeles with a B.A. in English in 2009 at the age of twenty. She currently lives in San Gabriel, California, with her husband, coauthor, and amazing partner in all things, Matt Carter, and their pet king snake, Mica.